Judy Garland, Ginger Love

Judy Garland, Ginger Love

Nicole Cooley

 **ReganBooks**
An Imprint of HarperCollinsPublishers

HarperCollins books may be purchased for educational, business, or sales promotional use. For information please write: Special Markets Department, HarperCollins Publishers, Inc., 10 East 53rd Street, New York, NY 10022.

FIRST EDITION

Designed by Joseph Rutt

ISBN 0-06-039251-7

98 99 00 01 02 ❖/RRD 10 9 8 7 6 5 4 3 2 1

For Laban—the future

She should have died at birth.
Cain killed Abel.
No twin should forget that.

—Jennifer Gibbons,
The Silent Twins

Acknowledgments

It is a pleasure to thank the many people who helped me with this book. I'm grateful to my early teachers at the New Orleans Center for the Creative Arts, Brown University, and the Iowa Writers' Workshop. Several people read and reread the manuscript and provided much-needed assistance. Jamie Weisman's enthusiasm and critical commentary were invaluable from the start. Pamela Barnett, Amelie Hastie, and Mary Leader provided encouragement throughout the project. Anne Marks and Ruth and Paul Cooley told me stories. Nora Dougherty showed me the long road home. I could not have written this book without my parents, Peter and Jacki Cooley, and my brother, Josh Cooley. And to Alissa Cooley, my gratitude is in every way enormous. Her presence in my life, both as a sister and a friend, has sustained me.

This book would not have been completed without summer residences at the Yaddo Corporation and the Ragdale Foundation, and a fellowship from The National Endowment for the Arts. Bucknell University supported my last months of work on the book. My sincere thanks also go to Ladson and Darlene Hinton, for providing time and space in their house for many years so I could write.

I am grateful to Judith Regan, and to Emily Sklar at the Regan Company, and especially to Dana Isaacson, whose careful critiques shaped this book into its final form. My agent, Sally Wofford Girand, has supported and encouraged me throughout the writing of the book. Her help and her faith in my work have been essential.

To my husband, Alexander Laban Hinton, who read and reread every word of this book, from its early drafts to the final manuscript, I owe the greatest thanks. This book was written with him, and now it is for him.

Prologue

On the screen, mother and daughter dance together in matching black top hats, raise their hands in the air in unison, their voices merging, impossible to tell apart.

The year my sister and I were born, 1964, Judy Garland and her daughter performed together in their first and only concert: *Judy Garland and Liza Minnelli, Live at the Palladium.* Our mother, Lily, watched the television broadcast from the New Orleans motel where the three of us began our life together as a family. She was seventeen. Madeline and I were four months old. My sister claims she can recall every dance step, every song mother and daughter sang. I know this isn't possible, yet Madeline becomes furious with me when I tell her I don't remember the performance because we were too young. She thinks I must remember if she does because we're twins, and she believes twins have the same body and the same mind. "Liza and Judy were as close as us, as sisters," she once said. "You're lying when you say you don't remember."

Lily had a record of the concert. She owned all of Judy Garland's albums. They were stacked in a box under her bed. If we promised not to touch the disks, we were allowed to look at the covers. I remember one where mother and daughter smiled widely, arms linked up. On that album, Judy Garland sings, "Well, hello Liza," to the tune of "Hello Dolly." It's as if she's surprised and happy to see her daughter on the stage beside her. I remember the stories

Lily told us about Judy Garland's life. Lily had seen every one of her films and knew all of her songs.

Years later, after Lily left us, I read a biography of Judy Garland. I found out there was more to Judy Garland than her life as a child star. There were canceled engagements, broken contracts, the time she was fired from MGM. Her daughters emptied her sleeping pill capsules, refilling them with sugar. "I'm going to kill myself," Judy Garland would state calmly as she passed through a room, and her daughters would be stricken with panic. Pills were sewn into the hem of their mother's dress. Then I began to understand what part of that life my sister had copied.

Dexedrine. Seconal. Nembutal. Bottles of Blue Nun wine. The first time my sister tried to kill herself was the night after I married Owen. Before that, she'd often threatened me with her suicide, but she had never done it, and I had begun to believe her threats were only a device to get my attention. I was wrong. The first night of my new life without her, I picked up the phone and heard her voice— slurred, low, unrecognizable words. "Linny, where are you?" I asked, but she'd dropped the phone.

The next time I saw my sister, she lay on a narrow stretcher, a tube running from her arm to a bag of clear fluid above her head. The emergency room was crowded; the nurses had been unable to find Madeline a bed so she lay in the hall. Her stomach had been pumped upon her arrival, and she was now out of danger, the nurse told me. The chart read "Accidental Overdose," but I knew she'd purposely swallowed the pills. Bottle after bottle were lined up on a shelf in her kitchen, displayed like a collection of antique objects. Xanax. Valium. Norpramin. I should have known my sister would not let me have my own life, apart from her.

The only drug I've ever taken is the Pitocin that flowed from the IV into my veins to start labor, the drug that didn't work. I lay in a bed in a private room, a television mounted high on the wall in the corner. I wondered if a person could overdose on Pitocin. I wondered if I took too much of this drug whether I would die, along with the baby.

I don't know much about mothers loving their daughters, but I know about sisters. Being a sister is the role in life I've always been best at, the one part I could play well. When I tried to become a mother, I failed.

The Pitocin dripped into my arm. And in my head, to comfort myself, I made Judy Garland sing one of Lily's favorite songs, "Meet Me Tonight in Dreamland."

1

This story starts before our lives—my sister's and mine—began. Twenty-nine years ago, our mother, Lily, found out she was pregnant and drank vinegar three times a day. She didn't want to gain an ounce. Since she was five, she'd taken ballet lessons, and after her graduation from high school she'd been promised a position in the touring company of the New Orleans Ballet, not in the *corps* like the rest of the ballet students, but as a principal dancer. In an assignment book with *Sacred Heart Academy* stamped on its cover in gold, she recorded what she ate each day: "4/7/63: ½ cantaloupe, ⅔ piece wheat toast, 1 poached egg." Her handwriting was neat and rounded, her measurements always precise. Lily frequently showed us this book when we were children.

This story actually starts with Agatha, Lily's grandmother, who taught her the vinegar trick. An immigrant from Hungary who came to the United States in 1933, fourteen years before Lily was born, Agatha raised Lily. Agatha's husband, Stephan, had died, and until Lily moved in, Agatha was alone. "I didn't have a mother," Lily said whenever she talked about her childhood, pronouncing the word *mother* with a pinched mouth. "I had Agatha." When she said "Agatha," her face relaxed.

Lily's parents had died in a car accident one night on their way to Pass Christian, Mississippi. Their Skylark smashed through the lake's guardrail, then sank into the water. It was Easter weekend. Lily was two years old. The night her parents died, she was watching *The Wizard of Oz* on Agatha's small black-and-white TV. She'd been at Agatha's house all weekend so Agatha could take her to church on Good Friday and Holy Saturday. On the Monday after Easter, her parents were dead, and Lily moved into her grandmother's house. When Lily told this story, I pictured her as a small, lonely orphan. But she didn't describe herself as sad. "I don't remember my parents," Lily told us if we questioned her. "Ask me about Agatha."

Although she'd left Hungary long ago, Agatha still appeared to live in the Old Country, wearing dark dresses, her hair in a braid that reached halfway down her back. Her rosary beads circled her neck even when she slept. In the 1930s, she'd taught herself English by reading movie magazines—*Modern Screen, Stars of Tomorrow, Motion Picture Weekly*. She'd acquired an enormous repository of facts about the stars, which she passed on to Lily. "Betty Grable had a tiny white dog she carried everywhere. That dog slept in her bed and sat right beside her every night at dinner." Agatha pointed at a twenty-year-old magazine, Betty Grable crossing her legs at the knee on the cover. Lily studied the magazine critically. Betty Grable was too fat to be a ballet dancer.

"Judy Garland was my first English teacher," Agatha always told Lily. The first English words Agatha had ever been able to read were from an interview with Judy Garland in *Child Star* in 1933, the year of the Century of Progress World's Fair in which Judy Garland performed. In those days she was nine and named Frances Gumm. Over and over, until she understood the words, Agatha worked through the column "Kiss-and-Tell." She saved that issue of *Child Star,* and showed its faded pages to Lily. Inside was an article titled "Baby Frances in a Star Dust Century." Agatha even liked to read the interview out loud to her granddaughter: "The Gumm sisters sang and danced across America with Mama in tow. Everyone was just waiting for Chicago. Baby Frances, you stole every show with your big-girl voice! What do you say to that, Baby?" Judy Garland's comments in the interview were short, orchestrated to sound like the perfect imitation of a polite child. "Yes, thanks. I sang 'When My Sugar Walks Down the Street.'"

Each Saturday of Lily's childhood she and Agatha walked across Magazine Street to the Prytania, New Orleans's oldest movie theater. The Prytania's weekend specialty was MGM musicals. The theater never showed new releases. The audience was almost entirely old women. Afternoon after afternoon, Lily and Agatha sat together in the dark and watched Busby Berkeley films. Agatha held Lily's hand, even after Lily became a teenager. Before the previews began, Agatha spread her big black shawl over their legs like a lap robe. "My sister Agnes and I had a robe over us when Father drove us through town. He didn't want the boys to see our legs," Agatha said. "The two of us sat just like this together." She pulled Lily into the circle of her arms.

Lily loved the films in which Judy Garland was a child star—*Babes on Broadway, Love Finds Andy Hardy*. They watched *Babes in Arms*, a line of children tap-dancing together, staging a vaudeville show to save themselves from the state orphanage. Mickey Rooney played the piano, Judy Garland sang. In the saddest scene, she sat alone without him and spoke to his photo. "I know I'm no glamour girl," she said.

Agatha elbowed Lily, pointed at the screen and whispered, "Don't believe it."

Lily saw *The Wizard of Oz* only once at the Prytania, when she was thirteen. The Prytania was nearly empty. Lily hadn't seen the film that made Judy Garland's career since the night her parents died. Agatha hadn't allowed her to watch *The Wizard of Oz* on television like all the other kids she knew. Seeing it at the Prytania was like seeing it for the first time. When she and her grandmother sat down in their usual seats in the second row, Agatha crossed herself. "Hail Mary, full of grace. The Lord be with you," she began. She finished the prayer with her eyes closed. Lily somehow knew Agatha was remembering the car accident that killed her parents eleven years before.

Agatha smiled, smoothing Lily's hair against her back. Agatha liked to fix it to look like her lost sister's, in a long tight braid. "My girl," she said now. She touched the corners of her eyes with her lace handkerchief, crossed herself again, then whispered, "Do you know there are four pairs of ruby slippers? MGM made four of every prop."

Whenever Lily described her second viewing of *The Wizard of Oz* to us, she only described one scene: when Judy Garland passes from one world to the next. "We've got to get away! We've got to run away!" Dorothy cried to Toto. But they were caught in the twister that blew the door off their farmhouse. Into the air the house flew, Judy Garland inside, images flashing in the sky. When she opened the door after the house crashed to the ground, the world was transformed to Technicolor.

That afternoon, as soon as they were home, Agatha turned to her. "You're old enough to know the family secret." She led Lily to the bathroom and closed the door. They stood together in the black-and-white tiled room for a moment, then Agatha said, "Watch me." She pulled her dress above her waist, over her underwear and the garters that held up her stockings, pointing to the outline of her clearly visible ribs. Her skin was pale, streaked with thick blue veins, but her stomach was flat, as flat as Madame Makarov—Lily's ballet teacher—explained a dancer's should be. "Look," said her grandmother.

Lily nodded, waiting for Agatha to go on. Excitement rose in her throat.

"I want to teach you our trick," Agatha said.

"What trick?" Lily's hands twisted the hem of her blouse.

"When I was a very young child, maybe five or six, I came down with scarlet fever, a bad case. The doctor told my parents I would die. He told them to leave me outside, under our biggest tree, for quarantine. He was worried I would infect the family. The village priest came to our house to perform last rites. He had liked me, and I liked him. He kindly read to me from the Bible about the crucifixion, the part where Jesus is on the cross and he calls out, 'My God, my God, why have you forsaken me?' Sour wine on a sponge is brought to him. The priest explained that sour wine is vinegar. I had an idea. I asked the priest to bring me the jug of vinegar Mama kept in the house, and I drank from it till it was empty. I was sick until I thought there was nothing left of me. But then I got better. I purified my body and drove out the fever because I'd prayed to God. For Jesus, vinegar was a punishment, but for me it was a cure."

"A cure," Lily repeated. Her heart fluttered in her chest.

"I taught my sister Agnes. Now I'll teach you. I keep a bottle underneath the sink. Reach down and get it." When Lily found the bottle, it was nearly empty. Agatha motioned Lily to stand beside her in front of the bathroom mirror and studied the reflection. "You look just like Agnes did when she was your age," Agatha said. "When I see you, I see her again." She took a long drag on the vinegar bottle, the muscles in her throat pulsing as the liquid ran down her throat. Lily stared, unable to turn away, afraid, as Agatha crouched, slowly and with some difficulty, over the toilet. She bent her head, and a bobby pin clinked to the tile floor. Agatha panted, as if she couldn't catch her breath.

"Are you all right?" Lily was terrified. She thought her grandmother was dying. Then she realized Agatha was vomiting.

Agatha stood up and carefully wiped her mouth on the edge of her lace handkerchief. "Your turn." She crossed herself and handed Lily the bottle.

Lily swallowed. The vinegar burned her throat. Her eyes filled with tears.

"Good. Now put your hand in your mouth." Agatha pushed Lily's finger to the back of her throat until Lily gagged. Without being able to help herself, she leaned over the toilet and emptied the contents of her stomach. Agatha released her hand. "Good girl. That's my girl." Lily couldn't catch her breath and her face felt damp. Sitting on the floor, she lowered her head into the space between her legs, one of her warm-up stretches from ballet class. Agatha was right: after the initial shock of the trick, she felt lighter, cleaner, cured.

From that day on, Agatha and Lily shared a pact. Lily went into the bathroom with Agatha every afternoon when she returned home from ballet, before she changed out of her leotard and tights. After they did the vinegar trick, they sat at the kitchen table, Agatha boiled them each a glass of hot water, and she told stories about Agnes. Agnes and Agatha were twins. When Agatha left for America, Agnes remained on the family farm in Hungary.

"When you have a daughter, you can name her Agnes."

Lily bit her lip. "Dancers never have children."

"Yes, children ruin a woman's body." Lily waited for Agatha to say something about her own child, Lily's mother, but she just poured more hot water into Lily's glass.

While her grandmother talked about her sister, Lily stood at the stove, using it as a *barre*, practicing ballet positions. She demonstrated steps as if she were Madame Makarov. First, second, third, fourth, fifth. Madame often smashed her cane to the floor to keep the girls in perfect form. She forbade the girls to wear brightly colored tights. "I cannot see your body!" Madame snapped the cane against the offending girl's legs. Once she told the other students that Lily's turnout was the model for the class. In the kitchen while Agatha talked, Lily turned her feet out again and again until her legs ached.

Before she chewed each bite for thirty seconds, timed, Lily cut her food into thirty equal pieces. "Count your chewing," Agatha said. "I taught Agnes to do that. In *Screen Secrets* I read that movie stars count too."

Lily was seventeen. She hated to watch other people eat. In the lunchroom at Sacred Heart, the nun on cafeteria duty wouldn't let her sit by herself. She was forced to eat with the rest of the senior class, and she was told she had to take a tray from the lunch line and put at least three items on it. Usually, she was able to get away with hot water, a slice of lemon, and a cup of ice. "The MGM diet," Agatha called it, one of Judy Garland's many diets when the studio executives decided she was too fat.

Lily listened to the clatter of a knife as it scraped a plate, the whispers of the girls who sat with her but didn't speak to her, and breathed carefully through her nose, trying to keep the timing of her bites precisely right. A roll crumbled on the front of Mary Kay Baldwin's blouse, and her lips were wet and oily from her malted milk. Sarah Harper ate her lunch quickly, her eyes fastened to her plate as if she were an animal at a dish. Watching the girls in the halls whispering confidences behind cupped hands, pinning up the hems of their plaid uniform skirts to show off their knees, Lily placed herself apart from them. She didn't care about their Sweet Sixteen parties or the debutante balls their mothers were already planning at the New Orleans Lawn and Tennis Club.

The world she wanted was at home: she and Agatha sitting at the kitchen table, with glasses of hot water and plates of egg noodles, timing their bites together. Or, upstairs in her bedroom, after dinner, when she leaned out the window, sneaking cigarettes, blowing smoke through the screen, into the crape myrtle trees. Smoking was her one secret from Agatha; the vinegar trick wasn't enough to kill her hunger. Each drag burned her throat and sent her into a fit of coughing, but she weighed ninety-seven pounds. "Ninety-seven is the perfect weight for a dancer of your height," Madame Makarov said. She said the word *perfect* in a voice of warning, as if Lily should be careful or she could become too heavy. MGM hadn't wanted Judy Garland to weigh more than ninety-five.

Lily poured herself a glass of water and took thirty sips, timed. Before she started her homework each night, she did her sit-ups, fifty, then seventy-five, then one hundred, two hundred, three hundred, her feet hooked under the bed frame, before she took a drink from the bottle of vinegar she kept in the closet under a pile of sweaters. She knelt before the toilet, a towel spread on the floor under her legs. Afterward, nauseated and exhausted, she could begin the work for school. None of it ever seemed to engage her, and she couldn't raise any of her grades above a low C. Each semester, her report card was filled with notations about her "poor effort" and "infrequent class participation."

Senior year, the guidance counselor at Sacred Heart, Sister Scott, called a conference in her office. "Isn't your grandmother supposed to be here?" the counselor asked as soon as Lily sat down. Sister Scott seemed barely older than Lily. Her blond hair peeked out from beneath her habit.

"She's sick," Lily lowered her voice. "She's in the hospital."

"Oh, well, I'm sorry to hear that, dear. Let's get started. I called you here to discuss your academic performance." Sister Scott twisted a piece of her hair and leaned across her desk. "So, Lily, isn't there one subject you like?"

Lily shook her head.

"Sister Dubonnet thinks you have some special talents in English class. Have you read any interesting books lately?" Her smile was still bright, unwavering.

"Reading is boring," Lily said. Sitting in a chair holding a book burned no calories.

"Have you made any decisions about college? You know, LSU's last application deadline falls next week."

"I'm not going to college. I'm joining the New Orleans Ballet."

"Is that really a wise decision, dear? Have you discussed this choice with your grandmother?" Without waiting for an answer, Sister Scott said, "Okay, let's talk about your friends. Are there any girls you consider to be special friends? Who do you pal around with?"

"I'm a dancer. I don't have time for friends," she said.

"You know, even if you aren't in the popular group—and I was a teenager once too, I know about the cliques—there are the girls who aren't *Catholic*," Sister Scott half-whispered, as if she were speaking an obscene word. "They always need friends."

"I don't have time for friends."

"How about boys, Lily? Is there a special boy in your life? You may not believe me, but it's not too early to start thinking about marriage. Lots of girls at Sacred Heart already have rings."

In the life Lily envisioned for herself, she was neither a mother nor a wife. None of the girls in Agatha's *Child Star* hoped for a ring given to them by a high school boy. None hoped to grow up, get married, and raise children. Alone, Lily imagined, she would travel the country on tour, dancing the principal roles in the best ballets—*Swan Lake, Giselle, The Nutcracker.* Each night, in a different hotel in a different city, she'd unwind the ribbons of her toe shoes and soak her feet in a clean white tub. Her feet would be hideous, callused, the toes crushed together and the toenails misshapen from years of being on *pointe*, evidence that she was a real dancer. The best dancer's bodies were beautiful on stage and secretly ugly.

The other girls at Sacred Heart would never understand. Dressing for gym class in their matching red gym suits, each name written on the shorts in curving script, the girls stood before the locker room mirror and looked at each others' breasts. "Mary Kay still wears a training bra," Sarah Harper said, "and you can see it through her blouse." They giggled and snapped each other's straps. Lily dressed and undressed silently, her body turned toward the wall.

The Health Class film titled *Your Womanhood* made her feel sick. Sitting on the gym floor with the other senior girls, as a woman's pregnancy unfolded in a square of light trained on the wall, Lily tried to imagine Judy Garland as the star of the film. Judy Garland would never wave good-bye to her husband from the bright front yard or stir fruit and sugar together for pie filling. Lily watched the woman's body grow, her pink dress expanding beneath the hands she clasped together as if she were praying. All Lily could think of was *Alice in Wonderland*, a book Agatha had read to her when she was little. Like Alice, the woman in the pink dress had no control over her body: it grew larger and larger without her consent.

The priest's voice-over said, "Your body changes to create your new family." The next shot showed the woman embracing an older woman who resembled her. Lily decided the older woman must be the pregnant woman's mother. Mother and daughter talked and smiled. The mother touched the daughter's hair. The priest continued, "Having a baby is a miracle of God when you're married." The baby's birth was never shown. The film ended with a pair of green-gloved hands placing a bundle in the woman's arms. She was fully dressed.

Sister Scott flipped on the overhead lights. "Any questions, girls?" She didn't wait for a response. "Good. You're dismissed."

On the gym stairs, Mary Kay Baldwin spoke to Lily for the first time. "Do they think we don't know *anything*? Like nobody would have told us by now? That's a totally eighth-grade movie."

Lily said nothing. What she knew about sex she'd learned from Agatha's magazines—in 1940 there was a doctor in Beverly Hills whose specialty was making movie stars not be pregnant, but the magazine did not tell how—and from Agatha's allusions to her own miscarriages.

All Lily ever told us about Reid Alistair, the man who was our father, was that he led a master class at the New Orleans Ballet when he was nineteen. No matter how often we asked, she refused to describe what he looked like. I made up Reid Alistair myself: wide cheekbones, large eyes, light-brown hair. Sometimes I pictured him as Nureyev or Nijinsky, the only male ballet dancers whose pictures I'd ever seen.

"I live in Mississippi," Lily heard him tell one of the other dancers. "Pass Christian." Her heart stuttered in her chest: Reid grew up in the city her parents had been on their way to visit when they died. All her life it had been a city that couldn't be reached, a place that didn't exist because her parents had never found it, like Dorothy's Oz. Reid Alistair had traveled to Germany, Austria, and Switzerland to perform, but he lived in his parents' house in Mississippi.

Her heartbeat quickened. From the side of the room, where she sat by the box of rosin, preparing for class, Lily studied Reid's body. Male dancers were not as thin as female dancers. His back and chest were laced with muscle under his T-shirt and his legs looked strong. During the master class, Lily danced well and hoped Reid noticed her. "*Tendu en arrière, tendu devant,*" he called, clapping his hands. Sweat trailed down her neck. She was exhausted. "*Plié. Plié. Plié.*" Madame Makarov stood at the *barre* with her cane, but for the first and only time, Lily didn't care what Madame thought of her dancing.

After the class, Reid approached Lily. Her heart banged in her chest. She couldn't breathe. "You're a good dancer," he said. His voice was low, melodious, with a slight southern accent. "Madame was right about you."

"Thanks." Lily tried to sound casual, but her voice was a whisper. She looked down at the floor.

"Do you want to get some coffee? A bunch of us are going to La Madeline."

Often, after master classes, the New Orleans Ballet dancers went out, always to La Madeline, a café in the French Quarter, but as a ballet student she'd never been invited. "Yes, thanks," she said, copying Judy Garland in the interview from *Child Star.*

Lily's story always stopped at this point. She never told us what happened with Reid Alistair after this moment: how coffee at La Madeline with a group of dancers turned into a sexual encounter. Instead her narrative resumed after midnight when she stood on the front steps of her house, fitting her key into the lock, and realized that Agatha had chained the door shut. Agatha hadn't put the chain on the front door since the night Lily's parents died.

Lily sat down on the steps and rested her head on her knees. She knew she should have called to tell Agatha she'd be late—more than nine hours late—but she also knew Agatha wouldn't have let her go to La Madeline, and she could never tell Agatha about Reid Alistair. He'd be her secret.

As she sat alone in front of Agatha's house, Lily remembered a story about Judy Garland she'd read in one of Agatha's *Modern Screens*. In this story, Judy Garland's mother abandons her in a motel room in a strange new city as a punishment, then returns when her daughter is sufficiently scared. First, the mother packs her suitcase, saying, "I'm leaving because you're bad." Then she walks toward the motel room door, while her daughter pleads with her to stay. Judy's crying makes no difference. When she leaves, the mother locks the girl in, then stands outside the locked door, listening. Finally, when her daughter stops sobbing, she returns. Then she allows Judy to beg for forgiveness.

Agatha wasn't standing on the other side of the door. Lily curled herself up on the steps, covering her legs with her coat, making her body as small as she could. She fell asleep.

February of her senior year: Lily stood alone in her room before the mirror on the door, checking herself, holding her breath. She'd been to Delta Women's Clinic on Airline Highway where a vial of blood was drawn from her arm. Then the nurse confirmed her fear.

In ballet class, during the warm-up at the *barre,* she practiced her movements and tried to ignore the panic that rose in her throat. Her body didn't yet display her terrible mistake. Lily told herself that she could stop what was happening. At home, each night, she did extra sets of sit-ups on her bedroom floor until her muscles burned. She increased the frequency of the vinegar trick. Instead of her finger, she used her toothbrush: by touching the back of her throat with the bristles she was able to vomit three times a day.

In her assignment book, her food lists became shorter: "2/6/64: 1 apple, ½ piece of toast." Lily was always hungry and constantly told lies. "I ate with the girls after class," she said to Agatha when she came home. "I already had dinner." On Saturdays, she said, "I just have too much homework to go to movies any-more." Agatha must have known something was wrong, but since the night when Lily was late, Agatha hadn't invited her to the Prytania, hadn't braided her hair to look like Agnes, hadn't touched her. Agatha barely spoke to her now.

Lily promised herself she'd make up the fight with her grand-mother as soon as she got her body under control. Leaning out the window of her bedroom, she smoked cigarette after cigarette. The new routine: ¼ piece of toast, cut into thirty pieces, chewed thirty times. She stopped drinking water: it added weight. Each morning, she sucked ten ice chips, then allowed herself five at night. Vinegar burned her throat. She hoped that if she exercised hard enough, if she felt enough pain in her muscles, her body would cooperate and she'd stop being pregnant. She couldn't tell Reid Alistair. After his master class, he'd returned to Pass Christian, but Madame Makarov said once that he was touring Switzerland with the Zurich Ballet. She couldn't imagine calling his parents' house in Mississippi and explaining what had happened.

Soon Lily couldn't stop herself: she ate. Despite the exercise, the smoking, the vinegar trick, she was unable to kill her appetite completely. All day, she could be good, eating only the toast and ice chips, but by midnight, she couldn't stand her hunger anymore. After she was sure that Agatha had gone to bed, Lily sneaked into the kitchen. She sat down on the floor in front of the refrigerator and always began with something small and negligible—a spoonful of mustard, a single egg noodle. Inevitably, she'd then turn to the more filling, dangerous foods, the ones she craved that she knew would add weight. She ate goulash out of the crock-pot with her hands. She drank milk straight from the carton. She swallowed cubes of butter. As she ate, she hated herself for it, but hunger won out. When she finished, she drank extra vinegar upstairs in her room and vomited.

In the third month of Lily's pregnancy, the New Orleans Ballet was scheduled to do a benefit at Women and Children's Hospital, a production of *The Red Shoes,* performed for the children's orthopedic ward. Madame Makarov had chosen Lily for the lead role: the girl who wears the magic shoes. "I want you for this part, Lily. We will see how you do." She tapped Lily's knees with her cane. "And I would like you to lose some of this weight."

"Yes. I will." Lily felt dizzy. She wanted nothing more than to put her head between her legs or to lie down in the corner of the practice room.

"Are you feeling well?" Madame asked.

"I'm fine." Lily forced her face into a smile.

That night, after she had done the vinegar trick three times and there was nothing left in her stomach, she weighed herself on the scale she kept underneath her bed. "One hundred and seven pounds," she said aloud. She lay down on the floor and pressed her face to the carpet. "No," she whispered, as if a single word could stop what was happening inside her body. "No! No! No!"

2

In Sarasota, this is the summer I wear Helen's clothes. Helen's closet spans the twentieth century. "Clothes are my memory," she told me. "I saved all the clothes I wore on important days. I still have the dress I wore when I was twelve on the day my mother died." Helen is my student. She is eighty-five years old. After I met her two weeks ago in the art class I teach at Beachaven, a nursing home on Siesta Key, she invited me into her room at the end of the hall. In her tidy, crowded room, she handed me a box. "New clothes, new life. Open it." The box was stacked with beaded angora sweaters, circle skirts, chiffon scarves patterned with roses. All 1940s clothes, the kind my sister and I looked for in trash cans when we were children. "I've been waiting for someone I could give these to," Helen said. I touched the sleeve of a pink taffeta dress. Helen didn't know I hadn't worn clothes like these since I left Madeline, since I married Owen and moved to Atlanta.

This morning, in the bedroom, while Owen sleeps, I dress quickly in the dark in one of Helen's outfits: a black cardigan, an organza skirt, pumps with rhinestones clipped to tiny pointed toes. I study myself in the full-length mirror on the bedroom wall. Nothing quite fits anymore. The skirt is tight around my waist, the sweater's pearl buttons strain over my breasts. In art school, the first class I took was Anatomy of the Human Form. I memorized a plastic model of a woman's body, piece by piece, in which everything was visible: organs, veins, muscles, bones. When I look at myself now I wish I could see beneath the skin. I wish I had proof that inside it's the same body I used to have, before the pregnancy.

When Owen and I moved back to Sarasota, I brought only one outfit, a striped sundress. Owen bought it for me after the baby died when I didn't want to leave the house. I liked it because it didn't remind me of anything in my life. I had worn it every day until Helen offered me her clothes. After several days, the sundress lost its department store smell and became wrinkled and damp with sweat. The straps wilted, the hem drooped. I knew Owen wanted to tell me I should change my clothes or at least wash the dress, but he said nothing. I know he was relieved when I began wearing Helen's clothes.

In bed, Owen stirs, turns over, and slides his hand into the empty space I've left. Asleep, he looks like a child, his face puffed, his red hair sticking to his forehead. I touch his arm gently, careful not to wake him. I want to touch him, to feel his skin against mine, but I'm afraid to do it unless he's asleep because I don't want my touch to lead to anything. On a pile of his linguistics books in the corner is the wood-block print I gave him for his last birthday, when I had just found out I was pregnant. I made a print of the three of us together—Owen, me, and our child. I modeled my first sketch on Käthe Kollwitz's prints, but the sketch looked too sad. In the final version, Owen is the only one of us who looks happy. The baby and I have melancholy eyes and tight, closed mouths. The print is the only piece I've done all year.

I tiptoe down the hall and into the kitchen. Our sublet house has an enormous kitchen, painted pink, with a table we could set for ten, as if we could have a huge family dinner. I open the refrigerator and stand inside the beam of light cast on the floor. On the three gleaming metal shelves is Owen's food—a cylinder of cookie dough and a carton of strawberry milk. When I first met him, I was charmed by Owen's love of children's food, food my sister and I had never been allowed to eat, food it had always been easy for me to refuse. This summer my refusals have become easier and easier, and I need harder tasks, greater punishments to test my control over my body. Shutting the refrigerator door, I kneel on the floor to find the bottle of vinegar hidden below the sink.

After Owen and I were married, until the pregnancy, I stopped the vinegar trick. But after the baby died this April, I drank vinegar every day. I didn't tell the doctors about this cure. I came home from the long afternoons at the hospital, the failed inductions of labor, and drank vinegar straight from the bottle. I wasn't trying to make myself throw up. I was hoping the vinegar would poison my body and start the delivery, release her. I was hoping I would not have to wake up another morning feeling her motionless weight under my ribs, her body crowding mine.

Now, when I take a long, slow sip, my throat burns. The vinegar drink does what Helen's clothes can't: it comforts me.

In Atlanta, Owen took apart the crib. From the doorway, I watched him unscrew the red metal bars. I couldn't enter the baby's room.

When I was pregnant, I spent most of the day in her room. I brought in my art supplies and sat on the bare wood floor, working. I designed a mural: a row of girl saints holding hands, dancing together like paper dolls cut from the same sheet of paper. I filled my sketchbook with faces of the saints copied from *A Girl's Guide to the Saints*, a book Madeline and I had been given in elementary school.

We planned to name her Frida, after the Mexican artist Frida Kahlo, and her middle name was to be Agnes, after my great-grandmother's sister. Owen liked the sound of the two words together. I wanted the baby to be named after my favorite artist and a woman in my family. I didn't want to call her Lily or Madeline. I spent months planning a Frida Kahlo mobile to hang above the crib: tiny self-portraits of the artist hung on wire suspended beside monkeys and parrots, all the images glued to wood and washed with blue and green, and beside them quotes from Frida Kahlo's diary pages. I used details from paintings by Frida Kahlo and Diego Rivera for the birth announcement. I planned to write the name, date, and her weight and height in calligraphy over a wood-block print of a door strung with bright, dramatic flowers: birds of paradise, spider mums, snapdragons. On each announcement, the flowers would be shaded a different color.

After the baby died, all my sketches and drawings were piled in a corner of the room beside the crib. "Throw that stuff away," I told Owen. "Please throw it away." My throat ached when I spoke.

He boxed the clothes we'd bought, undershirts and booties, sleepers, tiny knitted hats, and sealed the boxes with strapping tape. My eyes closed. I listened to the rip of the tape from the roll as he stretched it around each box. Finally he said, "What do you want to do with the boxes? Should I take them to Goodwill?"

I was surprised by my own answer. "Leave them in front of the house. Someone'll probably steal them." I pictured two children, twin sisters resembling Madeline and me, searching trash cans on garbage nights. I didn't want a pregnant woman to buy the clothes. I liked the idea that the baby clothes would be found accidentally by people who had no use for them.

"Alice, I don't—" But he didn't finish the sentence. "I'll be back in a little while." From the window of the baby's room, I watched him load the boxes into the car.

When Madeline called and said she needed me, Owen didn't want to come back here. We hadn't been back in three years, since we got married. "The last place you should be is Sarasota," he said. "You don't want to be reminded of the past now." I nodded, thinking of his word choice: in Sarasota I wouldn't be reminded of the past, I would reenter it. With Madeline, nothing was ever less than overwhelming.

The next day Owen cleaned out the baby's room while I watched him, and then he said, "Maybe getting away from the house would be good for us." I knew what he meant: we needed to leave the house in which we'd prepared the room, the world in which we'd made ourselves ready, planned for our future, imagined another life.

After the vinegar, I'm steady enough to drive. I gather my purse, my sketchbook, and the car keys. "I'm leaving," I call down the hall. Owen and I never leave the house without telling each other, but I don't want him to ask where I am going. I reach the front door, and my hand is already closing over the knob, before he finds me. He looks at my outfit but says nothing. Naked, except for a towel decorated with huge pink flowers wrapped around his waist, he looks tired and sad. For a moment, I want to drop everything I'm holding and wrap my arms around him, press myself against his body. A year ago, I would have done it.

"Hey," he says, "do you want me to come with you? Do you want to go to breakfast?"

As usual, I lie. "I already ate."

He doesn't believe me. Unlike my sister, I'm a terrible liar. Still I'm relieved to be engaged in a familiar conversation. Since the beginning of our relationship, Owen and I have always argued about food. "You're thin enough," he'd say. "Stop dieting." But I wasn't dieting. I was doing what Lily taught us to do: *fasting, starving, emptying*.

Owen runs his hand through his hair, a gesture of frustration I recognize. Suddenly I remember the touch of his hand running up and down my body, from my hair to my hips, his fingers grazing the surface of my skin. I bite the inside of my cheek. I can't let myself think about this.

He pauses, then asks, "Are you going to see Madeline?"

We came back to Sarasota because my sister had called and said she needed me. In the three years since I married Owen and moved away, Madeline had called me only three times, once each year on our birthday, three short conversations. Occasionally, she'd send me newspaper clippings or articles about twins. She wanted to punish me for leaving, but she also needed to remind me that the connection between us couldn't be broken, no matter where I lived. Now, every day for the nine days we've been back in Sarasota, whenever I leave the house, Owen asks me if I'm going to see my sister. I haven't seen her yet. I'm afraid to go to the house. Every day for nine days, as if she knows I'm nervous about seeing her, Madeline has sent me a Judy Garland postcard, her version of a warning. Nine postcards, one for each day I haven't gone to see her, postcards of Judy Garland as Dorothy, as Mickey Rooney's girlfriend, as Esther Blodgett from *A Star is Born*, and staged shots of her singing. Madeline never writes anything on the message side, and none of the cards is postmarked, so she must deliver them herself.

"I'm going for a drive," I tell Owen.

Owen sits down on the floor of the hall. The pink towel slips from his waist, and I avert my eyes. I'm afraid to look at his body now, as if one glance might lead us to another disaster. "It's just seven o'clock. Nothing's open, Alice. There's nowhere to go."

"I know. I can't sleep." I twist the strap of my purse around my wrist, hoping he'll give up.

"Try to sleep a little more. At least lie down on the couch." The suggestion makes my chest tighten. In our old life, Owen would never have suggested that I sleep on the couch. He would have called me back to bed with him.

"I can't." My voice is almost a whisper. "I really have to go." I want to kiss him. I want to draw him close to me, but instead I open the door and start quickly down the sidewalk. In the car, I force myself to take deep breaths. He's right: there's nowhere to go. I put the car in gear and start down Midnight Pass.

Before the pregnancy, Owen and I used to stay up all night working. "We're going to be a famous intellectual couple," I told him one night early in our marriage. "Simone de Beauvoir and Jean-Paul Sartre." He smiled at me and said, "Georgia O'Keeffe and Alfred Stieglitz." Wearing his headphones, he sat at the kitchen table transcribing language-acquisition tapes. Since he got his Ph.D. three years ago, Owen has been working on a section of the new linguistic atlas of the United States. It's a collaborative project, and he was assigned part of the South—Louisiana, Mississippi, and Georgia. At least one week of every month he spends on the road, interviewing inhabitants of small towns. His job is to interest them in any subject in order to record the speech patterns of the region. He hopes for certain phonemes or words that might be inflected differently in different towns. First he asks a question about cows or snake farms or summer storms, anything to start the people talking. Above the kitchen table was a large photograph of the mouth and throat with dotted arrows pointing to the essential places for his work: the pharynx, the uvula, the epiglottis.

I lay on the floor beside him and worked on sketches for my wood-block prints of Patty Hearst and the Symbionese Liberation Army. Lying down has always been my ideal position for drawing. When I glanced up from my sketchbook, I could see Owen's ankle tapping the chair, in rhythm with the rise and fall of the voice he had recorded on the tape. I had never in my life sat silently with Madeline. With Owen, I found those long nights of silent work strangely erotic. Owen suggested the title for my print series: *Silence I, II, III.* The first print is of Hearst Castle in San Simeon, California, with Patty and her sisters as children, playing freeze-tag in a marble fountain. In the second is the safehouse closet where she slept for months, different men breaking into the tiny room all night. The third depicts the Hibernia Bank robbery, with Patty disguised as Tania, her new identity, in a red wig. These prints are among my favorite work in my portfolio and the last project I completed before I became pregnant last fall.

"I like them, but they're pretty grim," Owen said when he surveyed the completed project. He didn't seem to understand the connection I wanted to make in the piece between childhood and danger. He could have been one of the children I studied carefully when I was a little girl living at the Star Dust Motel, a child who scattered his sand toys in an unfamiliar room, slept in a rented cot for a week, then left. Owen might have been one of the children I watched with envy when I played dress-up with Madeline between cars in the motel parking lot.

* * *

When I drive through Sarasota in the early morning, I look for places to start over, where no one will know me. I've been going to one trailer park each day. The trailer parks are full of families living temporary lives. If you rent a trailer, it's stocked with everything from sheets to forks and spoons. All you need are your own clothes.

This morning, I cross the Siesta Key Bridge on Midnight Pass, five miles from where Madeline lives. Midnight Pass is crowded with rows of trailers set on identical squares of land by the bay. I'm working my way through them in order. Beside a sign stuck in the sand—TROPICAL ISLAND TRAILERS WHERE YOUR TRAVEL DREAMS COME TRUE—I park the car and cross the grass to the rental office. A sign taped to the door reads COME IN, but no one answers when I knock. I knock again, and a woman opens the screen door a few inches and says, "Yes?" in an annoyed voice. She wears a bathing suit top and a plaid tennis skirt. Her cheek is creased from a pillow. I woke her up.

"Hi, I saw your sign out front. I just moved here from Atlanta. Do you have a vacancy?"

The woman opens the door wider. She studies my outfit. Her gaze rests on my rhinestone shoes. "Well," she says, repeating what she has obviously said many times before. "We rent by the week. Or the day, if you want. No parking. No pets. Why would you leave a nice place like Atlanta to move into a trailer down here?"

"A family emergency." Madeline would appreciate the phrase; it's both vague and dramatic. I lower my gaze to the sidewalk to make the woman wonder what's wrong in our family, a gesture borrowed from Madeline. "I'm looking for something more permanent than a week. I might be living here for a while."

She hands me a key attached to a rubber band from a rack behind her. "Take this and check out number seven. When you come back, you can pay me for the first week."

I study the walls of aluminum siding and the flat roofs reflecting the sun like mirrors held up to the sky. Inside trailer number seven, I shut the thin door and latch it, then find the bed that unfolds from the ceiling. Every trailer I've been in has one of these beds, bigger than a single but not the right size to be a double. I kick off Helen's shoes and lie down on the mattress, pulling my knees to my chest. If I lived here, I'd have one towel, one spoon, one plate, one book, like a hermit in a fairy tale.

Owen and I met at Happyland, the aquarium on Siesta Key. I was twenty-six and had been living alone with Madeline for eight years. Each afternoon, after my art class at the Ringling School and after my shift at the campus bookstore, I sat in aquariums working on sketches of starfish and sea bass.

The afternoon we met, Happyland was almost empty. On a bench in front of the indoor shark tank I drafted the outline of a fin. I felt the presence of another person on the bench and glanced over at the man who had sat down beside me. He held a small tape recorder against his face and a graph paper notebook in his lap.

For more than an hour, he and I sat in silence in front of the tank and watched the sharks. Finally he spoke. "Is that a sketch for a painting or part of a larger work?"

I didn't look up, and I didn't answer. I wanted him to know I wasn't the kind of woman who let strange men pick her up in aquariums. Madeline's boyfriends were all men she had met in this fashion—at the grocery store, on the beach, on the street in a passing car.

"Could I ask you something?"

I felt my face flush, my skin burned. This man was about to openly proposition me in front of the shark tank. Madeline would love him. "What?"

"Would you mind speaking one or two words into the tape recorder? I'm writing an article on children's language acquisition, and I've been conducting an experiment at a lab in Georgia using human voices. I'll tell you the words and you repeat them. Okay?"

For the first time, I looked directly at the man. He was tall, with a serious expression and dark red hair. Madeline and I had always wanted red hair. Our great-grandmother and her twin sister both had red hair. He wore gray pants and a T-shirt that said *Atlanta* in faded green script.

A few minutes later, I repeated his words. "*Boat. Street. Car.*" They were ordinary words, but when I said them into the tape recorder I pretended they were magic, rolling off my tongue, passing from me to him. I shivered, though Happyland was warm. All afternoon we sat together on a bench by the shark tank. During the conversation, he fixed his gaze on my mouth, not my eyes where I had always thought all men wanted to look. "You can tell so much about a person by looking at their mouth," he said. I imagined the two of us in bed, as he traced the outline of my lips, the tips of his fingers barely grazing my skin. "Lick your lips," he'd direct me, then he'd kiss the places where my tongue had been.

"I love your voice. Go on, say more," Owen said, in the same way that Madeline said men told her "I love your body." No one had ever told me to keep talking.

I was attracted to his loneliness. He told me he was an only child. "Isn't it awful not to have siblings?" I asked. "I can't imagine my life without my sister."

"I've never known anything different," he said. "Tell me about Madeline."

After that first afternoon we talked, I knew Owen was not like other men. No one in my life had ever loved the sound of my voice. Early in our relationship, Owen liked to record me. On the beach, while having coffee in a restaurant, or as we drove in the car, he'd suddenly interrupt. "Say that again. That's great." He held the tape recorder up to my face as I repeated my favorite colors of paint. "You should see the way your mouth curved when you said *indigo*. You sound so beautiful. Look in the mirror when you say that word." Later, when I watched myself speaking in the mirror, I saw nothing unusual, but I felt transformed. *Alizarin Crimson*. I moved under him. *Magenta*. Each word slid over our skin, smooth as a silk sheet.

After the trailer park, I drive to a Catholic church. I'm in time for the 10 A.M. healing mass. I've gone to a different church each day since arriving here, each one a name I found in the Sarasota phone book. Today I choose Our Lady of the Seven Sorrows, a contemporary church on Tamiami Trail, built with blond wood and few windows, perched on the side of the highway like an enormous flightless bird. I prefer the old-fashioned churches, with their spires and high ceilings, but I'm running out of Sarasota's Catholic churches.

In the vestibule, I walk straight to the statue of blue-robed Mary, Helen's shoes echoing on the stone floor. In high school, we were taught that prayers for lost children should be directed to the Holy Mother. I strike a match, touch it to the wick of one of the candles that circle Mary's feet. I try to formulate a prayer to her—"Think of it as a letter," the nuns told us in school—but I can't feel anything. I can't feel the presence of anyone I ever loved. Madeline. Lily. I want to feel Owen, but he's the hardest. Instead, I see the one person I never met, the baby that died this April before she was born. She floats on the surface of my eyelids, her arms like wings, her lips parted in a tiny, perfect smile. I see her moon face, blue eyes filling with water, reaching her huge arms out to me for a last kiss. Only in the churches can I let myself feel my daughter alive. Where is she—hidden in the recesses of the sanctuary, hovering at the edges of the stained-glass window, curled inside the silver chalice where she has made herself small?

"Whoever was the first to represent babies as cherubs or tiny angels was completely wrong. No one should have ever put Cupid on a valentine," I said to Owen as he sat with me in the hospital room at Georgia Medical Center this April. We had been told that the ultrasound now revealed no fetal heartbeat. All afternoon we waited for the other test results to confirm what we knew. I felt it was important to keep talking. If there was a moment of silence between us, one of us might cry. If we started to cry, we would be unable to stop. I had to keep talking. "Do you know that if a baby were eight feet tall, bigger than an adult, it could kill you?" The baby had died and I was told I had to wait three weeks until the doctor could safely induce labor. "A baby as big as an adult would have no morals and no sense of right and wrong but it would be stronger than you," I said. Owen nodded without speaking and covered my fingers with his hand.

I keep an aspirin bottle of vinegar in my purse for emergencies, moments when I remember the pregnancy and the baby's death. Now I twist off the child-proof cap and take a small sip. The mass begins. As in every church I've found in Sarasota, only old women attend the healing service. Heads covered in prayer shawls, they wait together in a line at the altar. I don't think they're praying for their children. They must be praying for their husbands, their friends, themselves. Touching their foreheads with the healing oils, the priest blesses each of them. I sit alone at the back of the church, Helen's black sweater pulled tightly around my breasts. If I knelt at the altar and swallowed the wafer, I would choke.

*   *   *

In our first session last week, my new therapist, Dr. Levy, suggested that I document the baby's life and death. "Make your daughter's life real," she said. "Women often find that in cases of miscarriage and stillbirth it's very healing to put together a representation of the event." Dr. Levy is a psychiatrist recommended by the doctors at Georgia Medical Center in Atlanta. I was told she specializes in "bereavement counseling." I imagine her sitting at her desk, facing person after person in a state of grief—father, mother, sister, friend. Yet she never looks tired. Her makeup is carefully applied, her silk suits ironed. Her nails are buffed to a perfect shell pink.

Before our first session, she administered a Rorschach test. "This is standard procedure," she told me. "Don't be nervous." I knew Madeline must have been given the Rorschach test when she was in the hospital too. Dr. Levy led me down the hall. Under a single window, which I suspected was a mirror, I sat at a table and stared at the ink blots. I could envision nothing but blobs of black ink, and I thought about how, early in our relationship, Owen pointed out the shapes of constellations in the night sky and I could see none of them, and I lied. "Here's a family of dead children," I said as I touched the edges of the paper. "Their mothers have left. All little girls no older than twelve."

"An art project?" I asked, unable to imagine myself taping lab reports, the death certificate, and the order form for the cemetery plot into a leather-bound book.

Dr. Levy continued, "Not necessarily a work of art, but a way to create meaning from the loss. As an artist, you may find this particularly helpful."

I nodded. I didn't tell her that I wasn't an artist anymore, that I found it impossible to paint or draw anything, that I didn't care if I ever worked on art projects again.

Instead of the scrapbook, I decided to make cakes of babies and children in different styles. A cake seemed better, easier, and after I made one, it could be thrown away. For ideas, I read library books on child care and texts about medieval illumination. Flipping through *Dr. Spock*, I tried to ignore the advice on mothering: don't let your child cry in her crib for hours to teach her a lesson, don't breast-feed after your baby is one year old. The book contained a few pictures, drawings of the stages of child development, but when I sketched, the children I drew looked wrong, their hands and feet twisted like claws, their faces frozen in tiny mean smiles. All I could envision were creatures out of Hieronymus Bosch paintings: small girls and boys with horns and forked tongues.

Once, Owen glanced at a drawing in my sketchbook, a baby with spiked teeth and claws. "I'm going to make a cake," I said. "It's Dr. Levy's idea."

"That's going to be an interesting cake. Don't bring it to birthday parties."

"I'm supposed to be mastering the trauma. Art as therapy." I turned the charcoal on its flat side to shade a baby's leg. The body resembled a chicken, the fine bones twisted into knobs. I sketched a line of feathers on the thigh.

"You don't believe in that, do you?" I heard the edge of disappointment in his voice. He paused. "Did you bring the slides you took of your thesis?" Owen had urged me to bring my portfolio to Sarasota so I could show it to art departments when I looked for a summer teaching job, but I'd left it behind. My M.F.A. thesis sits on our bedroom floor in Atlanta: a large wood-block triptych of Catherine of Siena, Joan of Arc, and Bette Davis. As a child, I loved the stories of the saints, stories of miracles and tortures. Ignatius successfully fought off wild beasts in the Colosseum, but I was always more interested in the pain and triumph of the women and the little girls: St. Rose growing weaker and weaker, starving in the garden to reach God, or St. Teresa proclaiming her desire for as many torments as possible—"Martyrdom! The dream of my childhood!"

My work used to be large, but now the world has narrowed, limited itself so much that all I can manage is a cake.

"Owen?" I call when I open the door to the house. There's no answer.

Our rented house belongs to a retired couple who spend their summers in Maine to escape the heat. In addition to the pink kitchen, it has two bedrooms, a kitchen, and a living room, all furnished in various floral patterns—damask roses big as dinner plates on the fabric of the couch, a grapevine snaking across the wallpaper in the front hall, plastic crocuses stuck in jelly jars on every windowsill—and a basement the owners had converted to a bomb shelter. In the cupboards that line the stone walls, they've stockpiled cans of soup and bottled water. Hurricane lamps illuminate small circles of light in each corner of the room. The closet is stacked with cement bricks and sandbags. I like the bomb-shelter basement. It's like a safe, soundproof campground, as if the owners of the house were preparing for what they thought the future might be like in the 1950s. Owen wanted me to take the basement as my studio, but I said no. Now I sit in the bomb-shelter basement and sketch my ideas for cakes.

Owen walks down the stairs. I turn my sketchbook over on my lap. I don't ask him where he's been and he doesn't mention my departure from the house this morning. "You got another postcard from Madeline," he says, handing it to me.

On one side of the card is the saddest photograph of Judy Garland I've ever seen. It must have been taken shortly before her death. Staring straight at the camera, she looks dazed, her hair thin and twisted over her ears. Her expression is a thin, false smile. Her skin is loose and wrinkled around her mouth and eyes. I flip the postcard over, expecting that, as usual, there will be no message. But for the first time, my sister has written a single line of text. I read *Madeline + Alice + Lily = A Family* written in careful cursive script.

Owen looks over my shoulder at the message. "What's this about? Why is she talking about Lily?"

I stare at that word *Lily*, our mother's name, the name of the woman who left us eleven years ago. And the other, *Family*. In the secret language my sister and I invented when we were children, the twin language, mathematical symbols linked our words together. We described the world in terms of *plus* or *minus*, *greater than* or *less than*. A family was a relation of three.

"I don't know. Tomorrow, I'm going to see her." I slip the card beneath my sketchbook. I've known for nine days that the cards signify danger. The tenth postcard confirms this. I can no longer ignore my sister.

"Maybe she just wants to be with you on your birthday," Owen says. The birthday Madeline and I share is in four days. "I bet that's it." He sounds as if he's trying to convince himself.

"I hope that's what she wants. I don't know why she'd mention Lily."

I haven't told Owen, but since the pregnancy I've been thinking about Lily too. When the baby died, I'd wanted my mother for the first time in years. After she left us, I'd trained myself not to think of her, but with the pregnancy, memories of her began flooding back. I can't talk to him about Lily now because he's the person I should want. He should be the one to help me recover from our loss.

*   *   *

My pregnancy was too easy. I'd read magazine stories about women who kept elaborate charts, using a basal thermometer, who checked their cervical mucus every day, who waited and waited for their bodies to change. But I became pregnant after only three months, and I believed I understood the dangers. "You already know your blood type is Rh-negative. The Rh factor should cause you no problems whatsoever," my doctor said during our first appointment. Owen and I sat side by side in plastic chairs in the examining room. "No one has to die from Rh disease anymore. A mother giving birth can only lose her own life if she's given a massive transfusion of Rh-positive blood." She smiled kindly at me.

"Can I have an amniocentesis?" I asked. I wanted to be sure we'd be safe from everything.

"We generally only do the procedure for patients over thirty-five. But if you feel you need it, we can do it."

The amnio confirmed what the ultrasound technician had said: the baby was a girl and she was fine. I'd hoped for a girl. Now, as Frida Agnes, she was real. The lab technician gave us a copy of the sonogram, a picture of her taken at nineteen weeks, and I put it in my wallet. For seven months, the baby woke and slept inside me. I rested my hand on my stomach and felt her body shift and turn. I could feel her movements; I guessed at her moods. *Frida, Frida, Frida.* Owen and I both talked to her, building an imaginary world for her inside my body.

Owen and I couldn't see what was ahead. We couldn't envision where we'd be, in the end: the waiting room of Georgia Medical Center's obstetrics and gynecology clinic waiting together for my IV sessions to induce labor and end the pregnancy that was already over. Three times, we entered a small windowless room, Owen helped me to unbutton my dress, tie on a paper gown, and steady my balance as I lay down and the needle dripped Pitocin from a bag above my head into my arm.

At twenty-nine weeks, the baby stopped moving. I didn't think this could happen. According to the medical facts my doctor had related, according to everything I'd read, the first child of a mother with Rh-negative blood should be unaffected by the factor. The rhesus gamma globulin injection is given within seventy-two hours of the first child's birth as protection for the future. I was sure this shot would make me safe. After the RhoGAM, my doctors had explained, none of my other children would be affected. My case was called "an extremely rare exception." My body was sensitized immediately, when my first pregnancy was in its early weeks, and began to produce antibodies, reading the baby's blood cells as foreign invaders. Finally, I was told, in my exceptional case, the shot of RhoGAM would've been useless.

At twenty-nine weeks, most babies have a good chance of survival if delivered right away. "A premature birth is not a death sentence," I read in one of my pregnancy books. "With current medical technology, we can save babies that weigh as little as two pounds." A baby at twenty-nine weeks, sixteen inches long, can weigh as much as three and a half pounds. At twenty-nine weeks, instead of a child, Owen and I were given a new vocabulary: *fetal distress, Rh incompatibility, exchange transfusion, bilirubin, high-risk.*

That afternoon, I start a birthday cake for Madeline. In my favorite illustration from *A Girl's Guide to the Saints,* the nail-studded Catherine Wheel was huge, dwarfing the child standing beside it, the magic girl who used the forces she found in God to turn her torture instrument to dust. Catherine's miracle has always seemed to me to be the best kind: at one touch of her body the wheel shattered on the ground. Overcome with amazement, her torturers gave up, and she was taken directly up to the kingdom of heaven.

Unlike a painting, when I make a cake I follow a strict plan. First, I conceive of the design, then make a preliminary sketch. To find the recipe, I study *The Cake Bible*. All measurements must be perfect and exact. I love the moments of anticipation best. The layer pans wait in a line on the counter, the silver measuring cup clean and ready. I smooth the sugar with a knife, cream butter to a froth with milk. Sugar glitters on my fingers. The smell of baking is so different from the smell of my studio in Atlanta and the class-rooms in art school. I used to love the smell of the studio: paint, turpentine, the green gel I used to clean the paint from my hands. The cake will bake and fill the kitchen with the sweetness of sugar and butter, a smell that sickens me.

I start Madeline's cake over three times. First, I find a recipe, a three-layer white chocolate cake. Next I draw the pattern quickly in my sketchbook, but it is difficult to make the shape of the knives that line the wheel look exactly right with small triangles of alu-minum foil. The figure of Catherine herself is also hard. Finally, at the end of the afternoon, I drive to a bakery in the nearby mall and buy a centerpiece designed for the top of a wedding cake. At home, I use the sharpest point of my X-acto knife to saw the two bodies apart. I throw out the black-suited groom. I set the bride alone in the middle of the cake.

3

"Are you feeling well?" Madame Makarov stood in the doorway of the dressing room, smoking, dressed in black silk for *The Red Shoes* benefit performance. She now asked Lily this question at least once every day. Lily tried to smile, uncomfortable under her teacher's gaze. "Is something wrong?" Madame's voice was sharp. Lily shook her head. She sucked in her stomach, waiting for Madame to comment on her weight, and smoothed powder onto her cheeks with a sponge. She knew her face was already pale, and her eyes were ringed with shadows. Although she'd stretched on the floor and at the *barre,* her muscles didn't feel loose. Her chest was tight. "Fifteen minutes to curtain." Madame tapped her cigarette against the door. She walked down the hall.

Lily couldn't speak. If she responded to Madame Makarov, she knew she'd cry. Madame could clearly sense something was wrong, and she could probably guess about Lily's secret eating. Lily sneaked into the kitchen every night now. She looked down at her breasts, which she'd tried to flatten with masking tape under her red leotard, and her stomach, which was puffed. As she laced her toe shoes, she tried to make herself believe she was nervous because Agatha was in the audience. In the three months since her grandmother had locked her out, they'd barely spoken. Agatha walked to the Prytania each Saturday alone, no longer asking Lily if she wanted to go. Her silence terrified Lily, who left as early as she could for school each morning and stayed at the New Orleans Ballet as late as she could after school, until Agatha had gone to bed. Lily told herself this new schedule was better. For hours each day, she'd taken class, gone to rehearsal, then practiced on her own, hoping to regain control over her body.

"The first mistake I made was looking at the audience," Lily told us later. "The kids distracted me." Children from the hospital filled the auditorium; many waited in the aisles in wheelchairs, some held crutches on their laps. When Lily entered the stage in the first *glissade*, she knew instinctively that her steps were wrong. Her feet moved across the floor, yet she was off balance. The orchestra's music thudded in her chest, but her movements seemed to have no relation to its rhythm. She kept dancing, counting off the steps in her head. *Glissade. Glissade. Glissade.*

Ten minutes into the first act of the ballet, when the witch turns the girl's bones to wood as punishment for her vanity, Lily lost her balance during a *grande jêté*. Her right leg slammed to the floor; she landed on her hip. She lay on the auditorium stage, one leg bent under her body. All she could think was that she shouldn't make a sound, that if she remained completely silent she could keep her secret. She squeezed her eyes shut, trying to focus on not crying. Her head ached. Agatha rushed to the stage, and the ushers yelled to the children in the audience, "Stay calm, stand back." When her grandmother bent over her, the sleeves of her black dress covering Lily like wings, for the first time since she found out she was pregnant, Lily began to cry.

She cried not from the pain but from her own failure, the secret she could no longer hide. Soon Agatha would know the truth. A paramedic lifted her from the stage onto a stretcher. "Easy now, that's a girl. You're just fine." Lily pretended not to hear him, acting as if she were unconscious because she couldn't bear to see anyone's face. She closed her eyes and hoped to die.

At Charity Hospital, on the psychiatric ward, the only place the doctors could think of to hide a pregnant teenager since the maternity ward was restricted to married women, Lily lay in a bed with slats on the sides that slid up and down like a crib. To keep from thinking, she focused all her attention on not eating.

Three times a day, candy stripers brought in a tray: cups of jello, slices of turkey, pale yellow dinner rolls. "I don't want it. Take it away," Lily always said. The candy stripers were all her age. Most of them were chubby. At night, when the ward was quiet, she pulled herself out of bed and did sit-ups and leg lifts on the floor, hoping that the combination of refusing food and continuing to exercise would end the pregnancy.

After two days of Lily's refusals, the head nurse carried in Lily's lunch tray. "The doctor has ordered an IV," she announced and slit open a package of needles. As she chose one to sink into Lily's arm, she said, "You can do whatever you want to yourself. We can't let you hurt your baby." She tapped the bag of fluid to start the flow of liquid. "Just so you know, the next step is an NG. It's a tube up your nose and down your throat. Everyone cries when we put it in."

Lily closed her eyes and tried not to picture a tube snaking up her nose and down her throat. Her body craved sleep, the blank kind, the kind without dreams. Every morning and evening, a nurse brought a paper cup of pills. With relief, she swallowed all the pills in the cup at once. On Demerol, she floated in and out of consciousness, surfacing as infrequently as possible in the dark water she imagined as her mind. Secretly she hoped the doctors would discover she suffered from a rare disease the clinic had incorrectly diagnosed as pregnancy. Or that she'd wake up and discover that the doctors on the ward had felt so sorry for her they'd solved her problem while she slept.

"Has my grandmother called?" she asked anyone who came into her room. The answer was always no. When she asked if she could make a call, the head nurse said, "There's a pay phone at the end of the hall, but you don't have phone privileges."

"I need to call my grandmother."

"What you need is bed rest. You're not allowed to get up. Some girls on this ward are locked in their rooms. I doubt you could get up and walk down the hall."

The head nurse was right: Lily didn't have the strength to rise from bed and drag herself down the hall. Each passing day, she felt more dizzy and exhausted. She stopped exercising.

One day, after she'd been on the ward for three weeks, she heard the door thud open, then shut. She closed her eyes so she wouldn't have to see the nurse.

The voice that spoke was not the nurse's voice. "Who is the boy who did this to you?" Lily sat up. Wearing a blue housedress, her face tired and drawn, Agatha stood beside the bed. She fingered her rosary beads. "I want you to tell me." Lily reached out to touch her grandmother, but Agatha stepped away. "Tell me. Tell me now."

"It doesn't matter," Lily said.

"It matters very much."

Lily pushed the blankets off her knees. "I don't care about him. I'm so glad you came—"

Agatha interrupted. "Marry the father. A respectable girl marries the father."

"I don't know where he is."

Agatha's mouth tightened. "Your mother would be disappointed in what you've become. She would turn over in her grave if she could see you. I'm glad she's not here." Lily was shocked to hear Agatha mention her mother, about whom they rarely spoke. "You've disobeyed the teachings of the Church, but that's not the worst part. You've disobeyed everything I taught you. I can't help you anymore." She dropped her rosary beads inside her sweater.

"I'm sorry——" Lily began. "Let's talk about something else. Tell me a story about Judy Garland."

"Those stories are over. I have a letter for you. Here." Agatha dropped a cream-colored envelope on the bed, turned from Lily, and left.

"Agatha!" Lily called. "Agatha!" Her grandmother didn't come back.

The note was from Madame Makarov, on the New Orleans Ballet stationery, two sentences telling Lily that the ballet could not hire her as planned. Included with the note was a clipping from the *Times-Picayune* society section with the headline "Girl Conceals Pregnancy to Be Ballet Star." To keep from crying about her grandmother, Lily made herself remember something Agatha had told her, a story about Judy Garland's first pregnancy. In the middle of filming *Babes on Broadway*, she discovered she was pregnant. Although she was married, MGM told her, "Motherhood does not suit Andy Hardy's girlfriend." The studio decided that it would be best for her career if she had an illegal abortion at Hollywood Hospital.

The day after Agatha's visit, Sister Scott sat beside her bed, her hand resting on Lily's arm. Her fingers were cool and dry. Her touch wasn't comforting. "You won't be coming back to Sacred Heart," she said. "We can make arrangements for you to finish high school through a correspondence course. Or you could get your GED. We'll decide that later. Right now you should concentrate on"— she paused as if she couldn't say the word—"the pregnancy."

"Graduation's in three months," Lily said.

Sister Scott smoothed her blond hair. "I'm sorry, Lily. I don't make the rules. The archdiocese believes girls like you set a bad example. Now, I do want to discuss something with you, as a friend, not as a teacher." She cleared her throat. "For a girl in your position, there's a course of action we can take if you don't want to be selfish. The church has set up certain homes where a girl like you can live until"—she paused again—"you come to term. We can find a good home for the baby."

"No," Lily said before she could stop herself.

"You must realize, Lily, that you're not ready to be a mother."

"No."

"Some married women can't have children. They'd give their eyeteeth to be you."

"Get out of here." Lily turned over in bed to face the wall.

The next morning, on the breakfast tray the candy striper brought in, folded between the plate and the cereal bowl, she found a brochure Sister Scott must have left for her. It advertised Mother Mary's House, a home for unwed Catholic girls in Baton Rouge, as if it were a summer camp, describing afternoons by the lake and barbecues. The word *pregnancy* was never used. In the single photograph on the last page, two teenage girls sat on the grass under a large oak tree, working on needlepoint pillows.

Holding the brochure up to her face, Lily studied the picture closely. The pillows were carefully positioned over the girls' laps so that nothing, no clue, was visible.

At the end of Midnight Pass, Beachaven looms beside the Gulf, a tall high-rise surrounded by weary-looking palm trees. I know most people would regard a job in a nursing home as the last resort after you've been rejected by the local colleges and every private high school in the state, but when Owen and I arrived in Sarasota I called all the retirement homes in the city to see if any of them needed art teachers. Without my portfolio of slides, my choices were day camps and nursing homes. Spending all day with other people's children might depress me, but old people have never made me sad. I hadn't planned to teach this summer. I thought I'd be at home with the baby, before starting my full-time job teaching at the Atlanta College of Art this fall.

There are no men in my class at Beachaven. All of my art students are women over seventy-five. Teaching at a senior center ensures that none of the women in my class will be pregnant, that I won't have to see a pregnant woman at all. Four days a week, I teach life-drawing. We work on a different part of the body each class, copying from *Gray's Anatomy* and Xeroxes I've made of Michelangelo's sketchbook. When I'm alone, I like to close my eyes, open the anatomy book to a random page, and look at an illustration, hoping for a different part of the body each time. With my students, I move through the body in order, starting with the limbs and moving inward. Looking at the illustrations in *Gray's Anatomy*, I'm amazed that anyone's body actually functions. So many things can go wrong. At the end of the four-week session, I'm planning to bring in a male model from the Ringling Art School to pose for us as a treat. No one in the class is especially talented, but all of the women work hard. I circle the room, giving suggestions, bending over their easels.

The first time I saw Helen, she walked into my class wearing a housedress and a Carmen Miranda sun hat, complete with a plastic banana. Her white hair hung in wisps around her cheeks. As she entered the room, several other women stared at her with disapproval and shook their heads. Helen ignored them and glided to an empty seat. She turned to me. "Like the hat?" she asked. "I got it in Barcelona sixty years ago this week."

My focus for the first day of class was the hand. During the class period, Helen wore the hat as she sketched index fingers; I tried not to stare at her. After class, she approached me as I rinsed brushes in the sink. "Have you got a cigarette?" I shook my head. "Do you know, I'm the only one of my friends who still smokes? Nobody even keeps ashtrays in their rooms anymore. I might as well have one small good thing left at the end of my life." I smiled, and she sat down beside the sink in a folding chair. "I grew up in the Catholic Home for Girls in Gainesville. I sang in the church choir three times a week. By the time I was thirteen, I was ready to dedicate my life to being a saint. The priest said, 'No one is a saint in the twentieth century.' I brought him the evidence—a children's biography of Mother Seton, the first American-born saint, from the orphanage library—and showed him the illustrations of the old woman performing miracles in small New England towns."

I set the brushes on the table and looked at her, wanting her to go on. She adjusted her Carmen Miranda hat. "Do you want some clothes? I bet you like old things. I've got stuff that'd look real good on you." After the second class, Helen started the real confessions: "I used to stand in front of the open window in the hall in the middle of winter, wearing a wet nightgown, trying to make myself sick. I got pneumonia and almost died." As a child, many nights Helen slept in the schoolyard by the chain-link fence to punish herself. When she was a teenager, the orphanage assigned the older girls charity work in the city: she delivered copies of *The Catholic Worker* to people's homes. She'd leave for her paper route at 5 A.M., taking the longest route around the city to make her deliveries, a tiny bottle of holy water in her pocket.

"Then I got married and forgot all that, including the idiot priest," she said. "I realized that life takes enough away from you without you depriving yourself. Like having children." When she said the word, I knew we'd be friends. Helen is childless, though she would never use that word. That word is supposed to describe women my own age. It describes me now, telling everything there is to know. The second time she stayed after class, the day she gave me the box of clothes, Helen said, "I couldn't have children. No doctor could figure out why."

"I'm sorry," I said, feeling it was a useless statement, one that had been made to me many times, but I didn't know what else to say.

"I had three husbands, and nothing happened with any of them, so I can't blame them. So don't ask me to show you baby pictures of my kids." She laughed and blew cigarette smoke through her nose.

Her voice grew more serious. "What I had was eight miscarriages. Every pregnancy got started, but I couldn't finish any of them."

The words were out of my mouth before I'd planned them. "I had a baby this spring. She died."

"Oh, honey." Helen touched my shoulder, then crushed her cigarette out on the floor. She hugged me. Her body felt light and fragile and I could have stood there with her forever.

Being with old people is a relief because they acknowledge death. The women in my class talk openly about it. To them, I learned, death was a simply a fact, inevitable as weather. "I'm glad I won't have to see the fighting over my jewelry when I'm gone," Marjorie Baker said. Jean Lewis picked her burial plot but later changed her mind. She didn't want to be buried beside her husband, because thirty years ago he'd cheated on her with a baby-sitter. Helen herself planned an elaborate funeral ceremony in the Catholic church where the priest told her she'd never be a saint, complete with an all-day open casket wake and graveside hymns.

Owen is relieved that I found a teaching job. He thinks it will help me. He's right: when I'm in the classroom teaching, at least I'm out in the world again. Standing in front of a class, letting other people see me, might be a first step toward the future.

In April, I still looked pregnant but the baby was dead inside me, and I didn't want to leave the house. At first, I tried to keep a normal routine, but inevitably, each time I ventured out on an errand or walked around the block, I was accosted by another woman, usually a mother, who'd ask, "When are you due?" or "Do you know if you have a boy or a girl?" The other women were excited about the possibility they believed lay in my body. There were no words to explain or describe what was happening to me;

I'd never heard of what happened to me happening to anyone.

If I told people the truth, their response was even worse. The head obstetrics nurse at the Georgia Medical Center whispered, "It's just as well that she died because she would have been severely damaged." She emphasized that word *damaged,* as if it were an obscenity. "It would be a lot worse if you had a four-year-old who died. That's what happened to my cousin." She told me that she had once had a miscarriage, after nine weeks: "The thing to do is have another right away." *I did not have a miscarriage*, I wanted to tell the nurse. *I carried this baby nearly to term.*

Finally, one afternoon, I told Owen, "I can't go out anymore. I'll go to the clinic for the labor inductions, but I'm not going anywhere else."

He said he understood. "You should be resting anyway. Why don't you get into bed?" For the next three weeks, I lay in our bed, and Owen was my ambassador to the outside world, bringing me library books, videos, and meals.

When I'd started showing, months before, in December, I'd realized that for the first time in my life I belonged. I was filled with pleasure when I saw that the world treated me as if I'd joined the ranks; I was suddenly part of the secret society of women. In April, I lay in bed thinking, *When you're pregnant your body is evidence. But can you be a mother without a living child?*

The day the baby stopped moving inside me and I telephoned the hospital for an emergency appointment with the doctor, Madeline called me for the first time. I'd never told my sister I was pregnant. We'd always believed we could share each other's pain, and she confirmed it. That morning as soon as I woke up, I knew what had happened, but I couldn't tell Owen.

I couldn't speak. I couldn't drink the cup of hot tea and milk, my favorite pregnancy drink, he'd fixed for me. We sat at the table eating breakfast. He smiled at me over his book on infant language development. Once he reached over and held my hand. I sat absolutely still, so if the baby began to move again, I'd know. *Owen,* I thought over and over in my head, *Owen, Owen, Owen.* I repeated his name until I thought I'd said it out loud. But I hadn't spoken. After Owen left the house to go to school, I walked the length of the living room. My paralysis had been transformed into a fear that if I stopped moving, something terrible would happen. I walked quickly, my hand on my stomach to check for the baby's motion.

When I answered the phone, I heard my sister's voice, "Alice, tell me you're okay."

"Linny." I spoke her childhood name that we invented, a word from our secret language. The word felt strange and unfamiliar.

"I miss you. I need you," she said, and my body filled with relief. Then she said, "What's wrong?"

"I was pregnant."

"Did you have an abortion?"

"The baby's dead." As soon as I said the words out loud, I bent over in my chair and dropped my head between my knees, still holding the receiver. I'd spoken the most horrible sentence in the world.

"Alice. Oh my God."

From that day on, my sister and I talked several times a day, as if we could erase the previous years of silence. When I'd return home from my sessions at the hospital to induce labor, all failures, or from my doctor's appointments, during which it was always agreed that there was nothing else we could do, I'd call Madeline. "Linny, it's me." For the first time since I left her to marry Owen, Madeline helped me. For the first time, she could comfort me. Owen waited with me in the hospital every week, he lay with me in bed each night. Every day he was excluded because I couldn't articulate what I knew was the truth about our baby on that first day.

Sometimes I dragged the telephone into the bathroom and turned on the faucet to drown out my voice so he wouldn't know I was talking to Madeline again. I didn't talk about Owen on the phone because I didn't want her to stop calling, and she never asked, but my sister had sensed the optimal moment to insert herself into my life again; she knew I'd be receptive to her advances. She could forgive me for leaving her to marry him if the pregnancy, which should have made me closer to Owen, brought me back.

Now, on the day I swore I'd see my sister, I visit Helen instead. The nursing home is decorated with the false cheeriness of a kindergarten. In the front hall, where men doze in their wheelchairs, the nurses have strung garlands of Kleenex flowers and pinned up fat paper suns as if to prove the season is now definitively summer. Next to the nurses' station is a toothpick model of Thomas Edison's winter home, built by a resident in another teacher's art class. I refuse to teach my students how to make crafts projects—useless, ugly objects to give to their grandchildren: popsicle-stick dolls, gum-wrapper chains, needlepoint covers for salt and pepper shakers. The nurses address the residents as if they're children—"How are we today, Helen? Feeling better?" They speak with exaggerated motions of their lips, as if the residents won't understand.

"Hey," I say, as I push open the door to Helen's room. She sits on the edge of her bed, pulling on white basketball socks that come up to her knees.

Helen jerks her thumb over in the direction of the other bed, circled with a curtain. "She kept me up all night again." Helen shares a room with a woman who is rumored to be a hundred and ten. I've never seen the woman because she never rises from the bed. "She was sobbing."

"Did you tell the nurse?"

"Nobody here can do a thing. If you live that long, that's what you get. But now you're here to rescue me. Go to the desk and sign me out." She studies my outfit. "By the way, nice dress. It looks real good on you. I wore that in 1952 when my second husband's mother died."

On the way out, we pass the Beachaven TV room. It's crowded with women in wheelchairs. Hung from chains on the ceiling, a television plays the soap opera *Another World*. A man and a woman are arguing on the screen. She is wearing a sleeveless green sequin-covered dress, and he is dressed in a white coat like a doctor. She says she wants more pills; he won't give them to her. The volume is very loud, yet no one appears to be watching the TV. Some of the women talk to one another, but most sit silently, heads bent to their chests, asleep.

On the phone, while I waited for the delivery, Madeline spoke in our old language, telling me stories about twins: jokes, anecdotes from newspapers and magazines. "Listen," she said, "it's from *The New England Journal of Medicine*. Now I'm quoting: 'The bond between twins is also reported when one of the twins has died either before or after birth. In the medical literature another phenomenon has been found, the vanishing twin. Although the ultrasound reports a twin pregnancy, only one twin develops. The other twin is absorbed into the mother's body. Born alone, the living infant is considered a surviving twin.'"

"Where did you get *The New England Journal of Medicine*?" I asked.

"In a doctor's trash. See, Alice, each of us is a split egg, a half-person, condemned to share each gene with the other."

On Madeline's good days, I loved the way my sister spoke. I let myself be enveloped by her voice, allowed my adult life to recede while our childhood bond took center stage.

"Listen," she'd say, "I just read in *Vogue* about a double wedding, a set of twins who married two men who were also twins. At the wedding, identical flower girls carried bouquets of chrysanthemums, and twin bridesmaids accompanied the brides. The guests were served two cakes, champagne from two punch bowls. The father of the bride walked down the aisle between the twin daughters. The couples honeymooned in Canada, sharing a room, a sheet strung up between the two double beds. What do you think?" I laughed, although the double wedding struck me as grotesque.

The only argument Madeline and I had during this time was when I explained about Rh disease and what it meant to have Rh-negative blood. She'd known her blood type since she was a teenager, but I wanted her to understand its implications. At the hospital, when my doctor found out that I was a twin, she wanted Madeline to come in for an appointment so she could explain the situation to her, but I said my sister lived in Florida and I would talk to her myself.

I urged Madeline to have an injection of RhoGAM, the treatment that would save her future pregnancies. "If you get pregnant, I want you to have this shot."

"I'm not pregnant. Are you asking me if I'm pregnant?"

"If you have an abortion or if you have a miscarriage, it's the same. You're sensitized as soon as you are pregnant."

"There's nothing I can do about it," my sister said. "If it happens to me, it will. I'll leave it up to fate. Anyway, I don't want to have children." Madeline sighed. "Mothering isn't in our blood." Her remark annoyed me. I knew she had said it for dramatic effect. I now hated any reference to the word *blood*. It reminded me of my failure.

After the delivery was completed in a single afternoon at the hospital, my conversations with Madeline underwent a perceptible change. I called from the hospital to tell her, but already the focus had shifted. "It's over," I said, my voice flat and exhausted. I thought I should tell her; she'd been waiting with me for this day.

My sister didn't ask how I was feeling. "I met someone," she said, excited. "His name is Jack. He just moved in."

Helen and I drive to our favorite spot by the Gulf on Siesta Key, which Helen calls the ugly beach. When the city planning board divided all of Sarasota's beaches into public and private, they left this spot out. It's always deserted. Prickly pear bushes and dwarf oaks stretch gnarled branches from the sand, and cigarette butts float at the shoreline. Red spiders crawl over the garbage on the rocks. I like this part of town because it has nothing to do with the postcard Florida, with manicured palm trees glittering in the sun or clean white sand. Today, as we walk on the ugly beach, Helen smokes the cigarette I've given her down to the filter. We eat Red Hots from a box she takes out of her dress. When I pour the candy into my hand, the red disks look like Madeline's sleeping pills.

Helen says, "You know why those old ladies in the TV room watch soap operas?" She always calls the other women old ladies but never refers to herself this way. "Because everyone's favorite stories when they're ninety are always about lost love."

"If I'm ever ninety, I won't be talking about it." I know I'll never live to be ninety. I may never turn thirty.

"When you first meet someone you love, when you're young,

you think, *This is it*. Then, after a few years with that person you can walk up and down the street in front of the house where the two of you live and you find out that there's any number of people in the world you could be happy with." She takes a drag of her cigarette. With the side of my shoe, I roll a tin can out of our path. Even the sand on this beach looks rusted. "Then again, have you gotten a good look at the men at Beachaven? There's only three of them, and I'll be happy to leave them to the old ladies."

I like to envision Helen as my great-grandmother's twin sister, Agnes, whom I never met. If she were still alive and lived in Sarasota, Agnes would have Helen's grace and energy. In the versions of Agnes's life I had been told by Lily, Agnes was the weak and sickly twin who stayed in the unnamed village where she was born in Hungary to live a life of misery and eventually die. In my own version, I revise Agnes's life to make her the vivacious, lively twin. She wears dramatic hats and smokes. She entertains friends with tales of wanting to be a saint.

Then Helen says, "Alice, have you thought about adopting a child?"

I stop walking, pretend to be staring at the flat surface of the Gulf.

"When I lived at the orphanage, people used to come every Saturday to pick out children and bring them home. Mother Superior stood us all in a line, in our best uniforms. Nobody ever picked me."

"The priest must have put in a bad word for you," I say, trying to turn the conversation into a joke.

"Well, I'm asking because when I look back at my own life it's what I should have done. I thought a baby wouldn't be mine if it wasn't my own. But I was wrong."

I can't tell Helen any more about the baby's death, about my doctor saying I could have more children if my next pregnancies were carefully monitored. So far I've only told Helen the briefest story about what happened: I was pregnant, I lost the baby.

We walk in silence for a few minutes. Then she says, "Is that doctor helping you?"

I don't know what to say. In the four sessions I've had so far with Dr. Levy, I've been practicing a lie: I talk about myself as if I'm Madeline. I always refer to myself as Alice but I think of myself as Madeline. Her life is easier to talk about than my own, and if I'm her, I can avoid the subject of the pregnancy. Dr. Levy's pen scratches rapidly across the legal pad flat on the desk in front of her. She never looks down at the paper as she writes; she stares straight at me. Madeline is me. I am Madeline. Madeline was the one who had the pregnancy, while I lived by myself alone in our childhood house in Sarasota.

I can't tell any of this to Helen, so I say, "When's your birthday, Helen? I'd like to make you a cake."

"You think I'm going to tell you the day I was born? Next you'll want to know the year." She takes my arm. On the way back to the car, Helen stops at the restroom in the abandoned concession stand. I sit outside on the steps. A little girl in a green sundress skips up and down the stone steps beside me, jumping up one, then down one, up two, and down again.

"Are you waiting for someone?" I ask. I've never seen a child at the ugly beach.

She nods. I wish she'd been cautioned about strangers in public places. She stares sideways at me, through her hair. "You know the lady who went in the bathroom?" Panic rises in my throat. Something has happened to Helen. I rise from the steps. "Is she your grandma?"

"Yes," I say, full of relief. "Of course she is."

"What's her name?"

"Agnes," I tell the child.

One night in May my sister called me again in Atlanta. "I want to see you."

"Come for a visit," I suggested. "You can stay with us."

She ignored my invitation. "I've been stealing things."

"You mean like we used to do?"

"No, I've stolen a lot," my sister said. "Expensive things. New clothes from stores. Good jewelry. It's not like when we did it. This is different."

"I want you to stop." I wondered how much Madeline meant when she said "a lot."

"I feel as if I could do something bad to myself, something painful." Her voice lowered. "I've hurt myself."

"What are you talking about?" Pulling the phone cord around my body, I hid behind the couch in case Owen walked in. "Have you taken drugs?" With Madeline, this was always my greatest unspoken fear.

"Alice, I've done things to myself. I cut a can in half and scratched my arm, and I couldn't even feel it. Last night I held a cigarette on my wrist, and I didn't feel anything. I looked down and I could see the burn, but if I hadn't seen it, I wouldn't have known it was there. It's easy," she said. "I could keep doing this, I think."

"Does Jack know?" I asked.

"He doesn't understand like you do."

"He's irresponsible." Anger sputtered in my throat. I felt rage for my sister's boyfriend whom I'd never met. I suddenly felt furious for all the boyfriends my sister had had in her life, all the men who'd refused to help her, who left her, who expected me to take care of her when they disappeared. "Let me talk to him."

"I have to go," Madeline said in a small voice like a child. She hung up.

I received a series of other calls like this, either very late at night when we were already in bed or waking us before the sky was light. Each time my sister sounded more and more distracted, farther away, and less like herself, or what I thought she used to be. "I have a shoe box full of aspirin. From a pair of Miss Wonderful red pumps." She paused. "How much cologne would a person have to drink in order to die?"

The next night, I answered the phone. "I bought a bottle of rubbing alcohol," my sister whispered. "I'm going to drink it, Alice. Here," she paused, "listen to this. I'm drinking it now."

"No! Stop it." I knew that what Madeline wanted most was my alarm, but I couldn't ignore her threat.

I remembered the night before our wedding, the last night I spent with my sister before I left her. She insisted that I sleep in our old house that night, and she said Owen could spend the night in a motel. In the middle of the night, my sister climbed into my bed in the dark. She sat on my chest; I woke up because I couldn't breathe. She leaned over my face so that her long hair brushed my skin. "Alice," she whispered. "Don't. Please don't." I never told Owen.

After I made her promise not to drink any more rubbing alcohol and swear she'd go to bed, I hung up, and I went into the kitchen to find Owen. I told him I had to see my sister. I explained to him that she had called me a few times recently, and she was acting strangely, but I didn't mention the suicide threat. "I'll go alone," I said.

"No," he said. "I don't want you to do this by yourself, especially now." He looked down at the papers scattered across his desk. We both knew what *now* meant. "I can finish my linguistic atlas project in Sarasota." I wondered if he was afraid of my being alone with

Madeline. "Three months," he said. "I'm willing to move there for the summer, but that's it. If she's not better, we can bring her back with us and put her in a hospital."

A hospital. When I heard the words, I felt a familiar panic, remembering when Madeline called me from the hospital the night after Owen and I got married. Madeline holds the hospital before me as a constant temptation: "If you don't stay with me, I'll go into the hospital." She likes to persuade me that I can save her from her-self. She wants to convince me she can be saved.

I told Owen, "She won't need that."

5

In the story Agatha told Lily, twins signified luck. Agatha said that in the unnamed village in Hungary where she and her sister were born, the birth of twins during a successful harvest was considered a good omen. The villagers attributed great powers to twins—they could forecast the weather, they could predict the fertility of the local women. But girls were bad luck, useless workers in the fields. They could never own land. Sisters meant nothing to the men in the family, even if they were twins.

Our great-grandmother Agatha was one of seven children, named after the saints, as was the Catholic custom in the village. The girls, from the oldest, Mary, to the youngest, Teresa, were a continual disappointment to their father, who wanted sons to till the land, the potato and bean fields he was so proud of. Agatha was also a twin. The birth of Agatha and Agnes in 1910 led to their mother's death from a hemorrhage that could not be stopped. From that time on, these girl twins were known as bearers of bad luck.

Agnes and Agatha were so alike that their father tied string of different lengths around their legs to distinguish them. For twenty-three years, the sisters never had a separate article of clothing or a pair of shoes of their own. When the twins were twelve, their father took them into the barn to talk to them. This was his tradition: each year, he took a different daughter to the barn for his announcement. He decided he might as well take the twins together. "You can stay here," the girls' father told them. "You can work here. You're never going to own any of the land." The twins nodded, solemnly.

After their father left, Agnes and Agatha sat together on the dirt floor. The girls were quiet together. They leaned against each other, eyes half-closed. They leaned together for support, solace, sustenance. They leaned together. That afternoon the sisters began to practice their trick. Agatha began it. She'd taught herself the trick the week the doctor had said she was supposed to die. For six days, as she sat under the tree alone, she cured herself. After the initial unpleasantness of the physical action of the contents of her stomach rushing up into her throat, the retching that made her gasp, Agatha found that the experience left her with an emptiness and calm that she enjoyed. She felt purified, filled with a strange peacefulness.

"Don't tell the others," she warned Agnes. "This will be our secret."

Lily often told us stories about Agatha and Agnes, the same stories Agatha had told her when she was a child. She may never have wanted the three of us to be a family, but she did make sure we knew the stories before she left.

6

"I don't want to see her," I say. I stop the car in front of Madeline's house on Midnight Pass and yank the key from the ignition so hard my wrist shakes. The words hang in the air of the car. Owen and I haven't spoken to each other since we got in the car back at our house. I wanted him to come along on the ride to Madeline's house to be with me. He agreed to drive back to our house and to pick me up later. I know that Madeline doesn't want to see Owen.

"Is it strange to see your house?" Owen asks.

"Madeline's house," I say. "It's not mine."

But it is mine, even now. I study the house where Lily left us. It's a Spanish-style house made of stucco with a red tile roof. Inside are three bedrooms, two bathrooms with claw-foot tubs, and a movie theater. When Lily found it, the house had been condemned. She bought it for almost nothing. When I last saw the house, when I moved out three years ago, it was beyond repair—the ceiling in the dining room fell down years ago, exposing bare pipes; a widening crack runs the length of the kitchen floor; and the heat no longer works in any room of the house. Rain fills the front hall during a storm. Entering the house again is not what makes me nervous; entering that life again is terrifying.

"Do you remember when I picked you up here for the first time and saw where you lived?" Owen says. "I couldn't believe you two actually lived here."

"I should go in," I say, but I don't move.

"Are you nervous?"

"I haven't seen her in three years."

"You've talked to her on the phone."

"It's not the same. Especially not with Madeline." My sister requires my presence, my full attention, and I'm afraid of what will happen when I walk through the front door of the house and begin to give her what she needs again.

"You'll feel better once you see her," he tells me. "You'll feel just like you always do with her."

I think to myself, *Yes, that's what I'm afraid of.*

Without looking at me, Owen reaches over and touches my arm. I know he's trying to be especially patient with me about my sister. "I'll pick you up in an hour."

I want to touch him, but I can't.

The day I found Owen at the aquarium, I did not go home to Madeline. The long afternoon turned into evening. It was seven by the time Owen and I walked out into the parking lot of Happyland. When we reached his car, he turned to me, his face expectant.

"I took the bus," I said, before he could speak.

"Do you want a ride somewhere? Do you want me to take you home?"

"Yes." I breathed the word before I realized that Owen was

offering to take me back to the house I shared with my sister, where I had told him that I lived. That was what he considered to be my home. I wanted to go to his apartment. Feeling bold, pretending I was Madeline, I leaned into him and wrapped my arms around his shoulders. I kissed him gently. I folded my body into his.

"God," he said, when he moved from my lips to my neck. He was speaking into my hair; his breath was warm against my skin. "I just met you. I've never done anything like this before."

"Let's go to your apartment," I said, and I kissed him again.

He stepped back and faced me. "Are you sure you wouldn't feel more comfortable at your own house?" he said. "Look, I don't want to move too fast here or do anything you don't want to do."

"I don't want to go back to my house. This is really what I want. Please."

In bed that night, he held me and I felt as if I were underwater. Not being dragged or pulled down, as I had felt so often in my life with my sister, but sinking slowly to the bottom of a clear, warm ocean where I would be safe. The ocean floor was clean, flecked with coral, completely still. The two of us could stay down there forever.

"Keep talking," Owen said, over and over. He rubbed my hands until my skin was burning. He smoothed my hair over my shoulders, across my breasts.

For three days, we lay like this, eating bread and fruit he brought to the bed on plates from his tiny kitchen, and I told him the stories from my childhood. I talked and talked. I told him the stories Lily had told us about our family. I told him about Lily and how she left us. These were stories I had never told anyone before. Owen lay beside me and listened. He asked questions that showed he was thinking about what I had said, questions no one had ever asked me before—"How did you feel when your mother left?" and "Why do you love your sister?"

For three days, we stayed in bed, turning toward each other, lying side by side, our legs tangled together. We reached for each other again and again. Long after Owen had fallen asleep, I stayed awake just so I could watch him. I studied his eyes with their pale, delicate lashes, the curve of his jaw, the hair that fell over his forehead glazed with sweat. I didn't want to sleep because I would miss the time with him beside me, but each time sleep overcame me, and when I woke from it, I knew I was safer than I ever had been in my life.

"We should get up," Owen said, turning toward me on the third morning in bed. I had no desire to rejoin the world. I had no desire to face my sister and explain my absence. I traced the outline of his face with my fingers, as if I were trying to memorize his features. I didn't want to sound like my sister: *Don't leave me, don't go away, stay with me forever.* I didn't want to beg for his attention. He moved closer and lay his arm across my back. "Alice, I want you to move in with me," he said. "Come stay here for a while. Bring your work."

I sat up in bed, pulling the sheet over my shoulders. The spell was broken, and it wasn't his fault. I'd broken it myself by remembering Madeline. For the first time in my life, I'd forgotten my sister. I'd thought only about myself.

"I have to go," I said.

Now, when I enter our house for the first time since I married Owen, I have to shove the door hard to move the cardboard boxes stacked against it. Bubble wrap and rolls of twine litter the front hall. The hall's wooden floor is covered with a pea-green carpet, frayed at the edges, and when I peek into the living room the few pieces of furniture I remember from my childhood, a scratched and legless armoire, a velvet chair with no seat, have been replaced with a card table and two folding chairs.

"Linny," I yell. "I'm back. I'm here."

As if in response, a man with long blond hair who I know must be Jack appears in the hallway. He's a large man with muscled shoulders, like all the men my sister has chosen, but his hair is long and sleek and shining. It falls to the middle of his back, giving him an oddly feminine appearance. When we were children, Madeline and I used to call this kind of hair Alice-in-Wonderland hair, the hair that is fine spun gold, the hair of fairy tales, the hair of every triumphant princess, the hair we had both desired. Lily had that kind of hair when we were young, while ours was dark. In her thirties, hers began to darken too.

A cigarette burns between Jack's fingers, no filter and a long ash. "Linny?" he says, pronouncing my sister's nickname with disgust. "Who the hell is that?"

For a moment, I feel better. If he's not aware of her childhood name, the name I invented for her, the name only I can call her, Jack can't be very deeply entrenched in my sister's life. Maybe it won't be hard to get rid of him. My sister has probably had the same thought about Owen.

"You're Alice," he says.

"Where's my sister?"

Jack jerks his arm in the direction of the movie theater. With the gesture, the muscle in his upper arm ripples. Madeline would find this appealing, but the show of strength leaves me feeling edgy. I wonder if he has hurt her yet. "Back there." He walks down the hall and past me. "Packing." He strides out the front door.

In the old movie theater, now her bedroom, Madeline stands bent over, her back to me, stuffing costumes into her suitcase without any arrangement, hats crammed on top of dresses, stockings strewn over the pile. I wonder if these are the clothes she has stolen. "Linny," I say again, and she turns around. She hugs me. Her dark hair is very short, above her ears, parted in the middle and straight. In my arms, her body feels light. She is thinner, more delicate, but she holds me as tightly as ever. She wears a green silk bathrobe, and I smell smoke and Shalimar on the fabric. But her embrace is the same, and as I hold her, I remember the past, the nights from childhood when we gripped each other in bed in the motel room, when we swore to each other that we would not ever need anyone but each other.

"God, I've missed you," my sister says. I can feel her breath on my neck when she speaks. "Don't ever go away from me again."

"You cut your hair," I say when we separate and stand looking at each other. For the first time, our appearances do not match: her hair is short and mine reaches nearly to my waist. For most of our life, men could not tell my sister and me apart. When we were teenagers, to confuse them, we used to dress up in identical outfits, then walk up and down the Siesta Key public beach, arms linked. Sometimes Madeline sat on the steps of the concession stand and watched me as I pretended I was her. She never pretended to be me. I have never stopped loving the thrill that ran along my spine when someone called me by my sister's name. Owen is the only man who has ever told me I look nothing like Madeline.

"Jack cut it. Did you meet him?" she says.

"Yes. What happened to the house?" I study the room, empty of the chipped dresser where we used to keep our clothes together and the mattresses where we slept on the floor. Now there is nothing in the room but Madeline, her suitcase, and a four-poster bed.

Madeline sweeps across the room, the movement of a movie star crossing a stage for the gaze of the camera. "After you left, I redid the house. I had to get rid of some memories of you. It's my house now, Alice." She delivers this speech as if it were dialogue from an old script, and I try not to find something false in it. I try, always, to believe my sister.

"I can understand that," I say, choosing my words carefully.

"Don't you have anything to say about Jack?" my sister asks. "You met him." Her eyes narrow. "What do you think of his body?"

I know from her expression that Madeline wants to tell me about sex with Jack, so I don't respond to the question. "Linny, where are you going?"

"Jack loves Judy Garland as much as we do," Madeline says. "He's seen all her movies too. He likes *The Wizard of Oz* best." She pauses, then says suddenly, "Did you ever ask Owen if he likes Judy Garland? I bet he doesn't. He doesn't seem like the type. But Jack's like us." She smiles.

"I am not like Jack. Linny, answer my question. Where are you going?"

The smile fades from her face. She turns away from me. "It was not a sudden decision. I want you to know we've been talking about it for a long time."

"What decision? What have you been talking about?"

"Jack and I are going on a trip," Madeline says. "We're going to look for Mother."

Mother. The word is unfamiliar. Lily herself refused it. *Lily,* the name her parents gave her, was the name she insisted we call her. It's now the name I choose for her, on the rare occasions when I allow myself to think of her.

I sit down on the edge of Madeline's four-poster bed. "How would you know where she is now?"

"She's in New Orleans."

"Linny," I say, "you have no reason to believe that. You don't know her. Why didn't you ever care about finding her before?" I want my sister to sit down on the bed beside me. I want her to tell me that as soon as she saw me she changed her mind and she isn't leaving after all.

Madeline stands in the center of the bedroom, tightening the belt of her robe around her waist. "I've been thinking about her. Jack and I have talked about her. He thinks I should try to look for her."

"How long have you known this man?"

"Three weeks. So what?"

"Linny—"

"Alice, how long did you know Owen before you married him? If anyone made a fast decision about a man, it was you."

I am silent. Owen and I were married after we had known each other for six weeks. Marrying him seemed at the time to be the only rash act of my life, although I know now that it was the right decision. I knew at the time that he and I had an instant connection, and I knew that if I waited too long, my sister would have time to break it.

"Lily would be old by now, Alice."

"She'd be only forty-six." I surprise myself that I know this.

"I need to see her."

Madeline isn't talking like herself. *Jack and I have talked about her.*

"Linny, I came here to be with you," I say. "I disrupted my entire life to come here. I disrupted Owen's life."

Madeline folds a beaded sweater and places it on the bed beside her suitcase. "I didn't tell you to do that."

"We came to Sarasota for the entire summer."

"Jack and I won't be gone long. We'll find Lily and bring her back. I wish you'd believe me about this, Alice. Oh, by the way, here's something I was going to send you." She tosses a postcard onto the bed. I pick up the card, anxiety filling my body. It's an invitation to our birthday party on Saturday, June 10. Our real birthday is June 7, but we haven't celebrated it on that day in many years. Lily changed the day for us. We'll turn twenty-nine together. The card spells out *Venezia* in silver letters over a picture of a boat floating on an unidentifiable body of water. On the other side of the card the caption reveals, as if this were a surprise, that the card does not come from Italy. On the message side is written June 10th, the word *noon,* and the name of a chain motel in Venice, Florida. The handwriting, large block print, is not my sister's. Jack must have written the card, but I can tell that Madeline contributed the message on the bottom of the postcard; in her tiny, crabbed handwriting she has issued a warning: *Don't bring Owen.* I turn the card back over quickly to the picture side.

My sister walks closer to me, steps out of her shoes, and stands on the tops of my sandals. When I feel her body edging against mine, I can't tell her again that she has ruined my summer. I can't tell her anything. She rises on her toes to wrap her arms around my neck. "I love you," she says. "I'm so glad you're here."

I see myself three years ago, waiting outside on the steps of the house for Owen to pick me up while Madeline watches at the window. Madeline wouldn't let me wait for Owen inside. Night after night, I sat alone on the front steps in the dark and thought about the two lives that intersected with my own as if I could balance them on a scale: *Owen vs. Madeline. Madeline vs. Owen.* I'd choose Owen and my sister would not forgive me. Even now I still hear the words my sister spoke, "Don't go, don't leave me, why are you always leaving me for him?" And my own excuses—"I'll only be gone for an hour or two, we're just going to a movie. I'll be home by ten, I promise"—as if I were a teenager begging to go out with my boyfriend for the evening and Madeline were my mother. Although I talked about my sister to Owen, my stories were carefully edited versions of the truth.

Then Madeline suggested I invite Owen to our house for dinner. "I'll cook," she said, placing a copy of *Fine Dining in Florida* in my hands. "Page thirty-three. I'm going to try the *coq au vin*. For dessert, page sixty-five, hazelnut white chocolate pie." For a week, my sister cut out pictures and recipes, shopped, and practiced making different dishes. My fears about the evening began to fade. I started to imagine Owen and my sister actually liking each other. Why, I asked myself, did I always force myself to imagine the worst?

The night of the dinner, Madeline called me into our room. "Easter Parade" blared from the portable tape player, Judy Garland's voice sounding bright and clear. It was one of her happiest songs, but I'd read in a biography that she'd had electroshock soon after the movie was filmed. My sister lay on her bed, wearing a white nightgown, a washcloth folded over her forehead. "I'm having a nervous collapse," she said. "I can't cook. I can't even come to the table. Sorry." She wouldn't come out of the room to meet Owen. "He can come in here for a minute," she said. "But only a minute."

Owen and I stood together at my sister's bedside. She lay still with her eyes closed. "I hope you feel better," he said. His voice was sincere. I tried to hide my embarrassment.

On the way out, he looked at me with a puzzled expression. I avoided his eyes. I waited for him to tell me our relationship was over. "You know, your voice sounds like hers, but you don't look much like her." I wanted him to say more. I wanted him to point out the specific differences between us, to show me why he could never love her but would always love me: the distance between my eyes was greater, my chin curved away from my ears in a different way, my shoulders were wider. I wanted a physical division between my sister and me that no one could notice except him.

After Owen left, I returned to Madeline. She was brushing her long hair. "Are you okay?" I asked.

"Of course," Madeline said. She wrinkled her nose. "Alice, you could do better than that."

7

In Charity Hospital, on bed rest, Lily quickly gained weight. At one hundred and seventeen, she couldn't stand to look at her stomach. One thirty. None of the clothes from her old life fit. She wore hospital gowns all day. One forty-five. Her feet swelled. She cut her slippers open on the sides as Agatha had told her old women in the village did when they could no longer walk. She'd been informed she was carrying twins. At night, when she couldn't sleep, she remembered her grandmother reading *Alice in Wonderland*. In the circle of Agatha's arms, Lily listened to the story. Alice grew smaller, larger, sipped from the dangerous bottle labeled "DRINK ME," ate the currant cake till she was so huge she couldn't fit inside the garden door. When Lily thought of Agatha, her throat closed with pain. After her one visit to the hospital, Agatha hadn't returned.

One morning in June, Lily felt a gush of liquid between her legs and screamed for a nurse. "I'm bleeding!"

A candy striper pulled the sheets off the bed, exposing Lily's bare thighs. "Your water broke, that's all," she said. She chewed gum. Lily stared at the gum, the strings of pink between the candy striper's teeth, and she kept screaming.

We arrived three weeks early. Lily's labor was thirty-seven hours long. For the first nine hours, she lay on a stretcher in the hall of the maternity floor, crying until her throat burned.

"Your contractions aren't close enough together," the nurse said. "Stop crying. You're embarrassing yourself."

"I want to die. I don't care if I die. Kill me. Get it over with!" In movies, women were always given drugs to knock them out if they were bad patients. But no one mentioned anesthesia. After twenty-two hours of labor, she dragged her fingernails over the skin on the inside of the nurse's arm, and finally a cone-shaped mask was placed over her mouth and nose. She inhaled the sweet gas she'd been given when she was a little girl at the dentist's office. For the remaining hours of the labor, she floated in and out of consciousness, in a weary haze, not caring what happened or if her body were ripped apart.

Lily's new room was on the maternity ward, as if the embarrassment of her pregnancy were now over. "You're very, very lucky," the obstetrics nurse told her a week later when she brought the babies in to see her. "It's a miracle both of them lived. You don't know how many sad cases I've seen involving twins."

We were wrapped in a single pink blanket. When the nurse parted the folds of the blanket to show us to Lily, we looked like small wrinkled sacks. "They're ugly," she whispered.

"All babies are at first. Soon you learn to love them and everything changes. Would you like to hold them?" Without waiting for Lily's answer—she was planning to say no—the nurse separated the two sacks and placed one in each of Lily's arms.

"I'm not feeding them," Lily said. "I told you to write that on my chart. I don't want to breast-feed. It's gross." *Gross* was a word that reminded her of high school, a word used by the girls at Sacred Heart.

"It's the natural thing, but you've obviously made up your own mind." The nurse flipped through a clipboard of forms, leaving Lily to continue holding us. "We need names for the birth certificate. Last name of the father?"

"Carson," Lily said, giving her dead father's name. She considered Bantorvya, Agatha's family name, but her grandmother would be ashamed at the use of the name for children who never should have been born. "Alice and Madeline." Alice after *Alice in Wonderland.* Madeline for La Madeline, the café where she and Reid Alistair had gone the night Agatha locked her out.

"Which gets which? We have to tag them." The nurse held up two clear plastic bracelets for our wrists.

"I don't care. You decide." Lily didn't see how it mattered which girl got which name. To her, the babies were exactly the same.

"So we'll call the one that was born first Alice and the other Madeline?" Lily shrugged. "You know, they say the twin born first will always be the dominant one. I probably shouldn't tell you that, because it's an old wives' tale, of course, not a medical fact. Alice weighs three ounces more, according to your chart."

Holding us in her arms exhausted Lily. She closed her eyes and tried to pretend she was the principal dancer in *The Red Shoes* again, but she couldn't arrange the fantasy, couldn't see herself crossing the stage in *jêté* after *jêté* in the red tutu and satin shoes. The vision was part of a life that she would never have any chance of living now.

In July, after more than five months in Charity Hospital, Lily was discharged. She sat in the wheelchair the hospital had insisted upon, the two of us wrapped up on her lap, pretending to wait in the lobby to be picked up. She had nowhere to go.

"No one to fetch you, dear?" The receptionist at the lobby desk had a British accent and a kind smile. "Where's the mister to pick up his family?" She made a clucking sound with her tongue, scolding Lily's imaginary husband. "We can't let you leave unless there's someone here to pick you up."

Lily's eyes filled with tears. "My grandmother's coming," she lied. "She said she'd meet me outside in a cab."

"Oh, good. When I was your age, I had a lovely grandmother too. Let me wheel you out so you can wait for her."

From Charity Hospital, Lily hitchhiked to Airline Highway. A family—a mother, a father, and two little boys—on their way to the airport picked her up. "Are you baby-sitting?" the mother asked.

"Yes," Lily said. "They belong to a friend of my grandmother's."

"Aren't they sweet?" said the mother. "I remember when these two were that tiny." She smiled at Lily, who closed her eyes and pretended to be asleep.

The Star Dust Motel advertised the cheapest prices on Airline Highway, but Lily always said later that she chose it for its name. The marquee displayed a woman dancing on a stage. Below, in sloppy handwritten letters centered on a piece of poster board, the sign read:

MEET THE STARS AT THE STAR DUST

VACANCY

FIVE DOLLARS A NIGHT

HELP WANTED

Built out of pink plaster with white metal balconies circling the parking lot, the motel mimicked the architecture of the Garden

District mansions uptown. All the rooms were identical, carpeted in red shag. They all smelled like a basement, the air heavy and damp.

The night clerk, a boy her age, hired Lily that night. "You can do the wake-up calls starting tomorrow. I've been doing them all summer because we don't have anyone to work," the boy said in a bored voice, before returning to the *Kid Flash* comic book open on the counter before him. "Be here at six."

Lily carried us across the parking lot to our room. Inside, the carpet was stained and torn in front of the bathroom, as if someone had stabbed it with a knife.

Nothing had prepared Lily for her experience of motherhood, for the unshakable exhaustion, worse than any she'd ever felt. Hours of the most grueling ballet classes hadn't ever made her body ache as it now did by the end of the day. "Children ruin a woman's body," Agatha had said. Lily could hear her grandmother's voice, giving her the warning.

Because Lily didn't own a crib, she put us to bed in the bags she'd used at the hospital. Madeline slept in her suitcase. For the first month of my life, I slept in her ballet bag, lined with pink satin. To keep us warm, she wrapped us in her old school uniforms from Sacred Heart, plaid wool skirts and white blouses. Neither of us would take the bottle. In the La Leche pamphlet the nurse had given her, Lily read: "Twins pose special problems at feeding times." The information was vague, but Lily understood that *special problems* meant *pain*. "Expect your nipples to crack and bleed."

"I put vinegar on my nipples," Lily told us later. "Then I held you to my chest and let you suck till you learned a lesson." She always seemed proud of her ingenuity when she explained her trick. "It worked," she said. "After three days, you two took the bottle."

For the first eighteen years of our life, the years we lived with her, Lily never grew tired of relating the story of our birth. Sometimes she'd make us repeat the story back to her, offering her own corrections. "No, Charity Hospital is on Canal Street." "You're wrong. I wore red tights." But what I always wondered was why she didn't give us up when she had the chance. Sister Scott had offered her an escape from the life we forced on her, and she didn't take it. Throughout my childhood, I told myself that secretly Lily had wanted us, though she couldn't admit it.

In the closet of our motel room at the Star Dust, Lily kept a scrapbook. On black construction-paper pages, she taped the important images of her life. Agatha had given her the scrapbook several years ago, but she filled it only when she left home. She put in images from her own life and photographs of Judy Garland. Side by side, on the same page, the two lives merged. There were pictures of herself before the pregnancy, photographs of Judy Garland when she was Baby Gumm on stage, a black-and-white print of Agatha from the 1920s, when she was young, a magazine clipping headed "Judy Garland's Secret Marriage Revealed By Louella Parsons," the small article about Lily's fall during the performance, Liza Minnelli's birth announcement from *Modern Screen,* a piece of red net from Lily's last costume, a photograph of Judy Garland in *A Star Is Born* helping a drunk James Mason off the stage, and on the last page, Lily taped our birth certificate, the conclusion of the story.

After a week at the Star Dust, Lily was promoted from telephone operator to maid. While she cleaned in the mornings, she carried us with her from room to room. We lay on different strangers' beds and slept.

At the Salvation Army down the highway, Lily bought a record player. It was from the 1950s, pink plastic, and it fit inside a broken case. She bought it because she had one album: Judy Garland's *When You're Smiling*, which had been left at the Star Dust by someone years ago and until she arrived had been hidden in the laundry room under a pile of yellowed sheets. Lily couldn't believe she'd found the Judy Garland record, couldn't believe the desk clerk let her keep it because he saw no value in it. She read the album as a sign, the first bright spot in months of fear and darkness.

Whenever the three of us were in the room together, she played the record. For the first few months of our lives, Madeline and I must have heard Judy Garland's versions of "Moon River" and "Lucky Day" over and over. Lily would sing along with "San Francisco" while she changed and fed us. Later Madeline would say that the music got into our blood, that the songs were imprinted within us forever.

When we were three months old, Lily changed our birthday to link us closer to Judy Garland. "From now on, you weren't born June seventh," she said. "You were born June tenth, the same as Judy Garland. We'll always celebrate your birthday on her day."

Once, a woman saw Lily carrying the ballet bag and the suitcase from room to room on her morning shift. The woman was leaving the motel, but she stopped and stared at Lily. She was smoking. She wore a tight black dress and orange lipstick. It was 7 A.M. "Be careful with them," she said. "My daughter had a baby, and her boyfriend stole it."

"I don't have a boyfriend." Lily walked past the woman to the next vacated room.

"You ought to fingerprint them. Get a record or something. Look, honey, this isn't the safest place." She gestured to the parking lot, empty as it was each morning, except for a pickup truck that belonged to a fisherman who had taken up permanent residence at the Star Dust. "The police would never believe you." She paused and stamped out her cigarette on the asphalt. "They don't believe girls like us."

In our room that night, Lily marked us. She pressed our fingers against the tip of her lipstick, the frosted pink called Broken Heart, and smeared the prints on an index card where she had printed "Alice" and "Madeline."

Then she undressed us and laid us on the carpet on the floor of the motel room, side by side, examining our bodies closely for the first time: the soft spots on our heads, our smooth pink gums, our knees, our toes, the space between our legs. No birthmarks or differences of pigmentation in the skin. Our arms and legs were the exact same length. Our bodies matched. Lily didn't think we looked at all like her. While her hair was blond, ours was dark. Her eyes were green, and ours were blue. Instead of resembling her, we looked like each other. We didn't cry as she worked her fingers into our ears and uncurled our fists to spread our fingers flat. Finally, she marked one of us. Carefully, Lily painted red nail polish on Madeline's index finger.

Whenever Madeline retells this story, she explains that at this moment, she and I ceased to be the same, forever. At this moment, she believes that she was set apart. Technically, as the nurse had told Lily at Charity Hospital, I was older, but the red polish Lily applied to Madeline's finger was what first removed my sister from me, creating a hint of glamour, mystery.

8

Owen and I stand in the roped-off kitchen of the Ringling house with the other tourists. On top of the Vulcan gas range is a loaf of false bread, cut and ready to be carried out to the dining room for an imaginary family meal. "I love that bread," I whisper to Owen. "You know someone in the art school made it."

John and Mable Ringling's winter residence, the CádZan house, sits on the edge of the bay. Now a museum, the mansion was built in 1926, a gift from John Ringling to his wife. I like to imagine the life the family once led in these rooms: the husband, the wife. Now the house is in a state of disrepair, the wallpaper peeling off the walls in enormous sheets, the furniture chipped and broken. Only the ceilings, painted with paneled murals, are still perfect. I study the ballroom ceiling, each panel containing a couple dressed in dance costumes, painted by the set designer for the Ziegfeld Follies.

Owen suggested that we come to the Ringling house today. We had often visited the house when we were dating. Our game was to pick our favorite rooms. I always chose John Ringling's closet.

Sealed off by a wall of glass, the closet is neatly arranged with the last remaining possessions of a dead man: his linen suits and wing-tip shoes, his hats laid out on the shelf, his suspenders hung from a metal bar. No one else ever seemed particularly interested in the contents of the closet, so we used to stand before it, uninterrupted, for as long as we wanted. Owen's choice was usually the playroom on the third floor. The Ringlings had no children. The playroom ceiling is covered with a mural depicting John and Mable Ringling in the center of a Venetian carnival celebration. Jesters, mimes, and women with masks dance around the Ringlings. The couple stands together in the center of the scene, dressed in formal evening clothes.

Today, I don't want to see either place. "Let's go outside." I lead him out of the house.

"Are you okay?" he asks.

I know Owen is feeling hopeful because we're visiting a place from our old life. Maybe he's right. Maybe recovery consists of repeating what you've done before. If I put myself through the motions of the life I had before the pregnancy, if I pretend long enough, I'll be cured.

When we walk out to the Dwarf Garden, I understand that this way of thinking is completely wrong. When we first knew each other, Owen and I loved this garden, full of stone statues of Italian dwarfs dressed in period costumes from different operas and Italian fairy tales. The dwarf statues are cracked, their legs chipped, scratches etched in their limestone faces like fine wrinkles. In the corner of the garden stands an especially petulant girl dwarf holding a scythe and a fistful of grass. All the statues resemble fat, discontented children.

*   *   *

Upstairs are the museum library's Special Collections. When I was a student at the Ringling School of Art, I loved to spend hours here, in the quietest room in the museum, studying monographs and rare prints. I'd choose a book to place in a wooden frame on the table in front of me. I turned the pages slowly, careful not to leave any fingerprints behind. The Ringling museum is famous for its collection of Italian Baroque paintings, version after version of the Holy Family. I studied *The Holy Family and St. Lucy,* in which Lucy proudly offers the Christ child her golden eyes on a plate. In *The Holy Family with St. Sebastian,* the couple hold their child while the saint looks on, his mouth set in a grimace of pain, his side pierced by long arrows. Mary touches her lips to her son's in *The Holy Family in the Garden,* as Joseph looks on sadly from a dark background. In most of the paintings of the Nativity he is excluded, hovering on the edge of the canvas, his body in shadow.

For three years I've been out of graduate school, and I miss the projects. I miss the assignments to complete on time, the deadlines. In my first semester of the M.F.A. program, in Painting I, the art teacher announced that during the semester we had to produce fifteen paintings and two pages of analysis on each. In addition, we were supposed to keep a daily journal of our work in progress. For that first semester, I was always painting. I set myself a schedule: each morning the alarm rang at 4:30. I started work in the dark. I slept in short periods in the afternoons, on the floor of my bedroom, asking my sister to wake me for dinner.

Madeline always wanted my attention. "Can't you take a break?" She stood in the doorway, twisting the long beads around her neck. "I feel like seeing a movie tonight."

"I can't," I told her.

"Look at this," my sister said one day, handing me a newspaper clipping. It related the story of a scientific experiment in France in which a woman moved into a cave with no electricity, no artificial lights, no clocks. For six months, she lived alone in the silent darkness of the cave. Scientists measured her heart rate and blood pressure, watching her vital signs. She spoke to them from the cave through a video screen, telling them she had made friends with the bugs and rats that were the cave's only other occupants. After a week, the Frenchwoman was staying awake for thirty-six hours at a stretch, then sleeping twenty-four to recuperate.

"See?" Madeline pointed to the last paragraph of the article. Two months after the experiment was concluded, after the woman had returned to the world of light and other people, she committed suicide. "Do you want to end up like that?"

In the Dwarf Garden, Owen stands behind me, rubbing my neck. We haven't slept together in eight weeks, since I came home from the hospital. I know he's thinking of how our bodies once fit and refit together and how if we could just touch each other again we could make everything better. His hands are gentle. I try to concentrate on the pressure of his fingers on my skin. He kisses my neck, and I want to say, *Give up, this isn't going to work, why don't you stop trying?*

To stay calm, while Owen runs his fingers up and down my back, I invent a new trick: I recite cake recipes silently over and over in my head. *A cup of sugar. Half a stick of unsalted butter. Five shelled walnuts. Two teaspoons of nutmeg.*

"Alice," Owen says. I shut my eyes.

I don't want to see the disappointment registering on his face. If he touches me, if we lie down together later, if he enters my body, I won't be able to bear it. And that moment is where his kisses, his embraces are all leading. I can't go with him to that place again. Sex is a room with a door I won't open, because I don't want to see what's inside, waiting.

The afternoon the baby died, after I'd told Madeline, I called Owen at the Georgia Tech linguistics lab. When he answered the phone, I couldn't speak. All I could say was "Please come home." When I first arrived at the Georgia Medical Center emergency room, everything happened fast. Three nurses crowded around the stretcher, hooking up an IV, checking my pulse, my heart. Above my head, the lights were bright and flashing. I was wheeled into a room for a sonogram and a pelvic exam, my lower body sheeted and separated so I could see nothing. Owen sat beside me. We both watched the fetal monitor's screen. I already knew.

"I don't hear a heartbeat," my doctor said slowly. "Let me check again."

Owen held my hand. He wanted to comfort me, but he couldn't. To comfort myself, I had my own trick. I left my body on the examining table, under the doctor's yellow gloved hands and the cold metal instruments. I flew somewhere up on the ceiling, fluttering like an invisible bird. I worked as hard as I could to make myself disappear.

Time slowed down, then stopped. And I was moved to a bed on the maternity wing.

My obstetrician returned to the room. "Alice, let me explain what's happened." She sat down beside the bed. "This is a case of intrauterine death." The words hung in the air. All I could think was that the term didn't name the person who had died, only the place where that death had occurred. "It would be too dangerous for you to dilate the cervix at this point. In a few days, we'll discuss inducing labor."

"I want an abortion," I said.

Owen stared at the floor and shifted his feet. "Alice," he began.

"You're too far along in the pregnancy. It's not safe," my doctor said.

"I want a cesarean. I want this to be over." My voice was flat, exhausted. All my energy was consumed by trying not to look down at my own body.

"Unless there are complications, we believe it's best to wait until you deliver naturally. For now, we'll just do what we can to keep you comfortable. Try to sleep." I couldn't imagine being comfortable now that I knew the baby was dead. "We'll keep you overnight for observation. You can go home in the morning. Owen, you can stay here tonight with her."

He nodded. His face was pale, his mouth tightened into a line.

"I'll check back later," my doctor said. "Call the nurses' station if you need anything."

"I'm sorry," I said to Owen as soon as she left, but I had to turn my face away from him.

"This isn't your fault." He set his hand on my wrist, squeezing my fingers tightly in his.

But I knew it was my fault. Somehow, it was linked to my family. A nurse came in. "Alice, what's your mother's blood type?" She was compiling a detailed medical history, in hope of an overlooked fact that might explain my exceptional Rh response.

"I don't know." I'd been asked this question before during my pregnancy.

"Well, is your mother deceased or living?"

"I don't know."

She smiled again, with an exaggerated patience, as if I were a difficult child. "Do you think you could locate her medical records? What hospital was she born in? Do you know that?"

"I don't know anything about my mother," I lied. "She gave me up for adoption when I was born."

Owen withdrew his hand from mine, a signal to me that he hated my lie.

All night, through the door of my room, Owen and I could hear the sounds of the nursery, the nurses' cooing voices, the babies crying. Then the reunions, one after another, going on all night: mother and daughter, mother and son, meeting for the first time outside of the mother's body, in the open air. I would never have that moment, the first grasp of my daughter's body, the presence of her weight in my arms.

"They never should have put you in the maternity ward," Owen said over and over. But at 3 A.M. he fell asleep in the chair beside my bed.

I dragged the sheets and blankets over my head and stuffed my fingers in my ears.

"I need more sugar for Madeline's birthday cake," I tell Owen on the way home from the Ringling house. As soon as it cooled, I threw the Catherine Wheel cake away and decided to make my sister what she'd want most: a Judy Garland cake.

At the Seven-Eleven on Tamiami Trail, Owen stops the car and slides a birdsong cassette into the tape deck. "I'll wait." He closes his eyes to concentrate on the rhythm and pitch of the birds' cries.

I walk up and down the aisles of the store and study the shelves stacked with frozen burritos, enormous soft-drink cups, and six-packs of beer. At the magazine rack, I flip through a copy of *True Romance*, staring at an article titled "My Lover Married His Sister!" written by a woman who found her fiancé in bed with his sister. I end up beside the dairy case, looking at the cartons of 2% milk stamped with children's faces: *Have you seen me?* I once read that most children who appear on milk cartons were kidnapped by a parent.

All I can think of is Madeline's last Judy Garland postcard before the birthday invitation. *Madeline + Alice + Lily = A Family.* The equation repeats over and over like a song. How did Madeline know that I too have been thinking about Lily since the pregnancy ended and the baby died?

"Alice," Owen says. He stands beside me. "I came to find you. You've been in here for twenty minutes."

The air from the refrigerated dairy tank chills my arms until goose bumps rise on the surface of my skin. *A Family.* I have to try to talk to him before it's too late. "Owen, I've been thinking a lot about my sister."

"Of course," he says. "We came here to see her."

"No, that's not what I mean. I've been thinking about my childhood too. I'm remembering all these things I haven't thought about for years."

"Maybe being back in Sarasota makes you remember. Alice, don't you think it's good that you're finally thinking about the past?"

I want to tell Owen that he's wrong, that remembering has nothing to do with being back, that the past is rushing in because we've lost the future. I'm terrified of what could happen.

In the autumn of 1965, Judy Garland came to New Orleans. Madeline and I were a year and a half old when Lily saw a notice in the *Times-Picayune* left on the floor of one of the empty rooms: "JUDY GARLAND LIVE AT THE ORPHEUM—ONE SHOW AND ONE SHOW ONLY!!" Lily remembered Agatha talking about how Judy Garland might perform in New Orleans this year; she and her grandmother had planned to attend the concert. Lily saved two weeks of her salary to buy the three of us tickets because she knew she couldn't leave two babies alone all night at the Star Dust. She didn't want to bring us along, she often told us later, but she had no choice.

In the weeks before the concert, Lily listened to *When You're Smiling* two or three times a day, as if she were practicing for the event. She hummed "I'm Nobody's Baby" as she vacuumed guest rooms, and once when the three of us were alone in our room, Madeline swears, she danced in front of us to "Toot Toot Tootsie," something I can't imagine Lily ever doing. Lily found three more of Judy Garland's albums at the Salvation Army down the highway and brought them home.

The New Orleans Ballet performed at the Orpheum. Outside the theater, Lily stood with us in her arms, gazing at the posters for the new ballet season. *The Nutcracker* would be performed at Christmas, as it was every year. Three years before, she'd played one of the children in the first act, a tiny role, but she'd been thrilled to be chosen to play a child when she was fourteen. Inside, since she'd had to buy three tickets, she gave us each our own seat, and she placed herself between us. Did Lily hope that she'd see Agatha? If the story were a fairy tale, her grandmother would discover her in the audience. Agatha would live with the three of us in the Star Dust.

I don't remember the concert, but Lily described it to us so many times that the evening is engraved in my memory. Madeline has tricked herself into thinking she remembers it. I try to separate what Lily told us about our lives from what happened.

The house lights went down, the curtains were raised, and Judy Garland walked out from the wings onto the stage. "There's Dorothy," a woman in Lily's row whispered, but Judy Garland was now much older. Her skin was pale and wrinkled, loose around her bones, her smile faint, and she was tiny, smaller than she looked on the screen, and more fragile. She was only forty-three.

First, she sang three of her old songs without faltering—"Zing! Went the Strings of My Heart," "For Me and My Gal," and "Poor Little Rich Girl." Then the MC announced, "Miss Garland will be taking a short break." The lights brightened. The audience murmured and whispered and rose from their seats. Lily sat perfectly still, waiting for the performance to resume. A half hour passed.

Judy Garland came back for "When My Sugar Walks Down the Street," but in the middle of the song she stopped, as if she had forgotten the words. She stood alone in the middle of the stage, motionless. The stage lights illuminated her expression of fear. The curtains swept closed around her.

10

In Venice, before I have a chance to knock, Jack swings open the door of the motel room. "You're late," he says. Then he laughs. He wears a white T-shirt, so ripped that it consists of strings hanging off his shoulders to his chest, and a pair of black tuxedo pants slung low on his hips.

I walk past him, walk straight to the bed where my sister sits. She's smoking a brown cigarette, wearing a black silk dress with roses pinned to the shoulders. Madeline has decorated the motel room: candles on the dresser, on the desk, in a circle around the bed. Flashlights are positioned on the nighstand, sending beams up to the ceiling. Towels are hung on the windows to block out the sun. On her lap Madeline holds a mirror, and she lights matches over the surface of the glass, watching each small flame burn out. Whenever Madeline is unhappy, she turns on all the lights in the house and removes the shades from the lamps to reveal the bare bulbs. Next she starts with the candles, sticking hot wax to the surfaces of the furniture, not caring if she ruins tabletops and chairs.

"Happy birthday, Alice," she calls to me. "Sit down."

"What's with the lights?" I say. "We're twenty-nine today, not thirty."

At least she laughs at my joke. "It was dark," she says, as if that fact explains her behavior. She sets the mirror down on the bed and drops the book of matches onto the carpet. "Would you like a cocktail? Jack, fix my sister a drink." I smile at my sister's words, *cocktail,* her outdated vocabulary drawn from the movies we watched when we were children. Judy Garland musicals taught her how to serve drinks, how to act with men. "Would you like a Singapore Sling? A Yellow Gin Fizz? An Orange Blossom Delight?" Then she laughs again. "Actually we don't have any of those."

Jack offers me a Budweiser. I take it from his hands without touching him. "Thanks," I manage to say, and I set the can down on the dresser. "Do you like my dress?" For our birthday, I'm wearing Helen's best organza cocktail dress, with a full pink skirt and a lace belt.

"How do *I* look?" Madeline asks me.

"She spent all day getting ready to see you," Jack says.

"Beauty is work. No pain, no gain," Madeline says, repeating what Lily so often told us, but when I look at her more closely, I see that her lipstick is smeared, as if she put it on askew, and her hair is tangled and matted on one side.

"Let me show you the cake." I want to turn the conversation to a safer subject.

"Have you ever seen one of Alice's cakes? Didn't I show you some of her photos? You'll love this." Madeline jumps from the bed. She grabs one of the upturned flashlights and shines a cylinder of light like a spotlight onto Judy Garland's body. "Alice, she's beautiful! I had a pair of stockings like that once. Do you remember? We found them in a trash can."

I nod, but I don't remember Madeline having found fishnet stockings in the trash.

"Her dress looks like a nightgown," Jack says. He pretends to lift up the edge of her dress above her crotch.

"This dress is a model of one of her costumes from *I Could Go On Singing*," Madeline says. "Am I right? The scene where she sings on the top of a piano in a bar?"

"Never saw it," Jack says. He touches Judy Garland's breasts with one finger and raises his hand to his mouth to lick off the red icing while he meets my eyes.

When Jack says that he hasn't seen the movie, I feel a small surge of pleasure. He can't love Judy Garland if he never saw her last film.

"Happy birthday, Judy Garland," Madeline says. "Now I want to give you *your* present. Jack, darling, hand me the boxes from under the bed." Jack follows her orders. "I have two things for you. I think you're really going to like this."

First, I open the shiny white box with *Burdines* stamped in gold on top and lift the tissue paper carefully to expose what's inside. The box contains pieces of a mannequin, a woman's head and a single arm, which has been separated, as if severed, from the torso. The hair on the head is lush and dark. The eyes stare up at me out of the box, blue glass. At the end of the arm, a wrist curves gracefully, the fingers open, permanently stuck in a fluttering position, the long fingernails painted red.

"I thought you could use it as an art model," my sister says. "What do you think?"

"Where did you get this?" I turn the head over and over in my hands. The mannequin's hair feels real between my fingers.

"The store where the box is from."

"Did you buy this?" I ask. "You didn't pay for this, did you?" I set the head back in the box. "Did you steal this from the store?"

Madeline does not answer that question. Jack says, "Open the other box."

The second birthday present is a peignoir set, a nightgown and a matching robe, white satin trimmed with lace. "It's from a bridal shop, but I thought it was beautiful enough to wear every day," Madeline says. "Don't you like it? Try it on."

"Did you steal this from the bridal store?" I ask.

Madeline sits silently, like an accused child.

"I don't think you're being very grateful," Jack says. "Maddie went to a lot of trouble to pick this stuff out."

That's not her name, I want to yell at him. *No one has ever called her that.* I say, "Madeline, they're nice presents, but you didn't buy them."

"So? What does that matter? Do you think I don't love you if I don't spend money on you?" She crosses her arms over her breasts. "You really aren't being grateful." She turns to Jack. "She usually doesn't act like this."

Being spoken about in the third person while I'm in the room makes me furious, but now it's two against one. I'm trying to stay calm. "I'm sorry. I don't want to have a fight. We'll talk about this later. Let's have the cake."

"I got you a card," Jack says. He hands me a pink envelope. Inside, surrounded by tulips, is the message, "To a Loving Sister." The card is unsigned.

Madeline smiles. "I was planning to give you the card myself, but Jack didn't have any present for you, so I let him give it to you." The birthday card reminds me of the sympathy card sent by the community college in Atlanta where I taught a painting class last year. All of the faculty in the Fine Arts Department signed it, in identical curving script, names bordered by small pink roses. The message was stamped in gold. *We would like to express our deepest sadness for your loss.* "Thanks," I say, without looking at Jack.

"I want to lie down," Madeline announces. "Let's the three of us lie down together."

"I'd rather sit here in this chair." I know her suggestion is a danger sign, and I don't want to lie in a bed next to Jack.

"Alice, it's our birthday. Do it for me. *Please.* I haven't seen you in so long!"

With reluctance, I lie down. Madeline is in the middle. Her elbows are crooked against our sides. She hands me her cake plate, and I rest it on my stomach as if it could protect me. Madeline and Jack have eaten half of Judy Garland's leg, her stocking, her high-heeled shoe.

"When Judy Garland was in the Austen-Riggs Center in Massachusetts, she performed in the clinic theater to help the other patients. I wish I could have been there with her," my sister says. "Don't you wish you were there too?"

Jack smiles as if the question were addressed to him. I already hate his smile. It spreads slowly across his face, resembling a leer, while his eyes remain expressionless, the color of dead grass. But I am more alarmed by my sister's statement. "Linny, you wouldn't really want that," I say before I can stop myself.

Jack sits up and his smile is gone. "Why are you being so nasty to your sister?"

I glare at him, but Madeline doesn't appear to notice. "You would too like to go there," she continues. "I know you would."

"Linny, you can take the last flower from her hair." I point at the cake on the floor beside the bed. Madeline shakes her head, sits up and lights another cigarette, looking around to see if we are watching.

Glad for an excuse to leave the bed, I cut the pastry flower into small pieces. I picture Madeline in a mental hospital theater, clapping while Judy Garland sings for a crowd of patients in blue hospital gowns. I picture my sister as one of the patients.

"Alice is bored. She's heard your old stories before," Jack says. He lights a cigarette for himself. He turns to me. "Why don't you go back to Atlanta?"

Madeline frowns and straightens the red silk band she wears across her forehead in the style of a flapper, a present I sent her for our birthday last year.

"Let's talk about something else," my sister says.

Jack's lips curl over his teeth in another version of his ugly smile. "I don't know why she's here."

"Jack. . . ," Madeline says in a voice of warning. She rises and clears the cake plates from the bed. Stepping over the candles, she carries the plates into the bathroom to put them in the sink. "The Judy Garland cake was perfect," my sister tells me as she returns. She blows me a kiss, with no enthusiasm. I wonder if she's thinking about my refusal of her gifts. "Now I want to talk to you about the search," she says.

"Linny, I'd rather talk about it when we're alone," I tell her.

"Anything you have to say to Maddie, you can say in front of me. Your sister and I don't have secrets," Jack says. "We're going to find your mother. I know you don't believe it, but we are." I ignore him, but he continues. "In Venice, there are four people named Lily Carson in the phone book."

I feel anger rising in my body. "You drove to another city to read a phone book? You can't come up with anything better than that?"

Madeline suddenly says, "I'm tired. Would one of you rub my back?" I don't move because I know Jack will get up first. I have seen this same scene played out with different men. Jack rises to stand behind Madeline, gripping her shoulders, his fingers moving up and down over her neck and in her hair.

"Did you bring me anything else?" my sister asks. "The pills?"

My sister always asks me for drugs, which, since I've started therapy, would be surprisingly easy to obtain. *Tofranil. Nardil. Nortriptylene.* The names roll off my tongue awkwardly, words in a language I never learned. Dr. Levy has a prescription pad in her desk drawer. Yellow capsules, small pink circles, blue tablets. I won't get the pills for Madeline, but she'll get them some other, unsafe way.

"Jack likes Prozac," she says. "Can you get any of that?"

"I'm not giving pills to Jack or you."

"You're uptight," Jack says, watching me over Madeline's head as he smooths my sister's hair. "Why can't you be more like your sister?"

"All I asked was a simple favor. Just some pills to help me sleep. It's not a big thing. I would do anything for you." Again my sister's voice sounds sleepy and far away. She closes her eyes. Suddenly it is as if my sister has left the room. I wonder if she has already found a way to obtain drugs on her own.

Jack takes advantage of Madeline's temporary absence from the conversation and leans across the bed to say, "We're leaving for Gasparilla Island tomorrow. We won't be seeing you for a while."

I pretend I haven't heard. "Madeline, can I take a bath in your bathtub? I love the bathtubs in motels."

Madeline opens her eyes and her face brightens. Only my sister would understand my request. *Bathtub* is a word from our childhood language. We played our Emerald City game in the bathtub. Now the word means *Come talk to me alone.* "Absolutely. Use my new black soap."

But as soon as I close the bathroom door behind me, I realize that the bath in my sister's motel room is not a good idea. Madeline didn't follow me in, and I don't want to be naked on the other side of the wall from Jack. The door has no lock. I pile all the towels against it to create an obstruction and sit down on the edge of the tub, resting my head between my knees in order to calm down.

Madeline bangs on the door. "Where are the pills? I know you have them," she yells. Her energy has returned. "Alice, answer me! Can I go through your purse?"

I push away the towels and crack open the door. "Come in, Linny."

"Can Jack come in too?"

"No! Just you." Madeline has an amazing ability to make an absurd request seem innocuous and my refusal of it strange. When she enters the bathroom, I quickly push the door shut behind her. "I want to know what you meant on the postcard."

Madeline climbs into the bathtub and lies down, propping her feet on the faucet. "What postcard?"

"You know, the card where you wrote *Madeline + Alice + Lily = A Family*."

My sister smiles. "What do you think I meant?" Then she opens her arms. "Alice, come lie down with me. We can pretend we're kids. Remember the games we used to play in the bathtub in the Star Dust? Remember—"

I've reached the limit of my patience with my sister. Instead of going to lie in the tub, I open the bathroom door. "I'm leaving, Linny. I need to go home."

Driving back to our rented house, I see that I must be making Madeline's thoughts my own. Her message didn't have the meaning I thought it had. I've been thinking about Lily, so I imagined that she must be too. Owen was right: she just wanted to see me on our birthday; with my sister, I want to read every action, every gesture, with alarm. I drive faster, hoping Owen will be home when I arrive, hoping he and I can salvage what's left of my birthday today and celebrate it without my sister.

Each year, on my birthday, Owen has made me a cassette tape. The tapes contain songs, bits of birdcalls from his work tapes, and his voice. Last year, he edited finches with Laurie Anderson and told a story about when he was a child and fell out of a tree. He ended last year's birthday tape by looking forward to next year, the year we've reached now, when there'd be three of us in our family. Remembering the tape, my eyes sting, but I don't cry. I force myself to stare straight out at Tamiami Trail. Last year, I listened to that tape ten times.

This morning, I woke up early and planned to spend my birthday with Owen, but when I looked at him, sleeping beside me, I felt panic rising in my body. In the kitchen, at 6 A.M., I found this year's birthday tape, but I was afraid to listen to it. What if he talked about the baby? What if he mentioned the life that we're never going to have now? I couldn't stand to hear him speak her name, and I slipped the tape into my purse, still in its plastic case, to save for later. Then I got in the car and drove around Sarasota until it was time to meet my sister.

As soon as I unlock the door of the house, the phone rings. Before I answer, I call, "Owen?" He's not home. I hope I'll hear his voice on the phone.

"I've been calling forever! Where have you been?" Madeline doesn't wait for an answer. "Alice, Jack left me."

First, I think *good*, then instantly my mood shifts to a familiar alarm about my sister's fate. I open the cabinet under the kitchen sink, remove the vinegar, and uncap the bottle. "Tell me what happened."

"He said I was impossible. He took the car. He said if I tried to stop him, he'd smash everything he could get his hands on in the room."

I take a long drink before I answer. "There's something seriously wrong with that man, Linny."

"How could he make this scene on our birthday?" For the first time, my sister is calling it *our* birthday and not just her own. But then she says, "I just took seven pills."

"What kind of pills?"

"I'm not sure." She begins to cry.

"Calm down," I tell her. "I'll be there in an hour."

When I pull into the motel parking lot in Venice, Madeline is standing by the neon sign advertising VACANCY, holding one high-heeled shoe in each hand, wearing a pink silk suit. She wraps her arms around my shoulders in a tight embrace.

In the room, the candles are extinguished, all the flashlights turned off. The air smells of smoke, and phone books are open on the floor. The cake plate is broken into pieces on the bed.

"I don't know what I'd do without you," Madeline says as soon as we enter the room.

"Where are the pills? Give them to me."

"What pills?"

"The ones you said on the phone that you took. I want to see the bottle."

"I said that? Oh, you mean the aspirin. I had a horrible headache." My sister is smiling. Now that I'm here, now that she's brought me to her side, Madeline is happy.

Looking at my sister, I can envision the rest of the afternoon: her weeping, my comforting her, and finally, at the end of the day, before dark, Jack's return. I'll vanish from my sister's sight as she and Jack wrap their arms around each other. To avoid this scene we need a plan. "Linny, I want to take back the bridal outfit."

"How would you feel if I took back your Judy Garland cake?"

"I didn't steal the ingredients to make it."

"If I had the money, I would've bought you a present."

My sister has never had a job. Ever since she was in the hospital, she's been eligible for a monthly disability payment, but it can't be more than several hundred dollars a month. I've always wondered how she gets by but have been afraid to ask. When I first married Owen, every month I cashed a small part of my paycheck to send to her and told Owen I spent the money on art supplies.

When I look at my sister now, her mouth is soft and sad, her lipstick rubbed off. Sometimes I see Madeline through the eyes of others and I'm afraid. For Madeline, it's the 1940s, a decade that was over long before she was born. She loves her hats with veils, her peplum suits, her lips shaped into a bow. She pines for the "old days," the days acted out in Judy Garland movies. But those days were before her time. She never lived in the past she covets. In any case, it's a past that doesn't exist, that never existed, the world of MGM musicals.

Now, as we get in the car, Madeline says, "Do you remember *The Harvey Girls*? It was one of Judy Garland's early films. Mother always liked that movie."

"Linny, don't call her Mother. She never let us call her that."

"She *is* our mother."

The word *mother* is hard for me to hear. If I call her *Lily*, I can keep her at a distance. In the eight weeks since the pregnancy ended, that distance has been collapsing. The pregnancy has brought her back, filled me with longing for the woman who left us twelve years ago, and I don't know why.

Madeline and I walk up Main Street in downtown Sarasota on our way to the bridal shop. We pass a poster advertising a missing girl, her face displayed on a telephone pole with DO YOU HAVE ANY INFORMATION ABOUT THIS CHILD? printed below.

"Look at that. She's been gone for five years. Why don't they give up?" Madeline says as we pass the sign.

"Maybe she ran away."

"Children that age don't run away."

"We thought about running away. We planned the whole thing." I am suddenly conscious that, for once, I am the one bringing up the past, asking my sister to remember.

"We were different." She walks on, ahead of me.

I remember our plan. We were eleven and wanted to go to New York, the city whose name Lily invoked whenever she talked about what her life could have been like if she'd gone on tour with the New Orleans Ballet, if she had not had us. She said Judy Garland used to perform in New York all the time. From what she'd told us, New York City seemed like the perfect place for two eleven-year-old girls to go alone. We found a Manhattan guidebook in a motel room and read it over and over. We never put the plan into action because we delayed for so long that Lily left us before we could abandon her.

My sister pauses in front of a display window, looking at a woman with broad shoulders and a severe expression, wearing a red jacket decorated with epaulets. "Do you like that?" She points at the window, crossing her arms over her chest as if she is considering her own question. In a conversation with my sister, my participation is not required.

In art school, I took a class in costume design and studied the history of the American mannequin. I remember a timeline of the mannequin's life, from her origins in the Industrial Revolution, a crank-up model that moved its arms and legs, to the fiberglass figures of today. In the twenties, wax women melted in the heat of the display lights. I picture Madeline with a papier-mâché face, strips of newspaper smoothed over wire bones, a body made of plaster, a *femme fatale*, a Judy Garland mannequin. I can kiss her red wax lips and take her hand. But I don't want to make that gesture of love. Instead I will separate her torso from her hips, unscrew her ribs. The rod that holds her spine in its straight vertical slips out. I will remove her eyes, ovals of glass, pull out her seed pearl teeth, one at a time.

"Here's the store," my sister says. The sign reads TOTAL WOMAN. The front window is crowded with mannequins at various stages of life: a bride, a bridesmaid, a pregnant woman, a bride's mother. White, newly painted, with a scrolled design over the front window, the storefront looks like icing edged on a cake. "I can't believe you want to return your present." She opens the door.

Inside, the store is divided: one half is a bridal store, and the other, behind a sliding wall, is a maternity store. When I see the racks of large pleated dresses with no waists and drooping bows pinned to the collar on the other side of the wall, I feel sick to my stomach. A few weeks ago, I had a closet full of dresses like that, until I asked Owen to put them all in a garbage bag and throw them away.

"Madeline, forget it. I changed my mind. I'll keep the outfit."

She flips through a rack of dresses labeled MOTHER OF THE BRIDE, peach and pink chiffon, with sleeves like wings. "We're going to get rid of your present. That's what you said you wanted."

A saleswoman from the bridal store approaches us. "Can I help you, girls?" she asks. She looks from me to Madeline, then back. "Who's the bride? When's the big day?"

Madeline looks at me. I look at her. I know she's about to lie. She says, "We're having a double wedding. October first." Lily's birthday.

I take a deep breath to prepare for my own lie. "Actually, I'm expecting a baby." It's easy, one simple sentence, oddly familiar. I'm used to practicing its opposite: *I lost my baby.* The saleswoman smiles.

In the maternity store, several women who are at least in their second trimester study the racks of clothes. I rest my hand, palm down, on my stomach, a protective gesture that makes a lump rise in my throat, which I tell myself to ignore. Madeline ties a pink pillow around my waist. There's one pillow for each trimester, and I have chosen the "six months" pillow, the most truthful, closest to how long the baby lived. I pull on a jumper that resembles a child's pinafore, with pockets over the hips. I stare at my reflection in the mirror. The only familiar part of me, the only aspect unchanged by the fact of pregnancy, is my long hair. I had been warned that hair sometimes darkens during pregnancy, but mine remained light brown, straight and thick, exactly like my sister's before she cut hers. Owen used to tell me he loved my hair. He used to say we should never let our daughter cut her hair until it grew to her knees like a child in a fairy tale. I wish I could walk out of the store in this dress, the pillow tied to my stomach. I wish I could live this lie forever.

But I'm not alone. The mirror reflects my sister, sitting behind me. She looks small, with her feet tucked under her, her hands folded in her lap. Her expression is sad. "Alice, do you remember the day we played French orphanage girls in the parking lot of the Star Dust? You told me, 'Let's pretend we're sisters?' 'We are sisters,' I said. You said, 'No, we're not. We're twins.' Alice, do you remember?"

"Yes," I say in a low voice.

"You know as well as I do that there are two kinds of twins. The blue-eyed angels, the twins from the Wrigley's Doublemint Gum magazine ads, with their handsome dates, their clean white teeth, their gleaming hair. You always wanted to be like that, but those girls aren't like us, Alice."

I already know what Madeline will say next.

"I can't go alone, Alice. If I go by myself, I'm not going to find her. I need you with me. Please come with me. She's our mother."

Mother: what I wanted to be and couldn't become. *Mother:* what Lily never wanted to be.

Madeline + Alice + Lily = A Family.

"I can't leave Owen."

"Doesn't Owen want you to feel better?" Madeline leans closer.

"Linny, stop."

"You know," my sister says slowly, as if she is carefully choosing her words, "you're thinking of Owen first, before anyone, before yourself. What about *you*? You were the one who was suffering this year." She pauses. "It was your experience. It was your pain. You carried the baby inside your body. He can't understand what you're going through now, Alice. But I do. Alice, remember, who was the one who called you the day she died? Who knew what had happened to you without being told?"

I'm walking faster than Madeline as we leave the store. "Alice!" she calls.

I know my sister is wrong. Owen wants to help me, and he feels the loss as acutely as I do, as ours, not just mine. But I can't help asking another, terrible question. What if Madeline is right: what if finding Lily is the key that opens the past and heals the present?

She catches up with me on the sidewalk and grabs my arm.

"Isn't Jack supposed to be going with you?"

"I couldn't care less about Jack," my sister says. "I don't ever want to see him again."

"Linny, I haven't said I'll go."

"We can leave on the last Tuesday in June. That would have been your due date, right?" She drops her voice. "Alice, I know how to make you feel better. I always have."

My head spins. Which one of us needs the other? I am Madeline. Madeline is me. The pull of her voice takes me back to the past, to the world of childhood. Without my daughter, without Owen, I find myself returned to my original family. I am Lily's daughter, not someone's mother. I am Madeline's sister, not someone's wife.

Madeline says, "I have something to show you." From her purse, she pulls a large square notebook, covered in blue velvet frayed at the edges, and sets it in my hands. It's Lily's scrapbook, the story of her life in the ballet world, ending with our birth, the story of Judy Garland she arranged through clippings and photographs, her own life and Judy Garland's merged into one story. I still know the contents of every page. Madeline moves closer to turn the pages. "See, Alice, she wants us to find her. It's a clue."

Lily's scrapbook begins with the stories of the first twins, small photographs of Agnes and Agatha when they were young, twin *cartes de visite*. Their faces are identical blurs, and Croatian words— their then names—are etched below the picture. There's no photograph of Agatha as an adult, only a yellowed clipping showing Judy Garland's mother, Ethel Gumm, standing in the factory parking lot where she later died suddenly one morning.

Finally, I see the piece of net from Lily's *Red Shoes* costume, faded to a faint red. I study the snapshots I've forgotten. Lily, age seven or eight, her long hair pulled back tightly from her face, wearing a black leotard and pink tights, standing in second position at the ballet *barre*. Her body is completely straight. Her mouth is set in a thin, grim line. A picture of *pointe* class a few years later: Lily's arm arcs in the air. Her head is turned to the right, eyes cast down to the floor, and I can't read her expression, but I know she's in pain. *Pointe* class hurt, she used to tell us, showing us her bare feet as evidence. Years after the classes, her toes were scabbed and calloused. She wears striped leg-warmers over her tights and a T-shirt ripped at the neck. Costume after costume—Lily as Giselle swooning on the stage, as Juliet poised at her window, as Gretel dancing through the woods, scattering bread crumbs behind her across the stage in the hope that she will be found.

Then Lily included the lyrics to several Judy Garland songs, from the soundtrack to *A Star Is Born*. "Born in a trunk in the Princess Theater. . . ." The typed letters are unsteady; she must have typed the words on the office typewriter in the Star Dust.

The book ends with us, with the newspaper story "Girl Conceals Pregnancy to Be Ballet Star," and with our birth certificates, side by side on the last page. "Girl Carson" is repeated twice because Lily hadn't yet given us our own names. When I see Agnes and Agatha preserved in the daguerreotypes, the birth certificates, the newspaper photographs of Judy Garland, and the words to her songs, I feel a wave of sadness. I remember Lily's stories about the other women in our family, the women from the past.

"Now, this." Madeline takes the scrapbook from me and sets another object in my hands, a thick black notebook. It's my sketchbook from childhood.

"Oh, God." My hands are shaking as I turn the pages. I haven't seen the sketchbook since we left New Orleans to move to Sarasota, when Lily had told me she threw it away. Here it is, now, eleven years later, a record of the life the three of us had together. I turn past my drawings of girls, to page after page of fathers. And then I find the sketches for the paper dolls with which Madeline and I made our magic world: Judy Garland and Ginger Love, the matching sisters, like us. For a moment, I feel as if I'm drowning, just as I used to imagine Lily's parents had drowned, as if dark cold water is closing over my head and an undertow pulls me down no matter how much I fight.

For the past few weeks since the baby died, I have heard Lily's voice in my head. I've remembered stories. Now I see all the images that accompany them, the records of the past, and my chest aches, my throat tightens, and I know what I'm going to do.

The past overwhelms the present. My childhood rushes back like a storm.

11

A single photograph documents Agatha's and Agnes's twinship, a photograph printed on a silver-colored plate of two identical children, *Agnes and Agatha* scratched in Croatian on the back. Of course, the family didn't have a camera of its own. A traveling photographer who walked from town to town would have taken their picture. In France and England, in the mid-nineteenth century, the portrait business was prospering. Queen Victoria was photographed for the first time, and her picture, reprinted as a tiny *carte de visite*, was sold on the London streets. No one had ever seen her real face before. A photograph, it was generally agreed, was authentic, while a painting was not.

By the early part of the twentieth century, in small villages in Eastern Europe, however, photographers were still very rare. Stephan Bantorvya, the traveling photographer who first came to my great-grandmother's village in 1920, was regarded with suspicion. Agatha's father allowed him to sleep in the barn because he needed another body to work the fields, since his daughters could not work as fast or as long as men.

Stephan's first specialty was pictures of dead children. He did portraits for family albums. He'd cut a lock of hair, then take the dead child's photograph. For an extra fee, Stephan made photographic jewelry, a round locket with the hair and the daguerreotype for the bereaved mother to wear around her neck. His other specialty was twins. He liked to pose twins together because he could practice symmetry. He wanted to make the girls as identical as possible. He took the photograph of Agnes and Agatha for free because the twin girls charmed him, and he gave the photograph to their father as a gift.

Inside the oval print, the sisters are posed in matching dresses, handkerchiefs circling their necks, their arms carefully crossed with their hands in the same positions in their laps. Their expressions are serious. Stephan was not accustomed to thinking about the intricacies of faces with changing expression, faces with movement, since he worked so often with the dead. Their hair falls in ringlets to their shoulders, matching curls they scorched with the iron.

For seven years, Stephan the photographer returned to the village every summer to photograph Agnes and Agatha. The bureau drawer in their bedroom was stacked with pictures of their identical faces. When she was seventeen, Agatha married Stephan the photographer, who would be our great-grandfather. The sisters spent a day dividing their clothing and possessions. How did Agnes feel on that afternoon when her sister gave up her handkerchiefs and dresses? Agatha was willing to surrender everything from her old life. She was moving to a tiny house on the other side of the river, a house on the edge of the land that belonged to her father and her brothers.

There are many photographs of Agatha after the marriage. She is always alone in these portraits. Agatha standing in the fields holding a scythe, Agatha, head wrapped in a red scarf, posed by the house on the hill where she grew up, Agatha on her way to church in a muslin dress. Agnes did not appear in any of these photographs. She had begun to have headaches that could last more than a day, and she lay in the darkened room upstairs, a cloth soaked in vinegar covering her eyes. In the early afternoon, the house was always quiet because everyone was outside working in the fields, and she could be alone. She felt exhausted. Her father looked in the door-way of the room, saw her lying in bed fully dressed, and shook his head.

12

Once we were big enough, Lily took us out of the suitcase and the ballet bag and let us share a single bed beside her own. When we were little girls, three, four, and five years old, Madeline and I slept with our legs hooked together, my knee on Madeline's calf, her ankle against mine. We slept like lovers. The year we turned five, Lily began waking us each night. Hours after she'd put us to bed, we'd be pulled from sleep by her touch, her hands on our shoulders shaking us, her fingers in our hair. Her grip was strong.

"Get dressed," she whispered. "Right now." Madeline sat up. Half asleep, I struggled into my sister's clothes. We only had one T-shirt, one pair of shorts, one bathing suit, a single dress. We alternated clothes, trading back and forth each day. The only thing I owned by myself were my shoes. Madeline always looked wide-awake, her eyes clear, her expression calm, as if she had not been asleep at all.

"Hurry up," my sister said, helping me lace my tennis shoes. I stood quietly in the dark, my eyes squeezed shut, while she brushed her teeth with the toothbrush we shared. Then I took my turn. Lily watched us, tapping her foot and blowing circles of smoke. I never saw her smoke any other time.

In the car, I climbed into the backseat while Madeline sat up front with Lily. I couldn't lie down across the seat and go to sleep, much as I would have liked to. Madeline was watchful, intent.

"Let's go," Lily always said to start the drive. She drove fast down Airline Highway, gunning the engine as we left the Star Dust behind. We always headed in the same direction: uptown, to the world where Lily once lived. The streets were empty, the houses shuttered and quiet. The tour never varied. We drove past the New Orleans Ballet first, a dark stone building. Second was the Prytania Theater, a brick structure with a rounded roof and a neon marquee. Finally, as if she'd saved it for last, we drove by Agatha's house, where Lily grew up. Lily drove most quickly during this part of the trip. The house was a blur of green paint and sidewalk. We were allowed to see it only in snatches. Each night I tried to see another piece of it, a corner of the porch or a windowpane, so that I could reconstruct a complete vision of it in my head.

"Why can't we go in?" I asked once. "Why can't we see Agatha?"

"Because we can't," Lily said. "She's dead. Now don't ask me any more questions."

Lights glowed behind the shuttered windows of the house. I knew Agatha wasn't dead. Yet it was her old house that always sparked Lily's stories. The first night we drove by it, as we crossed Magazine Street on our way back to the Star Dust, Lily said, "You girls have been good. I know I'm hard on you sometimes."

Then she glanced back at me through the rearview mirror and over at Madeline beside her. Lily's stories always began with Judy Garland.

"Judy Garland was a child with the voice of an adult," Lily said, as if this fact explained her fascination. Nearly all of the stories Lily told us were about when Judy Garland was a child star, in the years that led up to her role in *The Wizard of Oz*. Madeline and I listened intently.

"Judy Garland and her mother slept in the car all the way through California. They left the rest of the family behind at home." In those days, vaudeville theaters were fading out, fast becoming movie houses. Judy Garland was Baby Gumm, performing between shows, while her mother accompanied her singing on the piano in the pit below the stage. Or, Baby Gumm was dressed as an Egyptian princess, in a hat brimmed with tiny bells. A hatbox was carried on stage, and she jumped out.

Mother and daughter both wanted entrance to the elaborate false world of MGM—barns full of sawdust, klieg lights, cameras that were lowered on a boom. Judy Garland's mother taught her to act, just as later Judy Garland would teach her own daughter. Liza was eleven when her mother brought her out on stage during one of her own performances and made the girl sing all the songs she knew.

Lily said that in Hollywood, where Judy Garland had lived, flowers bloomed in the middle of winter. Pink oleander lined the walls outside the movie studios where the movie mothers brought their little girls for screen tests and callbacks. Lily had never been to Hollywood, but she knew all about it. The only flowers I saw at the Star Dust were the dandelions that grew through the parking lot's cracked asphalt.

Through Judy Garland, Madeline and I learned our family history. Starting with Judy Garland, Lily moved back and forth in time. "Liza stood on stage, terrified, but her mother knew she could sing. I was going to be the best dancer the New Orleans Ballet had ever had," Lily said. The stories were about Agnes and Agatha, then her life before she had Madeline and me. There were no men except for Agatha's husband, Stephan, whom she had never met, and Reid Alistair, of whom she rarely spoke.

I settled into my seat and looked out the window, into the uptown houses, imagining the families that lived within. They sat down to dinner together, wrapped themselves in clean towels after a bath, and read books at bedtime. I could imagine the lives of the girls. They slept peacefully through the night. But none of them had mothers who told them stories like ours.

On the nights Lily drove us through New Orleans, past the places from her old life, I felt safe and sure that no matter what else happened, the three of us—my mother, my sister, and I—were our own family.

After we turned five, Lily no longer took us with her while she cleaned. Instead, she locked us in the room where the three of us lived. "Don't touch this door," she said every morning on her way out to her first shift. "Alice, you watch Madeline. Madeline, you're in charge of Alice." We nodded solemnly. As soon as the lock clicked and Lily was gone, we climbed into the bathtub with the ice bucket.

The empty bathtub was Emerald City. The plastic bucket was a treasure chest we filled with small stones and shells from the parking lot. Madeline collected pieces of broken glass. "Amethyst. Ruby. Pearl." She pronounced each word slowly. We sat facing each other, our legs spread open, feet touching.

We emptied the ice bucket in the bathtub between our legs to start the game.

We set the jewels in a circle to make stage lights. In the stage set of the bathtub, Reid Alistair and Judy Garland were the stars. Reid

Alistair was a famous ballet dancer, and Judy Garland was a child star. They danced together, climbing the cold porcelain walls of the bathtub in a tango, a fox-trot, a chorus line of two. Judy Garland was very thin from the MGM diet Lily had described to us, and Reid Alistair could easily lift her over his head.

"Judy Garland only weighs three pounds," Madeline said, pointing to an imaginary figure in the tub.

"Nobody can weigh that little," I told her. "Not even a baby."

Madeline invented a sister for Judy Garland. Her name was Ginger Love. She was an unknown Gumm sister. She didn't perform with the other sisters in vaudeville shows. Instead, she worked for MGM in the costume department. Lily had told us Judy Garland had a friend named Ginger at the studio. As we envisioned her, Ginger Love wasn't glamorous or even pretty. She didn't have a husband, children, or even a lover. She didn't have a mother. And she was always alone.

Madeline wanted Ginger Love to be five, like us. "She never grew up," Madeline said. "She didn't want to." Ginger Love sucked her thumb all night and slept inside her kitchen stove. I pictured Ginger Love, her finger swollen from being in her mouth, her eyes closed. She was happy. She was safe. She would never leave the oven to get married or have children. She never ate. She never spoke out loud to anyone. "Ginger Love was a very good girl . . . ," Madeline sang as we sat in the bathtub. "Her hair was made of white and blue pearls. When she slept her dress would swirl." My sister dreamed up the best lines for the songs, so I let her take the lead.

I liked the game better when we let Ginger Love grow up. Sometimes Judy Garland and Ginger Love were in the Ziegfeld Follies. Lily had told us about them on one of the late-night drives. In sequined leotards, they performed high kicks on stage, diamond tiaras balanced on their heads. Reid Alistair watched from a seat in the audience. "He's jealous," Madeline said. "He wants to be like them." The sisters lived side by side in matching pink motel rooms in the middle of Emerald City.

"You need to start ballet before your bones develop," Lily said. "To have good turnout, you need to start lessons when you're five."

All our lives Madeline and I had heard about ballet. Lily had told us all about Madame Makarov, her old teacher, but we couldn't study with her because Lily said she was too expensive. My sister and I would take our lessons at the Airline Highway YMCA. At the Salvation Army, Lily bought us leotards and tights other girls had outgrown. Madeline and I spun and twirled, our arms arcing over our heads. Lily twisted our long hair into buns at the back of our necks.

The afternoon of the first lesson, we walked down Airline Highway to the YMCA. Lily walked quickly toward the building. "Hurry up," she said. Madeline and I followed her inside. The other girls, all older than us, were just arriving. Lily helped us off with our jackets, adjusted our leotards, then stepped back. I looked around to see if the other girls were watching us with Lily, if they could tell that she'd once been a famous dancer, but most of them had come with their mothers too. Madeline and I were the only girls who did not have ballet shoes.

The ballet teacher clapped her hands to get the students' attention. "Girls, assemble at the *barre*." Most of the girls seemed unsure of what to do, but Madeline and I had known what the *barre* was before we'd danced a single step. Lily sat down on the floor at the back of the room where I could see her in the mirror.

Class began with the five positions. Lily had already showed us the positions many times. We could move our feet just as the teacher told us. Then she explained how to put our hand on our hip and extend our right leg back. Lily had always told us ballet was painful. I cast a sideways glance at Madeline. She bit her lip. I could feel Lily's gaze on us in the mirror.

Until the third class, the following week, we were able to follow along. Then the ballet teacher announced that we were going to move away from the *barre*. She would demonstrate the *glissade* in preparation for the leaps that would be required of us later, when we were grown-up dancers.

"I can do it." It was my sister's voice. "Can I try?"

Madeline didn't wait for the teacher's permission. She ran forward, sliding as hard as she could toward the mirror. For a moment, I thought she'd smash the mirror, fall straight into the wall of glass. Then her feet skidded on the floor. Her ankle twisted as she went down. Madeline's eyes were closed, her face contorted with pain.

"Linny," I whispered, but she couldn't hear me.

Lily bent over Madeline. She had run to us from the back of the room.

The ballet teacher lowered her voice. "I think the problem here really is that the girls are too young."

Lily gathered our clothes and shoes. Madeline sat up, her body shaking. "I started when I was this age," Lily said, not looking at the ballet teacher.

Outside, Lily told Madeline, "Walk. I'm not carrying you." Beside me, Madeline limped along, her foot dragging behind her on the sidewalk.

We were never going back, and I'd never even had my turn. Madeline had ruined it for me.

At the Star Dust, Lily said, "Give me the clothes." We silently undressed. When I handed her our balled-up leotards and tights, she walked outside. From the window, I watched her throw the ballet clothes into the dumpster; then she slammed the lid.

That same night, we learned that Judy Garland had died.

Before bed, as Lily was switching the small black-and-white television from channel to channel in an effort to ignore us, she found the funeral service being broadcast. "Oh God!" She sank to the carpet where she sat, motionless, light from the screen flickering over her face. "Agatha," she said.

For a moment, I thought Agatha was dead, and it was her funeral on television. On the screen, a white coffin was piled with roses. Then I heard the taped voice-over: the child Judy Garland singing "It's far, far away—behind the moon, beyond the rainbow. . . ." A voice-over related the facts: Judy Garland had been found in the bathroom of her London home, an empty bottle of Seconal on the floor beside her. The coroner ruled her death an overdose. Everyone suspected *suicide*.

Madeline ran to Lily's side. Lily cried, the only time I would ever hear her cry, but my sister began to rock back and forth on the floor, pressing her knees close to her chest with her hands. Her sobbing was loud and continual and seemed to emanate from somewhere deep within her body.

Locked in her own private world of sadness, Lily ignored Madeline, as if she weren't there, as if she weren't crying, but I stared at her, helplessly. I was too young to understand what was happening to my sister. Excluded from the scene, afraid to move toward either of them and terrified of my sister's response to the death of someone she had never met, I sat on the bed by myself and stared at Madeline. I knew what my sister was doing: she could make up for her failure at ballet with sadness about Judy Garland. Her grief matched Lily's, a compensation for her fall.

I don't remember the television funeral. Madeline would later tell me that twenty-two thousand people walked past Judy Garland's white coffin. Thousands of others stood behind barriers outside. On a portable tape recorder beside the coffin, the song "Over the Rainbow" droned over and over into the room. Finally, she would be "laid to rest" in a crypt called Chapel of the Lilies, behind a huge glass window like a movie screen. Madeline says the white coffin was covered with yellow roses; star after star filed by—Lauren Bacall, Katharine Hepburn, Cary Grant—each placing a rose on top. Judy Garland wore a black crepe dress and silver slippers that no one could see.

The night of Judy Garland's death, all I could think about was my sister. Her sadness seemed out of proportion to the event. Her grief was somehow wrong.

When I was older, and I read biographies of Judy Garland, I read that her new husband found her in the bathroom after he broke down the door. She had been in there for most of the night, and her body was already stiff and cold. He also found the bottle of pills. More than one hundred were missing.

13

"Today, we're having a model," I tell the old women in my life-drawing class. "I want you to sketch me." The women don't know it's my last class. They set up their easels and pick up their charcoal pencils. In the center of the classroom, I unbutton my dress.

It's Helen's dress, chintz with a Peter Pan collar. I avoid her gaze and climb up on the platform quickly. I close my eyes. From Owen's tape recorder, which I brought with me for the occasion, Judy Garland begins "Meet Me Tonight in Dreamland," all bright trills and louder than I ever heard it. The women are silent, heads bent over their sketch pads as they sketch the outline of my body. I force myself to open my eyes and survey the classroom. Most of my students are too self-conscious to study me. Helen's stare is level, steady disapproval.

I've arranged my body on a bench draped with a brocade curtain, legs bent at the knee and pressed together like a pin-up girl from the forties. In the bathroom of Beachaven, an hour ago, I outlined my lips in dark red. Now that I'm on the platform, becoming a film star doesn't work, so I go back instead to *A Girl's Guide to the Saints*. I visualize St. Joan burning at the stake with an expression of repose on her face while the whole village watched. She knew what the men—the soldiers and the king—did not. My leg aches from my ankle to my thigh; my hip is tight and throbbing. I forget St. Joan and count, a trick Lily taught us: one Mississippi, two Mississippi, three Mississippi.

Charcoal scratches over the page, and Judy Garland starts "Cry Baby Cry" in a mournful voice. I concentrate on sucking in my stomach. What could I say about why I'm leaving? How could I explain myself? Unlike me, these women have children. Unlike me, they have outlived their original families. They wouldn't understand why I need now to turn back to that past. Their daughters are living. Their mothers are dead.

"Okay. Good job today. I'll see you Tuesday," I tell the class as I release my leg from its stiff pose and step off the platform. As quickly as I can, I dress, yanking the dress down over my hips. Of course, it's tight. I hear a faint tear in the fabric. The old women file out of the classroom. "Bye," I say. "Good-bye." They don't know they won't ever see me again.

In the parking lot, Helen stands beside my car holding her sketchbook. "I signed myself out. Want to go to the ugly beach?"

"I can't. I have some errands." The truth is, I have nothing to do to fill the rest of the afternoon, so I invent a task. "I need a car wash."

"I'll come with you." Helen opens the car door on the passenger side and climbs in.

In the car wash, Helen lights a cigarette, and smoke swirls in the dark space of the car. The huge blue brushes fill the windshield, flooding the glass with water. "I have to tell you something," I begin. "I'm going to look for my mother."

"You and Owen?"

I take a deep breath. "No, Madeline and I are going together."

A long silence. Then Helen says in a low voice, "Don't go."

Sheets of water pour over the windows of the car. Owen once told me he had been terrified as a child when his father took him to the car wash. He felt trapped inside the car, no possibility of escape. He calmed himself by pretending the car was a submarine and he was on a top secret and highly important mission. The image of Owen in his father's car feeling fear comforted me because I was afraid throughout my childhood. It was one of the few moments in Owen's life when he'd ever felt afraid.

Owen. I have not yet told Owen. Telling Helen isn't easy. Telling him will be impossible. I no longer leave on my drives each morning alone; instead, I lie in bed beside him and count the seconds that pass in my head, until I can safely rise from bed. During the day, I plan my drawing classes or sit hunched over my sketchbook, as if I'm working. When Owen's face brightens as he sees me pretending to work, I feel awful about my lie.

"Alice, I'm talking to you. What's wrong?" Helen says.

"Nothing."

"Why in the name of God did you make yourself the life-drawing model today?"

The green light in front us blinks through the dark, telling me it's time to drive out of the car wash. Helen and I drive in silence down Tamiami Trail. On a telephone pole, as we pass, I see a notice about a little girl who has been missing. In the newspaper, I recently read an FBI statistic: after a kidnapped person has been gone for more than twenty-four hours, there is a only a three-percent chance that that person will come back.

Helen breaks the silence. "Okay, Alice, if you're not going to talk to me, I have plenty to say. First, anyone could tell you that you're not going to find your mother. You haven't seen the woman in years. I doubt you'd recognize her if she walked up to the car right now." She pauses. "Second, I don't know what your sister has up her sleeve, and of course I don't know her, but I wouldn't trust her." She taps her cigarette in the air, knocking a trail of ash on her skirt. "Madeline simply wants to take you away from Owen."

We're driving in the open air now, beside the bay. I'm dazed, directionless, my perceptions dulled. There is only one thing I am certain of: the past is pulling me down like an undertow.

"You didn't tell Owen yet, did you?" Helen shakes her head. "Alice, don't do this. Don't leave here now."

"I'm sorry," I say. I turn the car around in the parking lot of Mister Donut and head back to Beachaven.

When we arrive at the curb in front of the building, Helen reaches into her pocket and pulls out a folded rectangle of paper. "Here. It's for you." A moment later, she disappears through the double glass doors of Beachaven.

I unfold the piece of paper. It's Helen's drawing from this morning's class. In the middle of the page, she has drawn me, naked, my knees bowed, my hands covering my breasts as if I am self-conscious, my expression sad. Beside me, she has drawn the body of a man. He is fully dressed, his right arm reaching out to me, as if to pull me toward him. I am turned away from him. She has outlined the man's body so that it's thin and dotted freckles across his face. His expression is sad. In his right hand, he holds a tape recorder.

The night before my sister and I plan to leave, I still haven't told Owen. Each time I prepare the words, formulate the speech in which I tell him I'm leaving Sarasota but want him to believe that I'm not leaving him, I can't do it. Each time I attempt to tell him, I decide not to go. I don't know how to explain my departure.

Tonight I dress in one of Helen's long white nightgowns. It buttons all the way up to the neck like the nightdress of a Victorian child. I get into bed with my sketchbook, balancing it on my knees. There is nothing to draw. Before the pregnancy, in that other life, I often used to sketch out new ideas right before bed. Then I would sleep and look at them again in the morning with fresh eyes.

But I begin to draw Lily, sketching her as a young mother, her long blond hair, her thin frame, the pink maid's uniform she wore at the Star Dust. When he comes into the bedroom, Owen drops his jeans to the floor. I turn my gaze away from his body. "Not another cake, I hope," he says.

"No." He dresses for bed in a T-shirt and shorts. Before the baby died, we always slept naked. I remember the feeling of his bare arms on my back, his leg thrown over mine, the way I once slept with Madeline. When the pregnancy ended, without discussing it, we both began wearing clothes to bed.

"Goodnight." I lean over and drop a kiss on his forehead, the kiss I'd give a child. Before he can kiss me back, I turn away from him and open the sketchbook, covering the paper with the crook of my arm.

When Owen and I were first married, I used sleep as a tool. I would sleep for fifteen minutes, hoping to find some images for a piece in a dream. In art school, small restorative naps never failed me. If I were feeling blocked in the studio at school and other students were around, I used to sneak into the staff bathroom at the end of the hall and stretch out on the tile floor for a while. In a book about the Surrealist movement, I'd read that Robert Desnos hung a placard on the door to his studio whenever he slept that spelled out ARTIST WORKING.

Art school. The studio. A book I once read. Words I once used casually that composed my life. As if every cell in my body has changed with the baby's loss, I'm no longer the person who spoke those words or who lived that life. *Owen.* Now I know I'll be awake all night. Immediately,

Owen falls asleep. I've always envied his ability to sleep. He'll climb into bed and drop right off, while I sit wide-awake beside him. When we first met, I watched him all night for three days. Now I touch the shock of hair that covers his forehead, pushing it from his face.

"Owen," I whisper. My voice cracks as if I'm going to cry. I wish I could start talking with the ease and fluency I had when we first met, when the stories about my past came easily to me. Now, although I've been thinking about those stories from the past more than ever, I can't begin to articulate the reasons why I want to look for Lily.

As I lean over Owen's body, my hair brushes against his cheek. He sighs. He pulls me closer, looping his arms over my shoulders. For the first time since the pregnancy, I let him hold me. I touch his mouth with my fingertips. We lie like this for more than an hour, as I watch the digital clock on the table beside the bed tick away red minute after red minute. Two o'clock. Two-fifteen. Two-thirty. Madeline and I are scheduled to leave at 6 A.M.

I can no longer lie in bed with him, pretending I'm not leaving. "I'll be back," I whisper, untangling myself from him. I pick up my sketchbook and head down the hall.

In the pink kitchen, shivering, I walk around the room, studying my body in the small reflective surfaces—the toaster, the pots hung on the wall, the door of the oven. Helen's white nightgown is broken into pieces. In none of these makeshift mirrors can I see my whole body.

Owen is at ease in his body—striding across a room, laying plates on the table for dinner, brushing his teeth. His gestures are confident. He never looks down at himself, never studies his ribs, his hips, the fine bones of his hands. He never checks his stomach to see if it is flat or round or wrong. He owns his body in a way that I never will own mine.

* * *

I pour flour and sugar into a bowl. *The Cake Bible* is open on the table, but I don't have a recipe in mind. I crack three eggs, separate out the yolks, pour the batter into layer pans, and shake the pans to remove air bubbles that might ruin the cake. I could make the cake and throw it out. I could make the cake, eat a piece, and do the vinegar trick.

Instead I begin to cry and throw the pans into the trash.

I run down the hall to the bedroom. "Owen." I push open the bedroom door, then lean over the bed. "Oh God, wake up. It's an emergency." I shake him hard.

He grabs my shoulders. "What is it? What's wrong?" I have a flashback of a time during my pregnancy when I was convinced that at any moment I might go into labor and kept a suitcase packed and waiting at the front door. We practiced waking up in the middle of the night as if it were a fire drill, setting the alarm for 3 A.M., 4 A.M. The drill became a game; we looked forward to pretending to go to the hospital in the middle of the night.

The noise of my breath rising and falling with a rasp is horrible, like the sounds of animal cries Owen once recorded in a lab and played for me, dogs wailing, cats howling, in an agony I knew humans would never understand. I hate the sound of my own crying, but I can't stop.

"What is it?" Owen repeats. He grips my shoulders. "Are you sick? Alice, what's going on?"

"Madeline" is the only word that I can say. I drop my head to my chest. "I'm sorry. I'm sorry."

Owen clearly does not understand because he doesn't back away from me. He pulls me toward him on the bed and smooths my hair, a gesture of consolation. Does he think I'm upset about my sister? Does he hope that I'm finally expressing my grief about the pregnancy? Before tonight, I haven't let him comfort me since the baby died. Maybe he believes I'll now allow him to help me.

Using all my energy, I push him away. I force myself to stand up. If he's touching me, I won't be able to tell him.

"Okay, Alice, don't make me keep asking. Tell me what's going on."

I flatten my back against the bedroom door as if to prevent my own escape. "I'm going away for a little while."

Owen stares at me, and his silence is worse than anything he could say.

I don't know what to say, so I go on. "My leaving doesn't have to do with you." Even as I start to explain, I know he'll never believe me. Why should he? My stomach cramps and closes into a fist.

Owen's voice shakes. "You're leaving me?"

"Of course not," I say, trying to sound reassuring as if I'm talking to a child.

"Do you want a separation?"

"No!"

"You never mentioned wanting to go away before."

"I've just been thinking about the past."

He looks at me, waiting.

"I need to know some things about my childhood."

The word *childhood* changes the conversation. I imagine an invisible rope drawing Owen back to the word I used earlier, *Madeline*. He makes the connection. "You're not going by yourself, are you? Are you going away with Madeline?"

"We're going to look for Lily."

Owen stands up and crosses the bedroom, then walks back to the bed. He runs his hand through his hair. "You want to see your *mother?* What makes you think she'd want to see you?"

"Madeline thinks she will. I don't know if we can find her, Owen. Since the pregnancy, I can't stop thinking about her."

"Have you talked about this with Dr. Levy?"

"No." I approach him, touch his arm, trying to turn him around to face me. His body won't yield to me. "I need you to understand."

"I don't think you need me at all. You want your childhood back."

"No." I should call my sister at the motel in Venice and tell her I've decided not to go with her. I should tell her she has to go look for Lily alone.

His voice is quiet now. "You're leaving me for your sister."

"Owen—"

"Alice, if you go on this trip, I can't promise that I'll be here when you come back."

"What do you mean?" Panic thuds in my chest. "Are you going back to Atlanta?"

"I can't wait in Sarasota all summer until you and Madeline decide you've had enough and you're ready to come back. I'm not just talking about going back to Atlanta. I have my own life too."

My own life. The words echo in my head, as if we no longer have a life together. I nod. Tears sting my eyes. Of course, he's right. He shouldn't stay here, in this house that isn't ours, that we moved to so I could be near my sister. I can't stay in the room with him because I'll change my mind.

I leave the bedroom. Owen doesn't follow.

I close the bedroom door quietly behind me. I pick up my sketchbook and walk down to the bomb-shelter basement, so Owen won't hear me crying. I turn on all the hurricane lamps and switch on every flashlight, tilting the beams up to the ceiling. I lie down on the cold floor. I want to close my eyes and leave my body behind. Everywhere around me, the concrete room is bright.

In my head, I promise Owen, when I come back after we've found Lily, I'll be cured. He'll see that I'll be much better, and he'll understand why I left. Lily will be my recovery.

I spread my sketch of Lily open on my lap.

I lost my daughter, but I'll get my mother back.

14

"Truth or dare," my sister said one morning the year we were six. We'd just climbed into the bathtub to play Emerald City. "Pick one," she told me. I didn't say anything. "Okay," Madeline said. "I'll pick for you. Dare."

The dare she offered was to go into a room of the Star Dust and take something to prove that I was there. "Steal Lily's passkey," Madeline told me. "That's the first part of the dare. Then you have to steal something and bring it back to show me."

That night, when Lily came back to our room to put us to bed, I wrapped my arms around her waist in an embrace, and Lily shrugged me off. "Don't you girls ever understand that at the end of the day I'm tired?" But already I'd slipped my hand into the pocket of her apron and closed my fingers over the key that could open the door to every room.

"Stay awake," Madeline whispered when we got into bed. We waited until we heard Lily's even, slow breathing. Then we dressed in the dark and sneaked from the room.

"Are you scared?" Madeline asked as we stood in the parking lot, preparing ourselves. She held the key, throwing it up in the air and catching it again.

"Of course not," I lied.

"We're not breaking the law," she said. "We already have the key. We're not trespassing, because we live here." Madeline's logic offered no reassurance that we wouldn't be caught and punished. "The people in 206 are out tonight." She spun around twice on the asphalt and pointed at a door. She placed the key in my hand. "Let's go."

I pushed the key into the lock on the doorknob of the room and slid the door open only far enough for us to crawl in. A wedge of light appeared on the floor, the moon's glare on cars in the parking lot. The light terrified me. Quickly, I shut the door. The lock clicked. The room was empty of people, but its inhabitants' possessions were everywhere, evidence of a family left in open suitcases. Madeline put her finger to her lips. Now that we were actually in the room, carrying out the criminal act, I was less scared. On our knees, we crawled through the room. I pretended I was a snake, sliding through dark water with my sister. I had no arms or legs, only a body that propelled me forward.

From the floor, Madeline tapped my leg. "What are you going to take?" she whispered.

"Why do I need to take something to prove I was here when you're with me? You know I'm here."

"That was the plan," she said. "You agreed."

I scouted the room, looking for a reasonable object, then I crawled to a suitcase that lay open on the floor. I pulled out the first piece of clothing I touched, a soft yellow dress. I stuffed the dress down the front of my shirt, over my stomach.

In the parking lot, Madeline hugged me. "You did it!"

I unfolded the dress. It was a little girl's party dress, the skirt an explosion of yellow and white lace. My sister and I did not own a dress like this. It resembled one of Lily's old ballet costumes.

"I should return this," I said. "This is a nice dress. Maybe she's planning to wear it tomorrow for a special occasion."

"We can't go back in there," my sister said, "and we can't wear it. Lily would notice. We'll have to hide it." She took the dress and led me to the dumpster in the back of the parking lot. She climbed the side of the huge metal bin. She swung her legs over the top. For a moment, she disappeared into the dumpster, and I felt a small stab of fear that she would not come back.

"I threw the dress on a pile of garbage bags," she said, when she reemerged from the dumpster.

Back in bed, Madeline fell asleep immediately. I lay awake beside her. We had stolen something from a little girl only to waste it. The little girl would wake up, find the dress missing, and she might cry. I pictured her mother consoling her. But another, shameful part of me felt a secret, terrible pleasure: Madeline and I had done the bad deed together. We had a secret that no one would ever know.

After that first night, my sister and I stole several times a week. I liked to wait until the guests checked out, but Madeline preferred to sneak into rooms while people slept. We weren't looking for anything valuable. If we found anything good, like the yellow dress, we always threw it away. We wanted things that we could steal easily, objects that would not be missed by their owners: pocket notebooks, curlers, packages of instant coffee. We slipped the objects into our clothes, inside the waistband of our shorts, wedged them into our ankle socks.

If we were caught, I hoped Madeline and I would be sent to prison together. Each night, I lay awake in bed beside my sister and envisioned it. My prison fantasy became a source of comfort, and I often used it to fall asleep.

Madeline and I would share a cinderblock cell with a bunk bed. We'd sleep on the bottom bunk together. For meals, the guards would give us stale Saltines three times a day. Other bad children would be our friends. In my fantasy about being captured with Madeline, I left Lily out. There were no adult women in the prison, only girl after girl like my sister who had done bad deeds and had little regret.

On the nights Madeline and I stole, I sometimes crawled out of bed and locked myself in the bathroom for a secret game. I climbed into the bathtub and made my own Emerald City into a prison. Judy Garland and Ginger Love were not just sisters; they were twins. They were Madeline and me. At first I couldn't decide who should be who. Then I let myself be Judy Garland, which would have made my sister mad. Emerald City was full of bad girls. I imagined them in a circle, dancing around the broken glass and rocks Madeline and I had collected from the parking lot. In my version of the game, I gave the bad girls their own song: "Ring Around the Rosy, A Pocket Full of Posey, Ashes, Ashes, We All Fall Down."

I had always watched families. Because the Star Dust had no air conditioning, and people left the doors and windows to their rooms open all day and most of the night, I had a good view from the parking lot. Mothers knelt in front of their daughters to smooth suntan lotion on their cheeks in quick, deft strokes. Mothers brushed their daughters' hair, slipped nightgowns over their heads, tucked them into bed.

When we started stealing, I began to be more interested in fathers. In the empty rooms, I saw their belongings, their razors and combs on the bathroom shelf, their underwear and socks draped over a chair. These unfamiliar objects fascinated me. I stared at men. The fathers arrived in station wagons or vans, came into the lobby looking for a cheap room, their faces lined and weary. They entered the Star Dust lobby alone, leaving the rest of the family in their car.

Often, the fathers complained about the price of the rooms at the Star Dust. "Five dollars a night for a room in this dump?" a man asked the desk clerk once, when I was within earshot, hiding behind a shelf of casino brochures in the lobby. "You're insane." The desk clerk shrugged, accustomed to complaints. The man handed over cash.

I heard fathers yell at their children in the parking lot. Once the families had moved their belongings into the room, the fathers often left. Sometimes they stood outside their rooms smoking or dropping quarters into the Coke machine. They usually looked unhappy, they always seemed exhausted, but they were in charge.

Once, I watched a man who yelled at every member of his family, one by one. "Get in the car," he screamed at his daughter after he emerged from the lobby with a room key. She was sitting on the hood of the car, swinging her legs, wearing red button-strap shoes that I admired. "Step on it. I mean now."

Then he turned to his wife. "Jesus fucking Christ, if you could learn how to read a map right, we wouldn't have to spend the night in this hellhole."

His son was last. The boy sat silently while his father berated him. "When we get back to Chicago, you're grounded for a month. And no TV."

If Reid Alistair lived with us, would he yell at us like that? Would his face grow red, his eyes narrowing when he saw us? I realized that I always pictured him as a teenager, the boy from

Mississippi who appeared briefly in Lily's stories. Despite its name, Reid Alistair would never stay at the Star Dust, even for one night.

Madeline didn't share my fascination. When I hid in the parking lot, she always came out to find me. One afternoon, as I sat between two parked cars, she approached me with both her hands hidden behind her back. "Pick one. Right or left?"

"I don't want to play."

"You have to. Pick."

I chose left, and my sister put a black spiral-bound notebook into my hands. "It's a present for you. I stole it from 10-C."

The pages were clean and blank, newsprint flecked with black and gray. I didn't know what I could put in the book, but I hugged Madeline.

She smiled. "Let's go to Emerald City."

In my notebook, I drew fathers. I sketched the outlines of their faces, bodies I could only imagine. Sometimes I drew them naked, with tiny, shriveled penises and knock-knees.

I knew what a penis looked like because Madeline had found a stack of pornographic magazines in the dumpster one night when we were throwing away a stolen doll. "Look," she said, her face flushed with the exertion of digging through trash, shoving the magazines at me. *Rubber Chicks*, *Peeping Tom*, *Girls in Love*. "Look." Madeline and I sat down on the asphalt and turned the pages of *Peeping Tom*. The pages were made of cheap, rough paper, the photographs slightly blurred. My sister held the magazine up close to her face: a kneeling woman gripped a man tightly between his legs while another man stood behind her naked back. His expression was mean.

"Be careful," I whispered to my sister.

"You're a baby," she said in her most haughty voice.

One cartoon caught my eye: a naked man standing alone in the middle of a crowded bus, his penis drooping between his legs. All the other passengers were crowded on top of one another, their bodies wrapped together. I didn't understand the joke, but the man looked lonely and sad.

I drew men with their children. Fathers and daughters. Dressed for a birthday party, a Christmas dinner, the men, in dark elegant suits, stood beside the little girls and held their hands. I never drew mothers. I hid my drawings from my sister, folding them between pieces of newspaper at the bottom of a drawer.

One afternoon, when I came in from the parking lot holding my sketchbook, Lily said, "Don't stare like that. Don't you know everyone thinks women who stare at men are asking for it?" She grabbed my arm and pushed me back into the room. "Keep the door shut. Look at your sister, just sitting there." Lily pointed at Madeline, who, in response to Lily's attention, hung her head listlessly, acting the part of the ignored playmate. "I ask you two to do nothing around here while I work all day. I'd like to tell you how lucky you are to have a sister. I never had a sister. What's the point of having two of you if you don't play together?" Without waiting for an answer to her question, Lily left.

I opened the bottom dresser drawer to check on my drawings. They were still there, lying flat beneath the piles of my clothes. I studied the pages carefully to make sure that no one had touched them.

15

By 1933, Stephan and Agatha had saved enough money for their passage on a steamship from Amsterdam to New York. The morning of their departure, Agatha dressed carefully, trying to wear every piece of clothing she owned: three pairs of stockings, extra knickers, an overskirt, two embroidered aprons tied around her waist. When she had finished, she felt fat and hot. Stephan filled a cardboard suitcase with his photographs.

On the ship, Stephan took more pictures of children—boys and girls sleeping on top of their bundles and suitcases, teenage girls boiling soup in the corner of the room, mothers brushing their daughters' hair and picking out the lice. The ship was dirty. Agatha washed every day with the bar of bear-fat soap brought from home, but her skin itched, covered with patches of ringworm, and no one could avoid the lice. Some afternoons while the boat rocked across the waves she sat on the floor and studied her arms, peeling off the pieces of dead skin as if she could heal herself. Sometimes she imagined Agnes sitting on the floor at home, motionless, aware of itching pain on her own unmarked skin. She hoped Agnes could feel it; she did not want the connection between them to be broken by the journey across the ocean.

She found it very difficult to practice her trick on the ship. She was never alone, and she did not want Stephan or the other women to know her secret. Occasionally, late at night, while everyone slept, she crept up to the deck and leaned over the railing to relieve herself of the food, but she was so afraid of being caught that the experience lacked the satisfaction it used to bring her, when she did it with her sister. Since she never walked or worked on the ship, she was sure her body was growing larger no matter what she did. She felt a rising panic about her weight that increased each day they were on the journey.

Stephan and Agatha slept on the floor of the baggage car of a train all the way from New York City to New Orleans. Like the ship, the baggage car was crowded. All their conversations were conducted in whispers, late at night.

"My body is disgusting," she told Stephan one night.

"We need to work on learning English," he said. "We can't live in a country where we don't know the language." She was left thinking he wanted to teach her a lesson: in our new life, some things are more important than your skin. He spoke without looking at her; he was studying an old copy of the *International Herald Tribune* and writing down unfamiliar words on a small square of paper.

On the train, in the trash bin, she found a copy of a magazine called *Child Star*, and she took it back with her to the corner where she and Stephan slept. All night, she sat up with the movie magazine, studying the photographs of Judy Garland and the interview accompanying them, "MGM: More Stars Than There Are in Heaven!" She sounded out the words and tried to make sense of the new language. "Mr. Louis Mayer has his own family of little movie stars."

New Orleans was the city Stephan had chosen because he had a second cousin there. Everyone else they had come over with on the steamer was headed for New York or Chicago. Moving across America for three nights on the train, Agatha lay awake in the baggage car and imagined her new life alone. Where was Agnes? In their old shared room, her body turned to face the wall, her head filled with pain? Agatha had done the very worst thing: one twin had left the other.

16

At Mater Dolorosa Elementary, Madeline and I stood alone together on the playground, at the edge of the schoolyard, watching the other girls. They formed a circle, hands balled into fists, choosing who was "it" for a game:

My mother and your mother were hanging out clothes.
My mother punched your mother right smack in the nose.
What color was the blood?
Red. R-E-D spells red and you are not It!

Their songs were dumb, I told myself, not like the Judy Garland songs Lily taught us. These girls had probably never heard of Judy Garland. I silently hummed "Over the Rainbow" and vowed that I did not need friends.

But when Lucy Armstrong approached me on the playground, telling me she wanted to ask me a question, my whole body filled with anticipation and even joy. One friend, I told myself, would make my life perfect. My sister and I could admit one girl from school into our secret world. Or, better yet, I could go off with Lucy alone. I could have something of my own that did not include Madeline.

"Is it true that you and your sister don't have a father?" Lucy asked.

As soon as the question was spoken, all of my happiness disappeared. Lucy's words hung in the air between us. "Where'd you hear that?" I tried to make my voice sound casual.

"Sister Louise. One day after school. She said your mother had sex outside of marriage, and that's a sin. Well," she said, impatiently, "is it true?"

"Our father is just away right now. He'll be back."

"Where is he?" Lucy stood on one foot, balancing a leg behind her as if she were practicing a ballet position. She was clearly showing off. I hated her for that graceful gesture.

"He's on tour in Russia with his ballet company. He has the lead in"—I couldn't think of the names of any ballets—"*The Red Shoes.*"

Lucy rolled her eyes. "My mother says it's a sin to lie."

I could never tell Lily what Lucy said. Everyone knew about our family. We had no father and we were poor. In the world of the Star Dust, we were no worse off than anyone else, and Lily taught us to believe our bodies were superior. When other families with girls our age came to the Star Dust, Lily would whisper to us, "Look at how much fatter those girls are than you."

At Mater Dolorosa, we were thin and it wasn't enough. Madeline and I qualified for "hot lunch," the free meal offered by the Catholic Diocese of Jefferson Parish. Other girls' mothers packed sandwiches wrapped in wax paper, thermoses of Hawaiian Punch, everything neatly arranged in a lunch box. When the other girls opened the boxes, I sometimes closed my eyes to inhale the smell of a delicious, fattening lunch from someone else's home:

bologna and mayonnaise, peanut butter, vanilla milk. My mouth watered. I dreamed of the food the other girls' mothers allowed them to eat. I watched them trade sandwiches and throw the fruit away. Sometimes after school I returned to the cafeteria and searched the trash for the other girls' leftovers. I never ate the left-over food, but I picked it out of the trash can and studied it. I touched white bread with the crusts torn off, half-eaten Twinkies, sticky soda bottles.

Each day at noon, five of us—the poor girls—filed into the cafeteria without looking at one another, a red stamp smeared across the top of our hands to indicate permission for the meal. Madeline and I always stood together.

"Hello, twins," Sister Ann said as we reached the head of the line. She smiled kindly and used the ice-cream scoop to deposit a perfect circle of mashed red beans and rice on each of our plates. I liked Sister Ann, although Madeline said she was fat and gave us extra food as a reward for being twins. She gave us squares of corn bread and two large dishes of collard greens cooked in bacon fat.

Sometimes Madeline refused to eat. "I'm sick," she whispered the first time she couldn't eat her lunch. "Get rid of this for me." She pushed her plate in my direction at the long table.

I thought my sister was conforming to Lily's rules again. Madeline's refusal annoyed me, further proof of the fact that she was the good child. "No," I said. "You have to eat it."

"You're not my mother. You can't tell me what to do."

"Just eat it and then go in the bathroom and do Agatha's trick," I said in a low voice. "You know how."

Tears welled in the corners of Madeline's eyes. "*Please*," she said.

"Okay." I dragged Madeline's plate over to my place and trans-ferred the uneaten portions to my own plate. I ate my sister's lunch quickly without looking at her.

Madeline's refusal inaugurated a new pattern in our relationship. I now ate twice as much as she did. I knew that soon I would be fat. Lily would notice. She would help me with my diet, admonishing me daily to eat less, circle the parking lot to burn off calories, do extra sit-ups on the motel room floor. I wanted to eat and eat until I became huge.

I even wished for "hot breakfast," the ultimate humiliation. Only the kids who were bused into Jefferson Parish ate this meal. I liked to stand in the doorway of the cafeteria and watch the poor girls eat. There was never enough time between when the bus arrived and when homeroom began for them to complete their meal, so they shoveled the food into their mouths quickly, large spoonfuls of Cream of Wheat and canned peaches. Over the PA system at the beginning of the school year, the principal had announced that students needed "parental permission" to have hot breakfast. I considered signing Lily's name, as I often did for field trips and raffle-ticket sales. But I knew my sister would never go along with the plan, and if she didn't eat hot breakfast, I couldn't eat it either. It was an unwritten code: neither of us did anything alone.

Lily taught us the MGM diet. "It's a family tradition. Agatha taught me," she said proudly.

Every Sunday, the three of us sat at the table in the middle of the motel room, each holding a glass of ice, sharing a bottle of vinegar. We'd drink, vomit, and then stop eating for as long as we could. "Let me see which one of you can drink more," Lily said, and Madeline always won the competition. Each week I swallowed from the bottle until my stomach burned, but I couldn't surpass my sister with Agatha's trick. I would never be pure enough.

After we finished the bottle, Madeline and I were sick in turn—hers, then mine. I never got used to the sound of my sister vomiting; her painful retching burned my throat, as if I were being sick along with her. Madeline and I each held the other's head in our lap as we waited for the nausea to pass. We lay together in the empty bathtub, legs pressed together, our backs resting on the cool porcelain, while Lily sat on the tile floor. I smoothed my fingers over my ribs, thinking of St. Rose, the beautiful young woman in the garden emptying her body to rise from the earth, but I could never become thin enough to leave my body behind.

When we sat in the bathroom, Lily taught us to control our breathing. If you take small, dainty breaths, then exhale with as much power as you can, she explained, your stomach stays flatter. A dancer's trick. I never could get it right: I hyperventilated every time and nearly fainted, but Madeline followed the directions perfectly. I stared at my sister's stomach, as flat as Lily's, then compared it to my own.

When we felt less weak and sick, when the nausea had been quelled, Lily would sing to us from *The Wizard of Oz.* Since Judy Garland's death, Lily's love for her had deepened in intensity. She no longer needed the albums because she had memorized every word to every song. Besides her story-telling on our late-night drives, the fasting afternoons when she sang to us were the only times in my life when I ever heard Lily sound carefree, almost happy, sound like a young woman, or even a child. "We're off to see the Wizard, the wonderful Wizard of Oz. . . ." Madeline clicked her bare feet three times as if she were wearing the ruby slippers. I imagined my sister as Dorothy, swept up by a twister, taken from her house in Kansas and dropped into the land of Oz. I couldn't picture Madeline happily marching down the yellow brick road to find the wizard who would help her return home again. I envisioned

Madeline collapsing in the Emerald City, doing nothing to save herself, hoping that Glinda the Good Witch would rescue her.

For the Thanksgiving pageant in fifth grade, our class rehearsed a play called *Geronimo Escapes to Louisiana*. Men's parts were assigned to the boys from St. Anthony of Padua, brought by bus to our school for rehearsals. All the girls were assigned the parts of Indians except for Madeline and me. Since my sister and I were twins, Sister Bettina gave us the roles of cowgirl sisters, dressed exactly alike in fringed skirts and buckskin hats. We had no lines, but we sat on a square of artificial grass on stage and performed a duet on the autoharp, an instrument neither of us knew how to play, a double-voiced version of "Home on the Range."

The boys from St. Anthony pulled their silver prop guns from their pockets in the locker room as they shouted "Stick 'em up" and lifted up our dresses. The violence of the pageant itself—the boys dressed as cowboys aiming their guns at the girls dressed as Indians—made me feel sick to my stomach. I hated the pageant. The other girls whispered behind cupped hands when my sister and I walked down the hall in our cowgirl dresses. They were jealous of us, I knew this, but knowing it did not help. What mattered was that we were never part of their group, no matter what we did.

Each afternoon, for the first three weeks of November, Madeline and I sat in the parking lot of the Star Dust until the sky grew dark, practicing our song with a rented autoharp from school. My sister and I were chosen for this performance because our appearances matched. Talent was not the point. We were like the scenery; as twins, we provided a symmetry on stage. We sat on Lily's car, wearing our cowgirl hats to get in character. Lily always told us that getting in character was crucial to practicing for being

on stage. "Home, home on the range, where the deer and the ante-
lope play. Where seldom is heard a discouraging word . . . ,"
Madeline sang as I picked the strings. I hoped her voice would
drown me out.

Madeline stole a box of Winn Dixie cookies from a room where
two children were staying, and we took them out to the parking lot
for our practice. We sat on the ground, and Madeline arranged the
box of sugar-sprinkled cookies shaped like angels between us. One
by one, Madeline broke all the angels into pieces. The box that lay
between us was now full of young girl angels with their wings
cracked off, their faces smashed. The cookies were too fattening to
eat; the pleasure was in breaking them.

"I hate this song," my sister said. "Let's do Judy Garland." She
began to sing "Over the Rainbow."

I felt a growing sense of nervousness, as Madeline sang "Why,
oh why can't I?" carefully matching Judy Garland's expression of
pain, her desire to return home. Madeline sounded more like the
recorded versions of the song from the years at the end of Judy
Garland's life than the movie version when she was seventeen.

From across the parking lot, Lily walked quickly toward us.
"Stop, Linny. Be quiet," I whispered, but Madeline ignored me.

"What do you think you're doing?"

"Practicing for a play," I said.

"What play?"

"At school," I told her. I pretended to laugh, a small nervous
sound. Madeline hummed the rest of the song, and I kept my fingers on the pick, plucking the notes.

"Neither of you should be in a play. Don't you remember what
happened with ballet?" Lily continued, "You never even asked me."
Then she saw the box of broken angel cookies. "What are you eating?"

"Why, oh why can't I?" Madeline sang, as if she were a scratched record, again and again. "Why, oh why can't I? Why, oh why can't I? Why, oh why can't I?"

"Stop it!" Lily said. "You don't know how to sing that song!" She yanked the autoharp from my lap. It crashed to the asphalt.

Madeline stopped singing and opened her eyes. She began to cry.

"You're too big to be crying," Lily said. "What's wrong with you?"

Slowly, Madeline bent down to touch the instrument, which had splintered on the ground. I stared at the part dividing her long straight hair, at her scalp, clean, pink, and identical to mine.

Suddenly my sister exploded. Her fists pummeled Lily's chest, smashed against her ribs, and Lily tried to push her away. "I hate you!" Madeline screamed. "I hate you so much!"

I stood alone, unable to move. When Lily finally shoved Madeline away, strings of tears and mucus clung to my sister's face. Her cheeks were a deep red, her mouth a slash of anger.

I said her name, but she didn't look at me.

"I hate you!" Madeline screamed. Then she ran across the lot, her body lunging and stumbling, slamming the door of our room behind her.

"Your sister's impossible," Lily said. She bent down and gathered the rest of the wood from the splintered harp. She brushed off her hands. It was the first time Lily had ever allied herself with me against my sister. I wanted her to tell me I was the good daughter, the easy child.

17

On the date the doctors projected as my due date, a day I thought I'd never live through, Madeline and I have a destination: the past. Our route to New Orleans goes up the coast, through the panhandle, the "Redneck Riviera," across Alabama, Mississippi, and then on to Louisiana. I've brought nothing with me but my purse and a suitcase of Helen's clothes. And hidden in the glove compartment, under a stack of maps where Madeline won't find it, I've brought the birthday tape Owen made for me last week. I still haven't listened to it, but I want it with me.

On the way out of Sarasota, Madeline drives. My birthday present, the mannequin, sits on the front seat between us. The car is a 1978 Skylark. I ask her where she got it.

"It's Jack's. I stole it for our trip. I'm sure he won't mind."

"You didn't ask him if you could take it? What if he called the police?"

"I hope he does," my sister says, flipping her hair. "That would be great."

Jack's car is powder blue and huge, with chrome shaped into shark fins and wire wheels. Inside, it's like I'm in a large sunken boat. The dashboard is flecked with cigarette ashes, and several beer bottles roll back and forth on the floor of the backseat.

"Maybe we should clean out the car," I say.

"You're supposed to have a junky car on a road trip. Anyway, at the end of the trip, we can smash the car into a tree, and we won't have to worry about it anymore. "

I know what she means. I've imagined it many times. Lily's parents, our grandparents, died in their Skylark on the way to Pass Christian. The car smashed the rail of the bridge and plunged into the water.

At a Texaco station outside of the Sun City retirement community in St. Petersburg, Madeline says, "Let's lock ourselves in the bathroom and I'll cut my hair."

Madeline's hair is now very short, barely covering her ears. She can't cut off much more of it. In our childhood language, *my* can mean one or both of us. Her statement translates as "Let me lock myself in the bathroom with you and cut your hair." I have always had long hair. I rarely even trim it because I like the weight of my hair on my shoulders and against my back. Sometimes I twist it into two tight braids and wind them around my head like Frida Kahlo in her self-portraits.

In the gas station bathroom, the door won't lock. I shove the trash can up against it. I don't want anyone to walk in and find us here. Madeline kisses the top of my head. We both know that she is going to cut my hair. "Ready?"

My sister works quickly. The scissors click again and again in the air around my head. Hair falls onto my dress, Helen's pink chenille, and onto the cement floor of the bathroom in large uneven pieces. "Isn't it strange that you don't feel pain when someone cuts your hair?" she says. The scissors snap. I consider telling my sister to be careful, but that might anger her and compel her to cut off even more of my hair.

When Madeline finishes, my head feels strangely light, as if relieved of some burden, my shoulders seem bare. I shake my head and nothing moves. "Look," Madeline tells me, pulling me against her in front of the mirror. When we stand together side by side, my hair is even shorter than Madeline's, chopped raggedly around my face. The short hair makes my face look small and wan. Owen had loved my long hair. As soon as I think of him, I want to turn around and run back to him.

"We match," Madeline says triumphantly. She hugs me to her breasts. "You could be me now."

But I look much worse than Madeline. Her short hair highlights and defines her features, even brightens her eyes. Mine makes my face look pale and dull. As in childhood, once again I am the plain twin, the ordinary girl. I am clearly the good daughter, the dependable one. No one would ever mistake me for my sister.

"We need makeup. Close your eyes," Madeline says, rubbing my lids with a dark shadow she has removed from her purse. "Now open." Then she holds my face in her hands to line the inside of my eyes. The kohl pencil is sharp; tears leak into my eyes. "You're blurring it!" Madeline says. "Stop." I blink and blink to clear my eyes and she wails, "Alice!"

"I couldn't help it. You hurt me."

"Okay, okay. You do me."

My fingers graze my sister's skin, a light touch, a trail across her face. I smooth foundation over her cheeks. "There," I say. "You're done."

"Oh no, I'm not. Don't you have a lipstick?"

I search through my purse, but all I find is an unopened tube of Alizarin Crimson oil paint. "Perfect," my sister says and purses her lips as if she is ready for a kiss. "Go ahead."

"It's poison. You need linseed oil to get it off. Don't lick your lips." I draw my sister's mouth in a neat bow. "Now you look like Louise Brooks," I say and she smiles. I've never been good at making up my own face, but I have always been able to do my sister's.

When we emerge from the gas station bathroom, men are staring. The station attendants and the customers at the gas pumps all turn around to look at us. The gaze that rests upon my sister and myself is a familiar one. Although I dislike being watched when I'm alone, especially by men, I'm used to it when I am with Madeline.

My sister takes my arm and we cross the highway to Winn Dixie. "We need provisions," she says.

She leads me to the toy aisle where she chooses two pairs of identical heart-shaped sunglasses and sets one on my face. The lenses are tinted bright pink, so the world of the supermarket appears to be suddenly transformed. I am studying the magenta ceiling when without warning Madeline drifts away. "I'm going to look for bottled water," she calls out, over her shoulder. "The purest best kind."

For a minute, I hear an exhaustion, an evasiveness I know signifies trouble, in my sister's voice, and I'm afraid. What if Madeline leaves me here in the grocery store? I picture her wandering at the side of Tamiami Trail, hitching a ride with the first man who drives by, returning to her life with Jack in nearby motels. If Madeline goes back to Jack, I can return to Owen. Then a fist of pain lodges in my chest: my being absent from our marriage for one day won't make any difference in our loss, the loss that now defines our marriage. My body shudders. I fix my eyes on the shelves of toys on the other side of the aisle.

I push the pink sunglasses to the top of my head, into my new short hair, and I study the red and purple plastic pails and shovels. Children's toys are always brightly colored; dolls never have sad expressions. I study a box containing a plastic castle, complete with a king, a queen, and a moat to keep their castle safe. A prince and a princess. On the back of the box, the directions explain that the castle hides a trap door on the top floor, so prisoners can tumble straight down into the dungeon. If we were given the plastic castle when we were children, Madeline and I would've thrown out the king and the prince. We would have made a new life for the queen and the princess alone in the castle. I turn to Barbie on the shelf below. Her hair is smooth and blond, like Jack's, her waist impossibly small. Barbie would never get pregnant.

Madeline reappears with a bottle of white wine vinegar. "Surprise!"

"No. That's over," I say, and my face flushes with the lie. Madeline doesn't know that I've been drinking vinegar alone since the baby died. Agatha's trick reminds me not only of childhood but also of the days when I came home from the hospital after the doctors failed to induce labor. I can't start drinking vinegar with Madeline again.

"We'll just drink a little, Alice."

"Linny, I said no." I cross my arms over my chest for emphasis.

"We have to do it together. We have to each take a sip." Madeline sighs, a long, protracted, staged gesture. "Alice. Alice. It's the baby's due date, the day you would have been a mother. Don't you think it's only right to start the trip off with it, in honor of you?"

Mother. My throat swells with pain. The word works on me every time like a charm.

At the first rest stop in Tampa, I barely touch my lips to the bottle. After she drinks a long swallow, Madeline says, "Let's get rid of all our clothes. I mean it, Alice. Let's throw everything out."

"I packed all of this," I say. "I brought what I need."

"You don't need anything. We're going to find what we need. We're going to find Lily."

The car fills up with heat. I watch a woman sitting on a picnic bench outside the building nursing her baby. "Linny, let's go in," I say. "We can talk about this later."

"No." My sister opens the car door and yanks out her suitcase. "You can watch."

In the rest stop bathroom, Madeline lays her suitcase on the floor, unzipping it. Inside are the stack of Judy Garland albums that once belonged to Lily: *Miss Show Business, You'll Never Walk Alone, I Could Go On Singing.*

"You're not getting rid of those, are you?"

"Of course not," Madeline snaps. "These records are the most important things I own." She sets the albums carefully on the bathroom floor and turns back to the suitcase. Under the albums are balled-up dresses, scarves, unmatched stockings. The suitcase is crammed full. Madeline fills her arms with clothes and walks into a stall. She shoves everything into the toilet.

"Linny! You'll mess up the plumbing," I say, alarmed.

"The plumbing isn't the point." Madeline crouches over the toilet, pushing the clothes down, packing them in.

A woman enters the bathroom. She stares from the open suitcase on the floor to my sister, bent over the toilet. "Is she okay?" she says, in a voice of both horror and concern.

I block her view of my sister with my body. "She's carsick," I say. "She'll be fine."

"I'll find another bathroom." The woman walks out. I can tell she does not believe me.

I ask five people, including the woman with the baby, to use another bathroom, apologizing to each. Madeline fills all three toilets with her clothes. She sweats, her face flushed, her hair stuck to her forehead, but her eyes are bright. She kneels on one of the album covers: a picture of Judy Garland in a sequined dress accompanied by bright red letters, JUDY GARLAND YOU'RE A STAR STUDDED CINDERELLA. JUDY, THAT'S YOU JUDY!

"Let's go," I say. "Please."

"One more thing. I'm doing this for you. I'm throwing out all my pills." She empties her pockets of six prescription bottles, then pours the contents of the bottles into the toilet on top of the clothes. "Are you happy?"

"Where did you get all those drugs? Come on. Let's get out of here."

"Alice, don't you have anything *you* want to get rid of? You have to throw something out."

"I told you, Linny, I don't want to throw out my clothes. They belong to Helen."

"Just some small thing. Anything."

"I don't have anything." I glance nervously at the bathroom door, waiting for it to open again.

"Hand me your wallet," she orders. "We'll find something you don't need." Madeline sits down on top of her open suitcase and begins to empty the wallet on the floor. Dollar bills and pennies spill onto the tile. I watch my driver's license drop between her legs. Then Madeline finds the sonogram, the image of the baby at nineteen weeks. "What's this?" She holds the small square up to the light. "An X ray?"

I told myself that I could carry the image from the ultrasound with me until I felt better, but since the baby died, I've been unable to look at it. I told Owen I threw it away because I knew it would be too painful for him to see it. The sonogram is the size of a photo-booth portrait, a small blurred white shape on black, like the daguerreotypes of Agnes and Agatha.

"I need to keep this," I say, reaching for the sonogram. My hands are shaking.

"Well, what else do you have?" Madeline's voice is impatient. And then she yanks out something I've forgotten. At the back of my wallet, hidden behind my library card, is a black-and-white picture of Owen as a child that he gave to me soon after we met, before we were married. The bottom of the photograph is stamped *27 September 1967*—he was in kindergarten. His hair is cut straight across his forehead and he wears a sweater vest and a tie. Before I can stop her, Madeline drops the image into the toilet. "It's time for you to get rid of this."

"Linny!" I bend over the toilet to retrieve the photograph. "How could you do that?" On the surface of the picture, the black-and-white streaks blur to nothing.

18

When Madeline and I were in middle school, the cast of Emerald City grew larger. We left the bathtub and moved outside to the pool at the back of the parking lot.

Long ago, the Star Dust's pool had been drained. Although the motel advertised the pool to draw guests, no one who worked at the motel remembered it ever being full of water. The grass around the pool was short, burned a pale yellow. A high chain-link fence circled the empty pool to keep children out. When my sister and I crawled down the ladder, hand by hand, into the shallow end one afternoon, we discovered the drained pool was a magic place. The high walls were painted green and were chipped, the floor sloped, and the drain in the deep end was a square black mouth.

"You could get sucked in," Madeline said. "If you stand on it, you could die." I walked a wide circle around the drain to keep safe. She stood on top of the drain, legs spread, one foot on each side.

Our new game was based on a library book I'd read. My favorite books were survival narratives, books shelved in the "young adult" section, designed for teenage boys. All of the books had vivid covers: men on life rafts, men in the forest being chased by wolves. In all of them, although there were many deaths, the main character, a boy or a man, didn't die. In my favorite, *Sole Survivor: A True Story*, a thirteen-year-old boy was stranded alone when a 747 crashed in the Atlantic Ocean. The rest of the passengers, including his mother, father, and sister, died instantly. For thirty days, the boy lived on a piece of fuselage from the plane.

The Coast Guard found him on the thirty-first day at sea. The novel ended on a triumphant note, with the boy's rescue. I wondered about the days that followed, after he left the hospital. Who took him in? I wondered about the rest of this boy's life. Did he dream about the plane crash and his days alone in the middle of the ocean? Did he ever wish that he were still out there, on the piece of metal, alone? The book was published in 1965. The boy was grown up now. Was he married? Did he tell his own children the story?

In the game Madeline and I played, Judy Garland and Ginger Love were lost at sea in the empty pool. They floated together on a piece of shirt cardboard one of the fathers had left behind. Because they'd been on the MGM diet for years, they were used to not eating. Having no food didn't upset them at all. To pass the time, they sang duets, the same songs Judy Garland and Liza Minnelli had sung together.

"Well, hello Judy. Well, hello Judy. . . ." Madeline did Ginger Love's part.

I played Judy Garland. "Well, hello, Ginger. . . ."

"You don't sound like her," Madeline said. "I'm better at being Judy Garland."

I was always anxious to include the third member of the cast of Emerald City. "Do you think Reid Alistair should save them?" I asked my sister.

"Alice, why can't we ever just have the two of them alone? You always want to bring in Reid Alistair. They don't need anyone to rescue them."

I sat on the silver ladder and read passages of *Sole Survivor* out loud to Madeline, who orchestrated the game. The book was written in the style of Agatha's old movie magazines and always addressed the reader: "Johnny caught fish with a coat hanger and fried them on his raft by rubbing two sticks together, a trick he'd learned in Boy Scouts many years ago. Did you ever learn that? Because he couldn't drink the salt water that surrounded him, he was occasionally forced to drink his own urine. Imagine that, boys!"

"You're going to ruin your eyes," Lily sometimes said to us when she walked by the swimming pool on her way to the laundry room during her shift. "Sitting burns only seventy-five calories an hour."

At thirteen, I still loved children's books: their naïive characters, tidy endings, and colorful illustrations. Besides survival stories, I especially liked books about orphans, lucky children who survived without a family. At the public library, I checked out children's books, pretending they were for my younger sister. Since teenagers up to age eighteen weren't permitted to carry an adult library card at the Airline Highway library and could only choose from the young adult section of the library, the librarian seemed to approve. "My, you're a good big sister, aren't you?" she once said. I blushed. My sister had no use for books or reading.

Lying on the floor of the empty swimming pool, I read *Alice in Wonderland,* the book I was named after. I loved the pool of tears Alice cried when she couldn't fit through the door to the garden because she'd drunk from the bottle labeled "DRINK ME." She was too large to enter the magic world. Then I read the whole series of stories about Nancy Drew and the books about the Boxcar Children.

I didn't like books in which children had parents. I stepped through the wardrobe with Lucy and entered the secret world of Narnia, known only by her and her brothers and sisters. The children in *Mary Poppins* had parents, but they didn't figure much in the plot. I read *Mary Poppins* three times. I pretended Mary Poppins was Agatha. Each time I read it, I was horrified by the part in the book when the old woman with candy fingers gave her fingers away to children in the park. She stood under a tree and cracked apart her hands and the children ate the pieces. The old woman with candy fingers was, however, a good trick to use to induce nausea so I wouldn't eat.

The swimming pool was the best place to read. In school, in our room, I couldn't focus on the words filling the page in their neat, clean lines. The letters blurred together. Emerald City was where I always concentrated best.

On every report card, the nuns noted my sister's poor performance in all her classes and threatened, "Madeline may have to be held back." Each quarter, Lily read Madeline's report card and shook her head. Instead of yelling at Madeline, however, she always talked to me. "You're the only one who can get through to your sister. Talk to her, Alice. Get her to work harder in school."

One day, in the swimming pool, after a game of Sole Survivor, I tried. "Just pull up your test grades in this class, Linny. I know you can do it. The first quarter you had A's on every test."

"Hmm." Madeline lay flat on her back on the pool floor.

I knew how to make her listen. "We won't be in the same class if you don't. If they hold you back a year, we won't go through high school together."

Madeline sat up abruptly. "That can't happen," she said.

Lily appeared above the pool, holding a pile of dirty sheets. I wondered if she had come out to see how my discussion about school with my sister was going. She said nothing about it. "How many times have I told you that girls who sit around reading all day are the ones who gain weight?"

I looked down at my stomach. My hipbones showed through my dress like a crest. Still, I ate my sister's lunch almost every day. I was heavier than Madeline. Her arms were thin and pale, no extra flesh anywhere. Her cheeks were hollow. She had followed all of Lily's lessons. Yet I was the one the nuns at school used to praise for my self-discipline. "Excellent attention," my report cards said. I could read or sketch for hours. Madeline never concentrated on anything for more than a few minutes. I didn't understand why I was the one who wasn't good at fasting, at starving, at emptying my body and becoming pure. Madeline could go much longer without eating.

At night, at least once a week, we took the tour of Lily's old life: the New Orleans Ballet, the Prytania Theater, and finally, Agatha's house.

When we came home from driving one night, the year we were thirteen, Lily taught us Agatha's trick. We'd learned about it from her stories in the car. For a long time, Madeline had begged Lily to teach it to us. "Please, please. I want to do it too!" Lily had always said we weren't yet old enough. She wanted to wait until we were the age she was when Agatha taught her, right before our bodies would start to change, before the signs appeared that we'd become women.

That night, by the time we came home from the drive, it was 4:30 A.M. Lily gave us a cassette tape. "I have a present for you two."

"Judy Garland?" I asked as she slid it into the recorder. I was exhausted. I didn't want to stay up listening to Judy Garland now. All the tapes Lily brought home were Judy Garland songs.

She shook her head. A woman's voice began, chanting over the clinking keys of a piano:

> *Give that chicken fat back to that chicken.*
> *Go, you chicken fat, go!*
> *Give that chicken fat back to that chicken.*
> *Go, you chicken fat, go!*

"It's an exercise tape," Lily said. "All you girls do is sit in that pool. I want you to get moving to burn some calories. Now is the most important time to watch your weight. I only want what's best for you, and you two fight me every step of the way." Madeline nodded. I tried to stifle my yawn. I wanted nothing but sleep. Lily and Madeline were behaving as if it were the middle of the afternoon instead of the middle of the night, as if exercising now was not only perfectly normal but required.

"I have something else, too." Lily opened her dresser drawer and took out a small leather-bound book. *Sacred Heart Academy* was stamped on the front in gold. "When I was your age, I started recording what I ate each day to keep track of my weight." She opened the front cover. "Come look." We sat beside her. The tape droned on about chicken fat. In the squares where Lily was supposed to record her daily school assignments, she had instead listed her food intake. I read, "5/3/61: 1 small piece boiled chicken, ⅓ slice pear."

Madeline inched closer to Lily on the bed, her face flushed with excitement. "5/4/61: 2 saltines, 3 pistachio nuts, ½ cup skim milk." Lily's middle school handwriting was neat and rounded.

Lily closed the assignment book. "Now, girls, I want the truth. Have either of you been bad this week?"

We knew what Lily meant. She wasn't asking whether we had stolen from guest rooms. She meant had we eaten too much.

Madeline was the first to speak. "Of course not! I've been good. Every day I only ate half a piece of bread at lunch."

"I can tell, Madeline," Lily said. She set her hand on my sister's stomach and smiled. "Good. Now, Alice?"

I didn't yet know the rules of the game. I wasn't sure if my sister was lying. I told the truth. "I ate three meals every day this week."

"Don't worry. We can fix that." Lily turned up the volume of the chicken fat tape. "Lie down on the floor. We'll start with sit-ups."

After we'd exhausted our bodies and listened to the tape three times, we did Agatha's trick. Lily led us into the bathroom and told us to kneel down. She unlocked the cabinet above the sink and took out a bottle of vinegar. "Alice, you go first. Listen to what I say. Drink just a little of the vinegar. Then take your toothbrush and touch it gently, do it carefully, to the soft red part of the back of your throat." As soon as I drank the vinegar, involuntarily, I vomited.

"Madeline, you're next." I watched my sister obediently follow Lily's directions. When she gagged, I couldn't look at her. I turned my head away. "Now listen, girls. Don't do this trick without me. It is only for emergencies." We nodded.

That night, Lily seemed to approve of us. She had given instructions, was pleased when we followed her directions. I made myself believe Lily loved us. I believed we belonged to her.

"I hate this game!" Madeline shouted one day as we sat in the pool playing Sole Survivor. "It's so stupid because they aren't really here."

"Who?"

"Judy Garland and Ginger Love, Alice. They don't exist. We're just faking everything."

"So let's make them real. I know what we can do. Wait here." I climbed out of the pool and ran to our room, pulled my sketchbook out from under the bed, found my colored Pentel pens and scissors, and ran back to my sister. She was sitting on the drain in the deep end, arms crossed over her chest. "Get off the drain, Linny." I sat on the pool ladder, opened the book, and began to draw. Madeline stood up and walked over to see what I had planned.

While Madeline watched, I drew Judy Garland and Ginger Love paper dolls. Judy Garland wore her *Wizard of Oz* blue and white dress. I dressed Ginger Love in the latest fashions, bell-bottoms and a midriff blouse tied under her breasts. I snipped along the edges of their bodies, folded a ridge of paper at the bottom of their feet so they could stand up, and handed the sisters to Madeline.

"I love them!" She threw her arms around my shoulders and kissed me on the lips. "Now, watch me." Madeline gave me Ginger Love, and walked to the shallow end with Judy Garland. "Red Rover, Red Rover. Let Ginger Love come over." I moved toward her, holding the doll.

Next we reversed: I called to her, "Red Rover, Red Rover. Let Judy Garland come over." Madeline walked to me.

The third time, I made a mistake. "Red Rover, Red Rover. Let Reid Alistair come over."

Madeline threw Judy Garland down. "Alice! We don't need him in the game!"

19

As she drives, Madeline leans out the car window, taking huge gulps of air. I haven't spoken to her since St. Petersburg when she threw away Owen's picture, and I know she wants my attention. I pretend not to care that she is leaning from the car. She lets go of the wheel, raises herself out of the car, supporting her body with her hands, and begins to scream. The scream fills the car; it rips through the afternoon sky. I grab the wheel and try to steer from the passenger seat while yanking her dress to pull her back inside the car. Madeline slides back into the car, but Jack's car skids, tires screeching on the highway asphalt, and we narrowly avoid colliding with a sign marking the distance to Tampa.

"You hurt me," Madeline says when she shoves my hands off the steering wheel. "Don't do that to me again."

"Don't do that to *me* again," I say. "You nearly killed us both!"

Madeline shrugs and stares at the road. We ride in silence for a while. I know she's trying to punish me by not speaking, just as I punished her earlier with my own silence. Then she says, "I'm sorry I got rid of your picture." Her voice is soft and small like a little girl's.

"You should be." I won't look at her.

"Alice, please don't be mad. I can't stand it when you're mad at me. Please. You know I'd never want to hurt you on purpose."

I use all my energy to ignore her plea. "Linny, I think we need to get something straight. What if we don't find Lily?"

"Of course we'll find her. After we find her, we'll take her home with us."

I realize that I haven't thought about what will happen after the trip, and I'm not sure what Madeline means when she uses the word *home*. I can't envision the three of us living together again— *Madeline + Alice + Lily = A Family,* as my sister wrote on the last Judy Garland postcard—in the house in Sarasota, but it occurs to me that this is exactly what Madeline wants.

"Alice, I love your clothes," my sister says. "Thanks for letting me wear your dress."

"It's not mine." Madeline wears Helen's black lace gloves and her red cocktail dress. Since she threw out all of her clothes, I have no choice but to share mine with her. Helen's dress fits my sister well. It hugs her waist tightly and settles on her shoulders and chest as if it were made for her. When I tried the dress on, it was too tight. When I see my sister wearing Helen's dress, I'm aware for the first time since I returned to Sarasota of how different our bodies have become in the last year. All my life I've been slightly heavier, but now the difference between us is clear. It's easy to tell who was once pregnant and who was not.

After a few minutes of silence, Madeline says, "Do you know I don't have a driver's license?"

"That's it. I want you to pull over, right now, Linny. I'm not letting you drive anymore." I knew I should have asked her if she had a license before I let her drive.

"Once you've been in a mental hospital, they take away your driver's license." When I hear the word *hospital,* my heart jumps in my chest, and I forget about admonishing her.

My sister never talks about the hospital. Her silence about those three months of her life is part of how she punishes me. It's the only experience of her life she will not share, because she still blames me. I had just moved to Atlanta when she called to tell me she had tried to kill herself. I called the Sarasota police long-distance and had them take her in a squad car to the emergency psychiatric ward of Sarasota General, told them to do anything they had to do to commit her. Owen and I had been married for one day when I got in the car and drove back to my childhood home. I made the drive in one night, arriving early the next morning to find my sister on a stretcher in the hall. She refused to speak to me.

"Of course, that's not all they take away from you," my sister says. "They take away your sanity, your integrity, and your will to live. And they think they're making you better."

I try to turn the conversation. "Well, I guess it's like being in any other kind of hospital," I say. "In April, when I was in the hospital——"

Madeline interrupts. "It's not the same at all. You have no idea what I'm talking about. Do you know the first thing they do to you when you're admitted to a mental hospital?"

"No." My sister and I are now on unfamiliar terrain. We've never once, in all our phone conversations in the past three years, discussed the time she spent in the hospital.

"Restraints. They tie you down. Then they take away your jewelry. The nurse comes into the bathroom, where they make you take a shower, with this green soap that has a very gritty lather, and she asks for your earrings, bracelets, necklaces, and rings. They are especially worried about the necklaces. Do you think women have hung themselves with their pearls?"

Madeline's version of events, I remind myself, is never reliable. When I went back to Sarasota, I talked to all the doctors. I told myself that they seemed kind and genuinely concerned about my sister. The ward she was finally taken to was freshly painted and well lit, and the nurses wore street clothes, as if they were no different from the patients. I think of the mental hospitals of fifty years ago, as I've seen them in old movies, with their electroshock treatments and straitjackets and cold packs, and a day room full of women in sacklike gowns talking to themselves and banging their hands on the wall in the hope of escape. It can't be that bad, I tell myself. Madeline is surely exaggerating to increase my guilt.

"Let me tell you what I did, Alice, when I was supposed to give up my jewelry. I swallowed it." She begins laughing, but it's not her usual expression of amusement. Her laugh is too high, too sharp, and goes on much too long.

I can't help myself: I picture Madeline naked in the shower room, placing her earrings and rings, one by one, on her tongue.

"I read about it in an article about women who escaped the Nazis. They swallowed their jewelry to sell if they made it out of the concentration camps alive. So when I die, I want to be cremated, and will you explain to the doctors that they need to get out my rings before they burn my body?" She hums "Sweet Sixteen," one of Judy Garland's happiest songs. "Remember that song? Lily loved it," she says, without waiting for my answer. "Lily had the most beautiful voice. Even when she talked, you could tell. I think she sounded just like Judy Garland, don't you?" She turns on the radio.

I don't think Lily sounded at all like Judy Garland, but I'll do anything to avoid the topic of the hospital, so I nod.

My sister and I listen to the radio. The first radio station is the Kingdom of the Living Jesus Broadcasting System. The host is a preacher, delivering a sermon on a show called "The Body of

Christ." He describes a group of children at a Pentecostal Church being slain in the spirit. "Then the whole row, all those kids, went down, down, down on the floor and into the water, and they were saved," he says. In the background, gospel music swells. Women's voices fill the air, praising the Lord.

"Let's switch." Madeline tunes in to a call-in talk show about crime victims. The host interviews a forensic dentist. "Teeth are forever," the dentist states. "Unlike fingerprints, they cannot be erased." He explains that many bodies have been identified by their teeth alone and suggests that everyone consult a dentist to have a mouth impression made.

"Teeth are forever," Madeline says. "Do you like that? Don't you think that would be a good line for a song? Ginger Love's teeth were forever."

An imaginary alarm sounds in my head. Madeline and I haven't talked about Ginger Love in years, since childhood. Ginger Love is a danger sign. We gave up Emerald City when Lily left.

When the sky darkens, Madeline and I check into the first motel on Tamiami Trail, a three-story building called Adventureland. Next to the parking lot is a tall, precarious-looking water slide and a pool that the desk clerk claims contains man-made waves. Behind the laundry room, you can play miniature golf. Our room is located on the second floor. Outside, on the balcony, an old man sits in a lawn chair with his feet propped up against the railing, smoking and stirring a spoon in a can of chili. Another man stands in the doorway, openly staring at Madeline and me. I avoid his eyes as we climb the stairs to the landing.

Madeline matches his gaze. "What do you think we are, TV?" she says, as we walk past him.

"That was good," I whisper, squeezing her arm. "I could never think of anything like that." She kisses me and squeezes my arm back.

But as soon as we enter the room, Madeline picks up her purse again. "I'm going out to explore." She doesn't invite me to accompany her. "Don't wait up. I may not be home till late."

From the window, I watch as Madeline wanders out to the pool. A few dispirited children straggle out clutching motel towels. My sister rounds a corner of the building and disappears. On the back of the bathroom door there is a small glass-plated warning: "Adventureland has very little fire protection. We suggest you plan your own escape route in case of fire." Our room contains one door, one small window equipped with metal bars.

For adults, the "adventure" in this motel must consist of the Pay-TV movies advertised in the booklet left open on the bed. For seven dollars and fifty cents, you can watch *The Love Thief,* a movie that tells the story of a blond woman in a black garter belt who hides in men's houses when they're not home and then is, apparently, seduced by the men from whom she steals. I turn the movie booklet face-down on the bed so I won't have to look at the picture: the thief in the act of creeping out of a closet while a man with a bare chest stands behind her, ready to attack. I change my mind and hide the movie booklet in my suitcase.

I can't admit to my sister that on our first day on the road, I want to call Owen. I want to go back. I slowly dial the number of our rented house in Sarasota. No answer. No answering machine. Owen either isn't there or he doesn't pick up the phone. I want to tell him I've a made a mistake. I shouldn't have left him.

But I've set this story in motion, and it has already become my sister's and I can't seem to stop it.

I dial the number of our house in Atlanta; no one answers. Maybe Owen is gone. Maybe he has decided he doesn't want to be married to me anymore. I feel a sudden panic that he has abandoned me. No, I have to remind myself, I'm the one who left.

What kind of mother would I be? During the pregnancy, I considered the question constantly, picturing myself with the baby in a series of different scenes. I always started with the birth. I visualized natural childbirth, which would be painful but bearable because I'd been to Lamaze classes, and Owen would be my coach. Then breast-feeding: I'd never give Frida a bottle. She'd move from the breast to drinking out of a cup. One image breeds another. I saw myself carrying her in a sling over my chest, her weight pressed against me. Later, I'd push her in a stroller through the park.

What I most often wondered was whether I'd become frustrated with her as Lily had with us, whether I'd be demanding or punishing or withholding of my love. I couldn't find an image to accompany this fear. If I could talk to Lily about the secret world of mothering, the world she wanted no part of, I might learn how not to be like her. But what is it that I want to know, now that the baby's dead?

Madeline would have been my baby's aunt. Part of me would have wanted to keep the baby away from her, yet I would need her. In our family, there are no mothers left. I'd want my sister.

I should look for Madeline. I should take Jack's car and search all the nearby bars; no doubt I would find her in one of them, sitting with a group of men, drinking and laughing, at the center of the table, tossing her short hair, flashing her eyes. As I did so many times when we were younger, I could rescue my sister from the men and take her home. I uncap the bottle of vinegar from Winn Dixie and take a long slow sip. The vinegar goes down like a punishment, a harsh burn.

I turn on *The Love Thief*. Besides her garter belt and stockings, the female thief wears a black mask that covers her eyes, like a glamorous cat burglar. In the first scene, she slips in the window of a mansion owned by a millionaire, fills her bag with gold bars from his safe, and lies down in his bed. I can't help thinking of Goldilocks and the Three Bears. The thief lies on the bed, her legs spread, in a helpless posture. She is waiting. When the millionaire returns home, he takes her in his arms roughly and begins to kiss her neck.

Madeline comes back to the room at 3 A.M.

I hear her shoes clicking on the stairs up to the balcony, and I throw open the door. She stands on the threshold, her hair matted and wet, Helen's cocktail dress torn at the shoulder. She smells like beer.

"Where have you been?"

"Out. I met a guy. His name is—" She laughs. "Well, I don't remember his name, but I think his last name was Sanders. Yeah, that was it. Anyway, I met him at this bar."

"You went alone to a bar? Oh, Linny, why did you do that?"

"We didn't stay at the bar, Alice. We went back to his apartment."

I grab her shoulders, shaking her. "Why did you go off with some man you don't even know? Don't you understand that's not safe?"

Madeline shakes me off. "I don't care about *safe*, Alice. That's your word. I've never cared about being *safe*." She crosses the room, away from me, then turns back to face me. "You're not my mother, Alice. Leave me alone."

In art school, while I was still living with Madeline, my first semester, I researched twins. I planned a huge installation, a mixed-media piece the size of a house, a museum of twins.

In the first room are the cave paintings, the museum walls rough stone, presenting the legend of the first fighting twins. The Huron Indians tell a tale about twins: Ataentsic, the moon goddess, tumbled out of heaven into the primeval waters. Her virgin daughter bore the first children of the earth, Isokeha, called the White One, and Tawiscara, referred to as the Dark One. The second twin, the Dark One, was not born in the usual manner; he came out of his mother's arm. Throughout their lives, the twins fought often, and finally the White One killed his brother with the horn of a stag and returned to the sky as the sun.

In the second room would be Castor and Pollux, the twin gods formed by an act of violence. When Zeus pursued Leda, in disguise, the rape of the pregnant woman by the swan produced two new children, identical children of different fathers. On a red-figure vase from the third century B.C., they recline on a bed, eating leeks and olives, worn out from their good deeds—guiding ships to safety, rescuing women.

Next, under a glass case, a coin, dated A.D. 200, with a double image, two heads, on one side and on the other, two figures on horseback. Identity of the figures unknown.

A medieval triptych, wooden panels carefully preserved. Romulus and Remus are suckled by the wolf, play happily in the forest, then are carried on a peasant's back into the village.

A pen-and-ink illustration from the book of Genesis, set in movable type from the fifteenth century, with the title *Rebekah wishes that her curse of childlessness had not been removed when Esau and Jacob begin to quarrel in her womb.* Rebekah's expression is bleak, her hands clasped over her belly. The inside of her body is visible through her skin as if illuminated. Inside her, the twin sons scratch and bite each other, two nations fighting it out in her body.

Here is a framed playbill for the display of Chang and Eng,

famous Siamese twins from Breklong, exhibited in the United States and France. For years, they were an exhibit in the Ringling Brothers Circus. In a celebrated double union, the twins married two sisters and, between them, produced eleven children, all American citizens.

The last room of my museum contains two small statues of women, carved from wood and decorated with strings of seeds, standing alone on a pedestal. In the Yoruba culture of western Nigeria, mothers practice weekly rituals of devotion to twins who died at birth or any time after. Twins are magic. They might be pure luck. Or disaster. If these mothers pray every week to the statues, they can save their families from the twins.

The project would end with photographs of the two sets of twins in my own family: Agnes and Agatha, Madeline and me.

The next day, at a souvenir emporium in Clearwater Beach, Madeline tries on hats. She spins in front of the small square of aluminum that functions as a mirror, admiring her reflection. She picks up fishing hats bound with string and tiny plastic fish, baseball caps for Florida teams. She fits a rubber bathing cap over her short hair.

Last night Madeline slept in the bathtub, but we haven't talked about our fight today. On the other side of the store, I pick out postcards. For Owen, I find a card depicting two monkeys in bathing suits on the beach, a mother and a father, with a baby monkey sitting on the sand between them. Above their heads are cartoon bubbles of dialogue: "Having Fun in Florida!" says the father. "Wish You Were Here!" adds the mother. In graduate school, when I first met him, Owen wrote a paper on primate language acquisition, so I hope he'll be amused by this card. The only problem is the baby monkey. I could cross out the baby, but the clear omission would be worse.

For Helen, I choose a postcard that reads "Spring Break '93, Having A Great Time!" from the half-price rack because this year's college spring break is already over. The Technicolor photograph depicts three teenagers, two boys and a pretty girl, lying on a raft. The girl's face is hidden by her hair.

I have nothing to write on the postcards. I turn them over, studying the empty message space, remembering the postcards Madeline sent to me when I first arrived in Sarasota—all blank on the message side. I understand her silence. There is nothing I can say to Owen now that would help him. I was unable to console him about our daughter's death. Instead, I left him. It's the single worst act I have ever committed in my life. Leaving Madeline to marry Owen was easier than what I've done now.

I approach my sister at the hat rack. "Linny, we need a plan."

She spins around to face me, a broad-rimmed sun hat shading her face, her expression a wide smile, her teeth gleaming and white. "What do you think?" She twirls again, holding the hat on her head with one hand, as if she were a runway model.

"I want to decide what we're doing."

"Aren't you having a good time?" Madeline drops the hat on the floor and walks away from me so that I have to follow her to keep the conversation going. "Isn't it fun to be together? Don't you like being with me?" She steps closer, stands against me, pressing her body into mine.

"We need to get to New Orleans faster."

She turns from me and studies a glass case, touching the edge of it with her index finger. Inside are odd glass animals: purple fish, an iguana, a two-headed turtle. Madeline reaches into the case and turns the turtle over and over in her hands. Her face is illuminated by pink light that emanates from the case. Her features soften. For a moment, she looks like her childhood self again. "Why?"

"To look for Lily," I say, unable to conceal my frustration any longer. "Isn't that why we're on this trip?"

"What's the hurry?" Madeline sets the glass turtle back in its place.

"Linny, I can't stay away indefinitely."

"Why not? What do you have to get back to?"

"I have a job. I have to go back to Owen."

"Alice, you wouldn't have left on this trip with me if your marriage was so important. I could tell things between you and Owen were falling apart. He doesn't understand you." She smiles. "Admit the truth. I gave you an excuse to leave." Madeline uses this final statement as an exit line.

I follow her outside. She sits on the hood of the car, her bent legs arranged in front of her in a pose, wearing the heart-shaped sunglasses from Winn Dixie and a sun hat I saw her try on in the store. "I wanted the hat, so I took it," Madeline says, as if she knows I'm about to demand an explanation. She shrugs.

"Don't steal anything else on this trip," I tell her. "I don't want to start that again."

"Don't pretend you're virtuous. You used to *like* stealing. I've known you your whole life, Alice, and you're not so very different from when you were a child. In fact, I'm surprised how much the same you are now as you were then." Madeline opens the car door and sets the sun hat on the mannequin's head. "Since you're so eager to get to New Orleans, let me tell you what we'll do. If you need to go to the bathroom, I'll stop at the side of the road. And we're not eating anymore. We simply don't have the time."

Jack's blue car glides down the highway. Madeline hums "Cry Baby Cry." The grass at the side of the highway is now lush and green, and the fields of kudzu that meet the horizon are slowly turning into swamps as my sister and I move closer to Louisiana.

20

Agatha waits on the dock in New Orleans. While logic tells her that Agnes will not arrive on the Mississippi, she waits for a ship to appear on the horizon. Each day, she goes to the dock, without telling her husband, to wait for her sister to suddenly, magically, appear.

Agatha sits quietly in a chair in the hall of the Hotel Dieu Hospital in New Orleans. This morning, she walked down Napoleon Avenue alone on her way to her appointment with the doctor, a secret appointment. On the avenue, the light is washed clean by rain. The neutral ground that divides one side of the street from the other is bright with flowers—bougainvillea, legustrom, trillium—flowers that are still unfamiliar to my great-grandmother although she has now lived in New Orleans for ten years. Ten years and five dead babies. One living daughter. Agatha misses the vegetation from her village in Hungary: potato plants, rhubarb, wheat, all ugly, useful plants that feed the children in a family for years until they grow strong. Healthy, robust children. They may not go to school or learn to read but they can run and jump. They breathe and sleep.

Agatha waits in the hospital corridor. She is alone but pretends that she is not afraid. What is there to fear? She twists the ring on her finger, proof that her pregnancies are sanctioned by the Church, respectable. If he knew, Stephan might have come with her to the appointment. Her last five pregnancies ended in death, and no one can tell her why. One child, her first, survived. She cannot take a chance again. She's heard that if you ask to have no more children in a Catholic hospital like this one, the doctor calculates a formula, your age factored with the number of children you already have. She knows her one daughter will not be enough. She knows preventing birth is considered a sin in the Catholic Church. After ten years of believing this, she flinches each time Stephan touches her because his touch, any communion between them, will begin the cycle of death again.

The nurse taps her shoulder. "Mrs. Bantorvya? You can come in now." She smiles kindly. Agatha feels relief. She will explain the situation calmly, explain how she cannot go through another pregnancy again, offer the lie that she and her husband have discussed it and have decided their family is now complete.

What is family? Family is blood.

21

To get rid of us, the summer before we started high school, Lily sent us to the movies at the Joy Theater on Airline Highway. "I don't want you around here all day where I have to watch you," she said. Madeline and I didn't argue, although we were teenagers and didn't believe we needed baby-sitting.

Lily told us paper dolls were babyish. "You're too old to be playing with dolls. Go to the movies." She still wanted to get us out of the swimming pool. She'd never seen Judy Garland and Ginger Love up close, and she'd never witnessed our games.

"They're not dolls," Madeline said, but I knew she couldn't explain our world in the pool or the secret histories of the girls to Lily.

Lily stood in the doorway, wearing her maid's uniform, holding a spray bottle and a sponge. "Will you two get *out* of here? I don't want to see you again until five. Walk on the opposite side to the cars. Men will do anything, even on the street in daylight," Lily said. "Don't talk to anyone and you'll be fine."

We started down Airline Highway. "I want to go to the Prytania," Madeline said. "That's where the good movies are."

"We can't go there. She won't let us. We can only see it at night." This was one of the unspoken rules of living with Lily: we were not allowed to go uptown.

During these summer afternoons, the Joy Theater was empty. Several old men who lived at the Airline Highway Salvation Army sat in the back and dozed, occasionally drinking from a paper bag they passed between them. Once in a while, a couple was there, holding hands or kissing, paying no attention to the movie, happy to be somewhere dark alone. During the week, despite the fact that it was summer, no children came to the theater. Sometimes the films were designed for children, animated Disney features like *Snow White* and *Bambi* or movies with children in them like *Willy Wonka and the Chocolate Factory*. Children's movies were always prefaced by cartoons. Wile E. Coyote tumbled off cliff after cliff. The Road Runner skidded to a stop and crashed, then stood up and smiled.

Other times, my sister and I sat through strange, frightening movies. Out of boredom or because she just didn't care, the woman in the glass ticket box admitted us to *Looking for Mr. Goodbar*. During the scene at the end of the movie in which Diane Keaton's character is killed, I had to force myself to look at the screen. Afterward, we walked home in silence. "Don't tell Lily," I said.

My sister flipped her hair over her shoulders. "I wasn't scared."

We watched that movie seven times, once each day until the program changed.

To keep me with her for the multiple viewings of *Looking for Mr. Goodbar*, my sister bribed me with secret candy—jawbreakers, sourballs, and Atomic Fireballs—which she kept hidden in her pocket. She held the candies in her open palm like jewels. "Pick one," she'd say, then close her fist quickly. I never knew how or where my sister got my favorite candy. Maybe she stole it. I sat beside her in the dark, cracking the shell of the hard candy between my teeth until my mouth ached with the taste of sugar. Madeline never ate candy. It was her trick to keep me sitting beside her, to make me watch what I didn't want to see.

The best films were the old black-and-whites, films from the twenties, thirties, and forties that were shown between the regular features on Wednesdays and Thursdays in the middle of the afternoon. These were the films that drew the greatest crowds to the Joy Theater.

"Pretend we're at the Prytania," Madeline whispered. "You can be Agatha and I'm Lily."

"No, you be Agatha," I said.

"I'm Agnes, Alice, and she's not in this scene."

The crowds were mostly women, most of them elderly, viewing the films of their young adulthood, years ago. The films themselves were in bad condition: the projector often stopped during the movie, the sound was full of static, and lines frequently marked the screen, across the actresses' faces.

"I want to be her," Madeline whispered, watching Theda Bara lounge on a tapestry-covered divan in *Cleopatra,* wearing a snake bracelet on her upper arm and a mocking smile. I wanted to imitate that expression, contemptuous and unafraid. Her eyes were heavy-lidded, darkened with kohl. I wanted to be her, too, but Madeline claimed her first. She also took Veronica Lake, with her smooth blond hair and her gaze, eyebrows lifted, that made men fall in love with her immediately in every film in which she appeared.

Once, whispering to me in the dark, Madeline said, "That's you." Mary Pickford appeared on the screen, a nice smile and a pale halo of hair.

"I don't want to be her!"

"You have to be."

Madeline and I waited for movies about sisters. One of our favorite movies was the silent film *Orphans of the Storm*, where Lillian Gish and her sister played two sisters, devoted to each other forever. The sisters lay in bed together, their long dark hair spread over each other's shoulders. During *Whatever Happened to Baby Jane?* I held my breath as Bette Davis pushed Joan Crawford down the stairs of their house and served her sister her own pet bird in a covered silver dish for dinner. There was always a bad sister and a good sister. The good sister and the bad sister fought until the end, but the bad sister always, finally, lost. In the end, the bad sister would die.

I didn't pay much attention to the plots of these movies. Instead, I leaned back in my seat and let the images wash over me. "Look," Madeline whispered in the dark and Marlene Dietrich crossed a room in a long tight dress, then draped her body over a piano. I wanted to close my eyes and hold the image inside of me forever. I wanted to imprint it on my brain. The experience was very different from reading a book. When I read, I focused on the page, on the lines of letters. I was methodical; I never skipped passages even if they consisted of nothing but description. At the Joy Theater, I sat beside my sister and watched the images on the screen as if they were appearing to me in one of my dreams.

To keep the images with me, I drew. I watched the screen and tried to follow the outlines of a woman's body with my pencil on my sketchbook in the dark. It was a game: the object was not to look down at my hand in the dark but to see what I could make without trying. I liked the movie stars from the past best. I set Bette

Davis and Greta Garbo side by side, as sisters, in white sequined gowns. I sketched a family of silent screen star girls.

The afternoon we saw *All About Eve,* Madeline and I fought.

As we walked along the highway, on our way home, I told her, "I just didn't like it. I don't know why."

"You can't say that," Madeline hissed through her teeth.

"Stop it, Linny." I stepped past her, but she grabbed my arm.

"You *have* to like the movie because I do. We have to like the same things."

"It's just a movie," I began but she didn't seem to hear me.

"You can't just decide you don't like it on your own!" She stamped her foot on the sidewalk. "You can't!"

I was frightened. Madeline thought I had overstepped the boundaries of our life together as twins by having my own opinion about Bette Davis. "Say you like it," my sister said. Her voice was sharp and commanding. "Tell me *All About Eve* is your favorite movie of all time." She yanked my hair until my head jerked back. My eyes burned from the pain. "Say it, Alice. I'm going to push you out into the highway if you don't. You think I'm faking? Look." Madeline forced my head in the direction of the highway. Through the tears that now blurred my vision, I saw the cars rushing by, three lanes on each side. "Do you want that?" her voice hissed in my ear. I shook my head, a tiny movement because she wouldn't let go. "Then do what I say."

I choked out the sentences my sister asked for. Then she released me, and I stumbled forward on the sidewalk. My neck ached where she had grabbed me. I knew that if I looked in the mirror I would see the prints of her fingers on my skin. Her grip was strong.

Madeline hugged me. "Thank you for doing what I wanted," she said, smiling.

Walking home on Airline Highway, I didn't talk to her. Madeline hummed an unrecognizable song. For the rest of the summer, as Madeline and I sat together in the dark, I told her I liked every film we saw.

Lily disapproved but we still played Emerald City with the paper dolls in the swimming pool. I drew a wardrobe of clothes for each girl, with small tabs at the top to attach to their shoulders. Judy Garland and Ginger Love had no ordinary clothes, the kind my sister and I wore. They wore movie star outfits. "Make everything match," Madeline said. We sat on the bottom of the pool, and she watched me draw.

I drew two of each piece of clothing: small feather boas, tiny sequined jackets, long, tight evening gowns. I made two pink trunks of folded paper where the girls could store their outfits. Each trunk latched shut with a paper clip.

"Make Agnes and Agatha now," Madeline said. "I'll tell you how."

"I can do it." I sat down in the shallow end by myself.

I cut Agnes and Agatha from the same sheet of paper. The sisters were linked by their hands. I drew them as children, the way they looked in Hungary, before they were separated. The only model I had for the sisters were the daguerreotypes in Lily's scrapbook, two blurred faces, so I made them up. I colored long red hair and made them each a single plain brown dress.

Madeline didn't know that secretly, one night in the bathtub when she was asleep, I'd made a Reid Alistair paper doll. I didn't tell her because she was never curious about him, and whenever I inserted him into Emerald City she was mad. I drew Reid Alistair in a *grande jêté* pose, his legs permanently arced in the air, and dressed him in a gold leotard. His face was pale and delicate like a child's.

In August, two weeks before we were supposed to go back to school, the Joy Theater sponsored a Judy Garland Film Festival in honor of the fact that it was 1979, the tenth anniversary of her death. As we left the theater after the cartoons one afternoon, Madeline was the first to notice the new poster by the ticket window: MISS SHOW BUSINESS LIVES ON! COME SEE ONE WEEK OF THE FILMS THAT MADE HER FAMOUS.

Madeline clutched my hand. "Lily will be so excited," she said.

Madeline and I went to most of the Judy Garland films alone. We saw *Broadway Melody of 1938*. Lily had told us that this film was Judy Garland's MGM feature debut. We watched Judy Garland try to save her racehorse while becoming a star on Broadway. She wore a wide-brimmed black hat and a dress with a starched white collar. Madeline sang along under her breath with the movie's best song, "You Made Me Love You." Lily often sang this song on our late-night drives, and my sister knew it by heart.

In *The Harvey Girls*, the first shot showed Judy Garland on a train, on her way to meet her new husband, a false landscape rushing by behind her while she sang with her hands clasped behind her back. Beside me, Madeline shoved her hands behind her back in imitation of the posture. We saw *Everybody Sing, Listen Darling, Andy Hardy Meets a Debutante, Ziegfeld Girl, I Could Go On Singing, We Must Have Music*. Madeline loved them all, but the Judy Garland film I liked best was *The Clock* because there were no songs. I became tired of musicals. In my sketchbook, I drew image after image of Judy Garland as a teenager, singing, kissing Mickey Rooney, drinking from a tall soda fountain glass. Judy and Mickey always had a plan; their characters loved to invent shows to prove their talents and save their parents' fortunes. I studied that face and body that Lily and now Madeline loved so much. "I like opera, I like swing," she sang, her face lit up and happy as she danced beside her partner.

Lily went with us to the theater to see only one film, *A Star Is Born*. The three of us sat in the dark together, Madeline and I separated by Lily. The Joy Theater showed the uncut version. The film was three hours long. I grew bored, but Madeline and Lily stared at the screen with rapt attention. The songs seemed endless. The film's Technicolor was so bright it hurt my eyes. Judy Garland's lips were a red gash in her white face as she sang "The Man that Got Away." I watched Esther Blodgett carry a scrapbook of her career around Hollywood, hoping for a part, and I wondered if this was what Lily had wished for once with her own scrapbook. Later, Esther would change her name, but her life held the same inner sadness. Judy Garland's arms were full of red roses, but no one knew what her life was like in secret, with her drunk, forgotten husband. "It's a new world," she sang, but I wondered if she meant it.

As we walked out of the theater, Lily said, "She lost the Oscar to Grace Kelly that year, and people sent thousands of telegrams to sympathize with her."

"That's terrible," Madeline said, her voice full of excitement. Her eyes were shining. I was aware of how strange it felt to be out in public with Lily, the three of us leaving a theater together as if we were a normal family who went to movies together all the time.

Lily took her hand. Lily touched her. The two of them walked ahead of me on Airline Highway, sharing their new, secret world.

"Maybe next time we can go to the Prytania," Madeline said.

I stopped walking before I even knew I'd done it. I waited for Lily's response.

She dropped Madeline's hand. "I'm not taking you there" was all she said.

As quickly as Lily had opened the door of that world to Madeline, she denied her access the next day. Lily never went with us to the Joy Theater again. "I'm busy," she said, when Madeline invited her to the next three Judy Garland films. "Did you forget I have a job?"

I turned away so I wouldn't have to see the disappointment on my sister's face.

When we returned to the Joy Theater without Lily for the last days of the Judy Garland film festival, Madeline wanted to steal. I refused to help.

"God, you're no fun at all," my sister said.

At the end of each film, during the credits, after the other moviegoers left, I put away my sketchbook and waited for Madeline to finish stealing. Madeline crawled up and down the rows of seats on the floor looking for what people had left behind. She wanted objects that had fallen from pockets or purses. Buttons, jewelry, knitted scarves. "This is way easier than sneaking into rooms at the Star Dust," she said. "This is so easy even you can do it."

My sister filled her pockets with lost change, lipsticks that had rolled on the floor to the front of the theater. Wile E. Coyote turned somersaults through the clean blue air, his body spinning in the wind as light as paper, and ended up intact. One sister smiled while the other set her teeth in an expression of hatred and prepared to ruin her sister's life. Judy Garland opened her mouth so wide the song exploded from her throat.

22

Madeline and I arrive in New Orleans after midnight. From the interstate, I see the Mississippi River, the Huey P. Long Bridge arching over the water, a path in and out of the city lined with lights. When I roll down the car window, the air feels as if it's filled with water. Madeline turns off I–10 and onto Airline Highway, the long road that runs from the center of the city to the airport, the street where Lily, Madeline, and I once lived.

Then my breath catches in my throat. We're here.

Madeline + Alice + Lily = A Family.

I haven't been back to New Orleans in twelve years, since I was a child.

Only a few cars move along the road. Most of the buildings, except for the bars, are dark. I study the motels at the edge of the highway: Paradise Inn, The Delta, motels notorious for prostitution, where men check in for an hour or less. Lily warned us about these men. Only the pickup trucks, rusted Cadillacs, and Peugeots in the parking lots testify to the presence of these invisible women offering their bodies again and again to men they don't know for money.

I want to go to the Star Dust. I want to see our old room again, open the door to the place where we spent our childhood, lie down on the bed where I slept with my sister each night. Maybe to see the motel would be enough. Maybe we wouldn't have to search for Lily if my sister and I could find what we're looking for at the Star Dust. What are we looking for?

Abruptly, Madeline veers off Airline Highway.

"Where are we going, Linny?"

She doesn't answer.

Madeline drives Lily's old route, uptown, to that forbidden world. We take the tour of Lily's life, the life we were allowed only to glimpse from the window of her car as she quickly drove past the places that once composed her life.

In front of the New Orleans Ballet, Madeline parks and yanks the key out of the ignition, but then she doesn't move.

"Let's go see it," I say.

My sister shakes her head, slumping over the steering wheel, her face turned away from me.

"Are you tired? What's wrong?"

Madeline says nothing. She flicks her fingers in my direction, as if to cast me out of the car.

"You drove us here, Linny. I know you want to see the New Orleans Ballet." I climb out of the car, leaving her behind because I refuse to let my sister ruin our first night back in New Orleans.

I never before stood in front of the New Orleans Ballet as I'm standing now, so close that I can run my finger along the window. It's made of frosted glass so from the outside no one can see in.

Pressing my face to the glass, I try to picture the characters in the story: Lily and Reid Alistair and Madame Makarov. I can't see anything. I study the sign hanging on a metal chain over the door, NEW ORLEANS BALLET, in curving letters. I read the chart of hours for a master class, for modern and jazz classes. The building's facade is closed to me, and I can't find out anything new about Lily's world. I return to the car.

"Let's go see Sacred Heart," I tell my sister.

Madeline remains silent, but she turns off St. Charles and drives down Nashville. We pull up at the edge of the wire fence that separates the school from the wide street, and I open the car door and leave her without saying a word. I circle the schoolyard in the dark, looking through the high wire fence, studying the jungle gyms and slides for the little girls, the lines chalked on the asphalt for hopscotch and four-square, the benches where the older girls must have sat to whisper about each other and gossip about boys.

Lily never would have sat on that bench, and neither would we. Our isolation from the world of other girls only mimicked her own. I imagine Lily in the schoolyard, during recess or a free period, sitting under one of the huge crape myrtle trees and writing in her Sacred Heart assignment book, recording what she'd eaten at lunch that day: *½ tomato, 1 poached egg, ⅓ piece of toast.*

Suddenly, I feel hands behind me gripping my throat. I whirl around to break free and find my sister standing behind me on the sidewalk.

"Fooled you!" These are the first words she's spoken since we arrived in New Orleans.

"Linny, you terrified me!"

"You're such a scaredy-cat," she says, using a term I haven't heard since elementary school. Her voice is light and mocking. "Follow me."

Madeline runs to the chain-link fence that surrounds the school-yard and begins to climb to the top, gripping the metal and using the spaces as toeholds. She hoists her body up. "Are you coming?"

Slowly, I climb up one side of the fence and down the other. My body feels heavy and clumsy; Helen's dress tears at the hem. I drop to my feet in the empty schoolyard. Madeline is far ahead. She's running. I try to keep up, but she's much faster. She scales the monkey bars and stands on the top, balancing herself on the metal bars. "Hey! Look at me!" The she jumps down into a pile of sawdust below and falls to her knees on the grass.

I'm startled by her energy; it comes from nowhere. I want to believe that our trip to New Orleans has filled her with enthusiasm and happiness, but something seems wrong. "Did you take any pills?" I yell across the yard, but she either doesn't hear me or pretends not to.

Madeline runs to the seesaw on the playground and jumps on. "Get on the other side, Alice."

Up and down. Down and up. My sister and I can't keep a balance. She goes up and I drift down, over and over. Madeline laughs, a shrill, loud sound that doesn't sound like her usual laughter. We push the seesaw faster and faster, up and down, pumping with our legs, as if we're on a bicycle. Sweat runs down my cheeks, and I push my hair off my forehead. My sister moves her side faster. Her legs touch the ground, then push her body up, over and over, and in one of her quick motions, I'm jolted off the board. I lose my grip and thud to the asphalt.

I roll over in pain. The right side of my body aches, and my knees burn from scraping the ground when I tried to break the fall.

"Alice!" Madeline runs to me. "Talk to me. Are you okay?" She cradles me in her arms, as if I'm a child. "Poor baby. For once it was you."

"What?" I look up at her, my eyes blurred with tears.

"For once you were the one that fell."

It's 4 A.M. We study the Prytania Theater from the car window. The building looks just as it did when Lily drove us past years ago: red brick, stone steps, and a marquee with several letters missing. I feel like I did when I stood alone in front of the New Orleans Ballet. I have no access to the past. The theater no longer shows MGM classics. *Pretty Woman* is now playing, though it was released two years ago. Instead of a poster of Judy Garland, there's a picture of Julia Roberts.

My body still aches from the fall. I'm too exhausted to try to imagine Lily and Agatha in the theater, sitting in the dark, while Judy Garland's voice breaks on the chorus of "Somewhere Over the Rainbow." More than anything, I want to sleep. "Linny, let's find a hotel and look around tomorrow."

"We have one more place to visit. You know that."

Madeline is right: we have to go to Agatha's house at the end of Constance Street. I remember that the cross-street is Jackson Avenue, but I don't know the street address. The location is imprinted in our memories, yet we've never looked closely at the house. Lily would never allow it.

Parking in front of Agatha's house feels odd. If the house used to be a shot from a movie, it's now a photograph. I'm used to seeing it in motion, a blur as Lily drove us by in the dark. The dark green paint looks chipped, but maybe that was always true. One of the front shutters is missing. The grass in the front yard is long and yellow, scattered with patches of dandelions and tangled weeds. The house where Lily once lived is tinier than I remember; I'm not sure if I remember it according to the scale of childhood, when everything seems huge.

"Emerald City," Madeline says, in a low voice. I'm not sure I heard the words. I don't want to hear them. I tell myself she didn't say them.

It's 5 A.M. by the time we check into the Crescent Court, the first motel we find on Airline Highway. I'm so tired I can't do anything but lie on one of the matching twin beds, but Madeline is still full of energy. She wants me to dye her hair.

"Red," she says. From her purse, she produces a box of Clairol dye, Miss Auburn, with a picture of a smiling redhead tossing her long hair over her shoulder. Madeline opens the box and sets the various bottles and brushes in a line on the bedspread. "I want to look different." She switches the TV on and off, without looking at the picture on the screen. "I want to look like someone else so I can hide."

"There's no reason to hide, Linny. No one cares we're here." No one cares that I'm gone, except Owen, or maybe Helen. Whenever I allow myself to think of Owen, my chest tightens.

"Jack could come after me," she says, yanking at her hair with rapid motions, as if she wants to pull it out of her head. "What if he showed up and broke down the door?"

"I told you he was dangerous."

"I want you to dye my hair, Alice. I want to look like Agatha. Do this for me, *please.*" My sister's voice is pleading, the tone I remember from several years ago: *Don't get married. Don't leave me. Don't do this to me.* "Please."

"Are you high?" I ask her suddenly. I don't know where the question comes from, but once I ask it I know I should have asked her when we first left on the trip.

Madeline's voice is sharp. "What kind of sister are you? I'd never ask you that."

"Did you take something?"

She sits down hard on the bed opposite mine, her legs bouncing, and lights a cigarette. "God, Alice. Jack gave me some speed, okay? Yellow mollies. They're in my purse if you want one."

"I don't want any speed. If I dye your hair tonight, will you swear to me you won't take any more drugs on this trip?"

She nods, her face solemn.

"I'll do it. Give me the box so I can read the directions. Go wet your hair in the shower."

"Want to do yours too?" my sister calls from the bathroom as she rinses her hair.

"No!"

She reappears, naked. "Remember when we dyed Lily's hair? She wanted to have dark hair like us. We gave her a black rinse. First we bleached all the natural color out of her hair with peroxide. For an hour her hair was perfectly white. She looked like a princess. Don't you remember?"

"No." I have no memory of this incident at all.

"As soon as we finished, she wanted it changed back. We didn't know how to fix it. But she wasn't mad." Madeline leans over to embrace me, her bare arms tight around my shoulders. "I promise if you dye my hair, I won't ask you to change me back."

As Madeline bends over the sink, I pour the contents of the little plastic bottles on her head. She insists that she doesn't need to cover her eyes. The dark liquid runs down her face, over her ears, staining her skin. The dye resembles blood, as if my actions above Madeline's head are violent, as if I'm causing my sister pain.

Light rises over Airline Highway a little after six. By eight, I've finished Madeline's hair, and she's in the shower for a final rinse.

I want to call Owen and tell him about our trip, but I can't. Instead I call Helen.

"Who the hell is this?" she says.

"Alice." My voice is a whisper.

"I've been worried. Are you okay? Where are you?"

"We're in New Orleans at the Crescent Court Motel on Airline Highway."

"Owen called me, Alice."

Behind the bathroom door, Madeline sings "Be a Clown." The only words she seems to remember are the chorus, which she repeats over and over like a chant: "Be a clown. Be a clown. All the world loves a clown. Be a clown. Be a clown. . . ."

"Don't you want to know what he said?"

I want Helen to tell me every word of the conversation. I want to question her about the tone of his voice, his inflections, whether or not he's sad without me. Yet if I ask about the conversation, I won't be able to stay in New Orleans with my sister looking for Lily. I'll want to give up and go back to Sarasota.

"He wants—"

Gently, quietly, as if the hand performing the action is not part of my body, I hang up.

"Be a clown. Be a clown. Be a clown."

A scene I don't want to remember flashes in my mind. In Georgia Medical Center, the afternoon the pregnancy ended, when the fetal monitor was removed from the room and the ultrasound equipment was rolled back down the hall, Owen set his face in his hands and cried. Lying beside him, I watched him, but I could not comfort him. Never before in the three years I'd known him had I ever heard Owen cry.

My sister interrupts the memory by emerging from the bathroom, her new red hair wet and stuck to her forehead. She wears Helen's small fur stole around her neck. Naked, she stretches out across the unmade bed. Her head leaves a faint pink stain on the pillowcase. "I think I'd like to be sick. I could lie in bed and you would bring me cool washcloths and chips of ice. In the hospital, they have this treatment called a cold pack, where the nurses wrap you in freezing sheets and leave you on a bed until you can stay calm. I had that treatment at least once a day."

I flinch when she says *hospital* again, but I tell myself that the story about the cold pack could have been taken from an old movie. She looks at me with a dreamy expression, and I feel nervous. Madeline steps into her underwear, red lace, and hooks her bra. She smooths her hands over her breasts, her hips, as if she's checking the size of her body. Then she lies down again.

"Let's go to the Star Dust," I say.

"Why do you think I wanted you to dye my hair? I didn't want to go there without a disguise. One more thing, though. Would you shave my legs? Please, Alice. I'm so tired. I don't have any energy. If you shave my legs, I'll feel much better." She pauses, then says, "As soon as you do them, we can go."

"Okay. Anything to get the day started. Hand me the razor."

While Madeline leans against the headboard of the bed, her legs outstretched in front of her, I smooth her skin with baby oil. Gliding the blade slowly up the bone, close to the surface, I'm careful not to hurt her.

"When you're done with my legs, I want you to keep going." Madeline gestures up her body, to her stomach, then touches her inner thighs. "I want you to do me here."

I set down the razor on the bed. "I'm not going to shave you there," I say. "Forget it."

"Say the word, Alice, I can tell you're afraid of it. Say 'I don't want to shave your *cunt*.' Tell me why you don't want to do it. Are you afraid to touch me there?" Her voice is taunting.

"Have you ever been shaved there?" I ask. "I have. They shave you there before you have a baby."

I remember the way the nurse held the razor against my skin before the labor. I wish I had been told you needed to be shaved before a birth. It was one of the last procedures before we went into the delivery room. Owen stood beside the bed and held my hand. "This won't hurt a bit," the nurse had said, as if she were talking to a child. But it wasn't the physical pain that upset me; it was the humiliation. Afterward, when I looked down at my body, my pelvis looked like a little girl's, framed by my swollen, pregnant belly.

Madeline gazes up at the ceiling. "What's wrong with Owen?"

"Nothing."

"Why hasn't he come looking for you? He knows where you are."

My body stiffens; my head jerks up to meet Madeline's gaze.

"Alice, I can't stand watching you. You can't see the truth."

"The truth?" The razor is heavy in my hand.

Madeline curls her body close to mine. "Don't you see I love you more than he ever can?" She smiles. "I always got Jack to shave my legs."

"What made you think of Jack?"

"I've been thinking of him a lot. I don't tell you everything," my sister says. "I might call him and ask him to meet us here."

"Linny! I don't want Jack here with us."

"Why? You'd rather be back with Owen. I'm not allowed to miss Jack?"

"It's not the same." I struggle to find a better explanation. "You barely know him."

"You think you know Owen so well? Honestly, Alice, he's probably off with someone else right now. I know a lot more about men than you. He could get rid of you like that." She snaps her fingers.

I'm so tired my eyes burn, and my right side still hurts, but I know Madeline and I have to get out of this room. "Get up." I stand, shaking off her grasp. "We're going to the Star Dust."

I pull one of Helen's housedresses over my head, noticing that it's still slightly tight around the waist, and brush my hair, with fast, furious strokes. Brushing short hair is a strange sensation. The brush keeps hitting my shoulders as if I'm missing my hair. I remember how Owen used to brush my hair at night, before we went to bed. His touch was gentle, his hands smoothing my hair against my back.

"Give me the car keys," I say, trying to refocus my attention on my sister. "I'm driving."

She stands up and hands me the keys. "Some people would be glad to have a sister like me."

"I *am* glad to have you as my sister. Now get dressed."

Madeline spends more than an hour trying on Helen's clothes. First, she dresses in a yellow wool suit and a pillbox hat. "Too hot." She unbuttons the jacket and throws it on the bed. Next she puts on capri pants and a cardigan sweater, but when she studies her reflection in the mirror above the dresser, she says, "I can't wear this either." Then she tries two different dresses, one striped, the other a flower print, and removes them both immediately before she's buttoned them up the back.

I sit on the edge of the bed and watch her, growing more exhausted with each costume change. "Linny, just put something on."

"This is a big moment. I have to look good. Alice, this is like my screen debut. Tonight I've got solo-above-the-title billing. Remember that? Judy Garland had it for the first time with *For Me and*

My Gal. On the marquee her name was above Gene Kelly's and the title. Now I've got my hair right, but I can't find the perfect thing to wear."

Finally Madeline settles on Helen's evening gown, a strapless dress with a tight bodice and a black crinoline skirt. I can't imagine Helen ever wearing it. The dress is in terrible condition, worse than any of the other clothes. The zipper is broken and the hem held together with safety pins.

"Ready." She twirls in front of me like a fashion model.

"You look great. Let's go."

"Can I wear your black shoes?"

I remove Helen's pumps to give to her and lace up my old tennis shoes. Now my sister and I are dressed as opposites: she looks like a movie star, and I resemble a housewife. She's dazzling and I'm exhausted. All that links us is our short hair, and hers is bright red.

In the car, Madeline and I are quiet. From the Crescent Court, the drive to the Star Dust is only four or five miles, but I drive as slowly as I can, as if to prepare us. I pull up on the edge of Airline Highway where the fathers used to park their cars when they weren't sure their families could stay at the Star Dust for the night.

The motel is gone.

Madeline pushes open the car door and jumps out. In her long black dress, she runs toward the empty space where the Star Dust once was. "Linny!" I follow her.

For a moment, Madeline stands in the middle of the expanse of blank ground; she stretches her arms, holds out her fingers as if she's balancing herself on a thin wire. Then she collapses in the dirt. She falls down in one quick gesture, and I run to her. Her eyes are shut. "Linny." I bend down and shake her shoulders gently. I can't decide if Madeline has fainted because she's so distraught at the motel's absence or if she's faking. "Say something."

Madeline's eyes flutter open. "I think this would have been our room."

I sit back on my heels. "How do you know?"

"I just feel it." Madeline arcs her arms above her head in the dirt, as if she's making a snow angel. "Do you think there was a fire?"

"No. I think someone razed the place to the ground." On either side of the vacant lot is another motel. I can't read the signs from here, but I see the same cars that we used to see in the parking lot: Cadillacs, pickups, an occasional motorcycle.

I yank Madeline up, dust off Helen's dress. She points past me, and I turn to look.

"It's still here," she whispers. She takes my hand and we walk.

The pool is all that remains of our old life.

Madeline and I stand at the edge and look down at the green cement walls, the drain, the ladder. The bottom of the pool is filled with rocks from the parking lot and dead leaves.

"It looks the same," I say, but I can't make sense of the reversal: can our home be gone yet our magic world be intact? My sister grips my hand tightly. Together, as we've done so many times before, we climb down the silver ladder.

Madeline and I stand in Emerald City, and for the first time since we came back to New Orleans, the differences between us disappear. We're like we were when we were children. I look at Madeline and I see myself. Despite the gingham housedress I wear and the evening gown my sister has put on, as we stand in the empty pool I'm more conscious than ever of our resemblance. It's a reflex: I look at her, I look down at myself. I look at her, and I see myself. I am Madeline. Madeline is me.

My sister walks into the deep end, slowly, as if the pool is filled with water. She stands on the square mouth of the drain, one leg on either side, just as she used to do as a child. She closes her eyes.

"There's no place like home. There's no place like home. There's no place like home." She clicks the heels of Helen's pumps together three times like Judy Garland did.

But then she turns to me. "Alice, we're home." Her makeup is smeared. Tears glitter in the corners of her eyes. "We're home."

"Judy Garland," I whisper, before I can stop myself.

She says, "Ginger Love."

Then my sister breaks the spell. Madeline grabs my shoulders and forces my mouth toward her own so my lips cover hers. She opens her mouth. She breathes into mine, her breath filling my mouth, then she kisses me, hard, smashing her front teeth into mine. Blood leaks into my mouth, as if she's cut my tongue.

I pull away from her.

The vision of our old magic world dissolves like an image on a movie screen. I hold my hand to my mouth.

I shouldn't have said it. *Judy Garland. Ginger Love.* I know I shouldn't have said it.

The closer we move to the past, the more my sister comes apart.

23

All summer, Agnes tells her father she is too sick to work in the fields. Each morning, she uses Agatha's trick. She throws up in the slop jar under the bed. It is the third summer of Agatha's absence, and Agatha's absence now determines the history of her sister's life. Agnes is in bed, a cloth soaked in vinegar folded on her forehead.

The vinegar cloth is Agnes's excuse. To her other sisters, the cloth signifies sickness, which means she will be left alone all day until the sun goes down and everyone returns for supper. She is even absolved from cooking because she is so sick. Agatha would have known immediately that the cloth was a lie, but Agatha is not here to offer a protest.

Agnes is writing letters to her sister. Onto pages made of woven fabric, she glues the photographs Stephan took of the two of them, which she has cut into diamond shapes and triangles. She searches the bedroom for other memories of their life together to include in the letters. On her hands and knees, she looks on the rug on the floor for Agatha's long red hairs, holds them up to the late afternoon light coming in from the window.

Before she can stop him, their father sells the rest of Agatha's clothes. Agnes would like to have kept them. Agatha owned beautiful clothes, which she had made herself—embroidered overskirts, lace aprons, sashes in red, blue, and gold silk. She took none of these things with her when she left, and Agnes knows her sister intended to leave the clothes for her as a gift, an inheritance. But her father gathers up the clothes and sends them away to be sold in town.

"With the money from the sale of the clothes, we'll get five new chickens," he announces one night at supper. Agnes's stomach turns. She is filled with disgust.. "A man wanted them for his daughter's hope chest," her father continues. "His wife is dead and his daughter can't sew."

"If she comes back, she won't have anything to wear," Agnes says.

"You are an idiot," her oldest brother says, his mouth full of potato. "She's never coming back."

"Don't speak to your sister that way," her father tells him, but he doesn't correct her brother.

"We don't need chickens," Agnes writes that night on a piece of fabric she plans to include in the letter to her sister. "I need you."

24

The year Madeline and I were seventeen, the late-night drives with Lily changed.

Before, she'd always drive quickly by Agatha's house, but she'd linger in front of the Prytania and the New Orleans Ballet. Now she drove so fast we made the tour of her old life several times each night. But the biggest difference between our old drives and the new was that Lily no longer told family stories. We sat in the speeding car in silence.

One afternoon in Emerald City, I tried to discuss the situation with Madeline. We sat in the shallow end, making Judy Garland and Ginger Love tap-dance. Madeline hummed, "I Like Opera. I Like Swing." In the middle of the song, I set Ginger Love down on the pool floor. "Have you noticed that she drives faster?"

"Ginger Love doesn't know how to drive."

"I'm talking about Lily. She's acting strange."

"You're imagining it. I know her better than you," my sister said. She tossed her long hair over her shoulder and searched through the pile of paper doll clothes. "I lived alone with her before you were born."

"You did not! What are you talking about?"

"Alice, you think you know everything about me, but you don't. You don't know because you weren't there." Madeline held Judy Garland up and attached a fur jacket to her shoulders. "I like opera . . ." She reentered Emerald City without me.

One night, on the fifth trip by the Prytania Theater, Lily spoke. "We're getting out of here." Her voice was flat. "We're leaving New Orleans."

"Are we going on a vacation?" Madeline asked. The word was unfamiliar, but I knew what she was thinking: normal families, ordinary families, went away for a week or two in the summers for relaxation. For years, my sister and I had seen families on vacation at the Star Dust. I couldn't imagine the three of us staying in a motel for a week off, sunning ourselves on a beach, eating in restaurants, sleeping late.

Lily drove through a red light. "We're moving."

"Why?" Madeline said.

"It's time for a change," Lily snapped. "What does it matter why we're going? We're going."

"What about school? What about our friends?" Madeline said.

"You can go to school anywhere. You two don't have friends."

"When are we leaving?" Madeline asked in a low voice.

"I told you. Now."

For the first time since we'd gotten in the car, I spoke. "We can't go now! You didn't tell us we were leaving when you woke us up to drive tonight! We don't have any of our things."

Lily turned to look at me, and one hand left the steering wheel so she could shake it in my face, a gesture of warning. "Let me tell you something, Alice. I'm your mother. I make the decisions. I'm in charge of you. It doesn't matter whether or not you think what I've decided is fair. You don't have a choice."

Beside me in the backseat, my sister began to cry. I put my arm around her in an attempt to comfort her, but she shrugged me off.

"You don't have anything worth saving, you know, if that's what you're crying about," Lily said.

"What about our paper dolls?" I asked. "What did you do with them?"

She glanced back at us in the rearview mirror. "I threw them away, Alice."

"How could you do that? You didn't even ask us! Those were ours!" I said.

"You two are too old to be playing with paper dolls. Little girls play with dolls. You and Madeline are in high school, and it's time for those games to stop." She spoke firmly, not looking back at us again.

I was afraid to look at Madeline.

Her tears were over. Her body was rigid. She reached into the front seat and grabbed Lily's hair, pulled it, hard.

Lily yelled, "Get off me!" Madeline didn't let go. The car skidded. A car behind us honked. Lily stopped the car in the middle of Airline Highway.

Time slowed down so there was nothing but my sister hurting Lily, while I did nothing to stop what was happening. I couldn't move.

Madeline released Lily and began to scream. I had never heard any sound like that scream. It filled the car, high plaintive shrieks that made my ears ache. It didn't sound like the voice of a teenage girl. It didn't sound like anything that could arise from my sister's body. Madeline screamed in short bursts, one after the other, like notes of a song, like breaths. Her screams burned my ears. The sound would never stop.

"Alice!" Lily yelled, as if I were the one screaming.

In the backseat, beside my sister, I sat silently, my hands folded together in my lap. I pretended I was Judy Garland on the life raft in *Sole Survivor*. I prepared a meal of salt grass and water I scooped up with my hands. I would spend the time singing my old songs. Days and days would pass before anyone would find me.

Lily interrupted the fantasy. "Alice, I'm talking to you. Help your sister."

I couldn't speak. There was no room for my voice in the car. I wanted to go back to the life raft in the ocean, where I could be safe and alone. Being someone else was easier. Then Lily leaned over and slapped Madeline's face hard. The screaming stopped. My sister held her hand up to her cheek where a red mark was rapidly spreading over her skin.

Lily had never hit either of us before.

"We're going to the airport." Lily spoke in a quiet voice.

"Are we taking a plane?" I asked.

"We're going to the airport so I can figure out what we're going to do. It's a safe place where we can sit all night without anyone bothering us." Lily turned the key in the ignition and started the car.

Madeline stared straight ahead, not looking at either of us, her hand cradling her cheek. "Linny," I whispered. "Linny, please say something. Let me see your face. I just want to make sure you're okay." I touched her hair.

She jerked away from me, covering the slap mark with her hand.

*   *   *

In the New Orleans airport, Lily and I sat on a black leather bench in the arrival area. Madeline sat by herself, her body slumped on a separate chair. Lily picked the skin around her fingernails, her mouth set in a line. I wondered what plans she was formulating. Madeline's face was blank, her eyes red from crying. She stared at the people walking through the airport, but her gaze rested nowhere. None of us spoke, as if what had happened in the car made talking impossible.

For hours, I watched people in the airport greeting one another, their faces filled with expectation and happiness. Probably, I decided, they would soon be furious with one another. Then they would be back at the airport, looking appropriately sad at their separation. I pretended that we were waiting for our father to come home. Maybe Reid Alistair had been on tour with the ballet company for weeks, and Lily had brought us to keep her company at the airport while she waited for her husband.

Everyone who saw us must have known that we had been waiting too long to be waiting for a plane.

It was almost 4 A.M. I was exhausted. I knew we had to stay awake, however, for safety. Madeline's chin bumped her chest, then rose again as she drifted in and out of sleep. If my sister was sleeping, I knew I had to stay awake to watch over Lily. Lily showed no signs of fatigue. I pinched the thin skin on the inside of my elbow over and over to stay awake. I couldn't fall asleep and leave Madeline alone with Lily.

Finally Lily spoke. "I brought some of your stuff." Her voice had lost its strident tone. She sounded weary.

"Where is it?" I said.

"In the trunk of the car. I picked out what I thought you would need. I'm sorry about the paper dolls, Alice." She glanced at Madeline, who was now asleep. "You're too old to be playing with them. I'm sorry, but it's true. It's not you I worry about. It's Madeline."

Lily and I were talking in an unfamiliar way. The balance of power had shifted between us. Like me, she was worried about Madeline. "You should have told her we were leaving," I said.

"You saw how she acted tonight. Look, Alice, I was fired from the Star Dust."

"What happened?"

"The manager said I was stealing. I denied it, but no one believed me. Guests were reporting things missing from their rooms. They questioned all the maids, but the rooms with the thefts were those on my shifts."

My throat closed. I tried to swallow. Madeline and I hadn't sneaked into rooms in at least a year. Or at least, I hadn't. Madeline had been stealing from guest's rooms by herself, playing her own secret games without me.

"I hate the Star Dust, but I wouldn't steal from the guests." Lily shook her head. "Now I want to tell you something, Alice."

I waited. My heart thudded in my chest.

"Your sister's in trouble."

"She's just upset." Even as I said it, I didn't believe it.

"No, Alice." Lily was saying my name in this conversation more than she ever had in my life. "Your school called me last week. I talked to some woman, Sister something-or-another, the vice principal. The school wants her to see a psychiatrist, Alice. A psychiatrist." She pronounced the word slowly. "Do you know what I'm talking about?"

I knew about psychiatry from Lily's Judy Garland stories. Lily had once told us that when Judy Garland was a patient at the Austen-Riggs Center, the clinic had a little theater where the psychiatrists told her she could perform. I pictured Madeline in a hospital, dancing and singing for an audience of doctors. I twisted my fingers in my lap, waiting for her to go on.

"They said she could take a drug that would calm her down. I wouldn't let her do it." She paused, running her hand through her hair. "They think I'm a bad mother, that's what's really going on here. Do you know what psychiatrists do? They blame the parents. They especially blame the mother. I don't need to be called into some doctor's office to hear what I've done wrong." We both looked at Madeline, then gazed at the floor, as if to avoid each other's eyes. "I want you to promise me you'll look out for Madeline. She needs you, Alice."

"What about you?" I asked. "Why can't you take care of her?"

There was a long silence.

I asked, "Where are we going?"

Lily pointed across the hall at the only other person remaining in the arrival area, a cleaning woman wearing a T-shirt that said *Ringling Brothers and Barnum and Bailey Circus Museum, Sarasota, Florida, 1981.*

"We're going to Sarasota, Florida," Lily said. "Wake up your sister. Let's get back in the car."

25

Madeline and I sit on a bench by the Mississippi River on the edge of the French Quarter. We haven't slept in three days. It was my idea to drive down here; I thought coming to the French Quarter would help us decide what to do because it's a new place, one we never went to when we were children. Though it's July and the afternoon is sunny and warm, I'm shivering. At the edge of the water, two teenage girls with matching short purple hair share a joint, passing it back and forth between them, with no attempt to be secretive. They laugh as they smoke. One girl takes out a bobby pin to finish the short end of the joint.

"Do you think they're sisters?" Madeline asks.

"They're sitting too far apart."

"You're right." As she says it, Madeline inches closer to me on the bench, her thigh pressing against mine.

I draw my knees up to my chest, making my body smaller. I think of Agatha reading *Alice in Wonderland* to Lily, the nights in her childhood she described to us, and I wish I could sip from a magic bottle and become so small I'd disappear.

Madeline and I haven't talked about the visit to the Star Dust or our kiss.

I try again and again to make my sister think about how we'll carry out the search for Lily. When I look up, the girls who aren't sisters are gone. A barge drags down the river, toward the bridge; a long, low horn sounds across the water.

"You don't want to go back," Madeline says.

"We are back. We're in New Orleans."

"You don't want to go back to Emerald City."

She knows I don't want to reenter the made-up world of our childhood. I don't want to speak through paper dolls as we used to do. What I want is to look for Lily. Madeline, who has always wanted the past back, who still lives in our childhood, might be less interested in finding Lily than I am. Madeline might not care if we find Lily at all as long as we are here, in New Orleans, alone together.

Three men walk by us, sharing a bottle wrapped in a paper bag. I feel their eyes on our bodies as they pass. My sister shifts her position on the bench, hiking Helen's dress over her knees to expose her thighs. I yank the dress down over her knees.

"I slept with Owen," Madeline says, staring at the river. "I should have told you a long time ago. I wanted to tell you. He asked me to keep it secret."

I only experience a few seconds of alarm before I realize she's lying. "No you didn't, Linny. Owen wouldn't sleep with you."

"Oh, Alice, you don't know him like you think you do. It was the night before your wedding. He crawled into my bed. I couldn't stop him."

"The night before my wedding, *you* came into *my* bed. You sat on me until I woke up. You couldn't have forgotten that, Linny."

"God, why do you always refuse to see the truth? I worry about you." She pushes closer to me on the bench so that our bodies are pressed even tighter together: knee to knee, hip to hip, arm to arm. "You know what else? I never told you this. I might have gotten pregnant that night."

I shove my sister away from me. "Stop it!" I can listen to her lie about Owen, but I can't stand it when she talks about a made-up pregnancy.

"I was pregnant for at least a week. I could feel the baby kicking." Madeline closes her eyes and stretches her arms out on the top of the bench.

"I'm not listening to this anymore." I rise from the bench, untangle my body from hers, and walk toward the steps that lead up to the street.

"Because you don't want to go back to Emerald City," she shouts after me.

I walk quickly, telling myself I don't care if Madeline follows or not, turning onto Royal Street. The pregnancy was the one thing in my life that I could own apart from her. I won't let her take it away from me with more of her lies. When I hear Madeline in Helen's shoes running behind me, I duck into the first building on the street, the Reality Flea Market.

The flea market is an easy place to hide. I can pretend I'm searching for something: dishes to match a set I already own, a cigar box of pirate coins. I could be anyone, a woman studying a framed map on the wall, trying on old clothes. I walk to the back of the flea market where Madeline won't see me, to a display of antique children's toys. Most of them are old and broken. A red metal caboose for a train with no engine. A doll with one glass eye. A year ago, in my old life, I would have bought one of the old toys, brought it home to show to Owen, saved it for the baby, set it on a shelf in her new room, ready and waiting for when she came home from the hospital with me.

She never came home from the hospital.

I sit back on my heels and hug my arms to my chest. My whole body aches. The baby isn't here. She'll never be here. Without meaning to, I start rocking back and forth, as if I can comfort myself with the action. I close my eyes, but I can't shut out the vision of the baby's room: the unfinished Frida Kahlo mural I'd drafted on the wall, the crib. Nothing blocks the image, no matter what I do.

When I leave the flea market, Madeline is standing outside at the door. She reaches for my arm. I blink away the tears in my eyes and walk past her. She follows, trailing behind me.

Farther down the street is a laundromat wall covered with writing and hand-drawn tombstones, their edges outlined in red spray paint: "RIP MARK," "RIP SCOTT." The wall is filled with dead men's names. Each outlined grave bears a different name. The wall is a memorial. I stare at the names, painted in curving letters. At the top of the wall is written "DESIRE MURDERS, 1993." Desire is a public housing project, the most dangerous place to live in New Orleans. All I can think is that those dead men had mothers who must have loved them once.

At the Desire wall, Madeline catches up with me. "I'm sorry, Alice," she says. "I shouldn't have said it. Forgive me?"

I can't block out anything anymore. I let my sister hold me as we stand there on the street.

"We're out of vinegar," Madeline reports as soon as we're back in Jack's car. "Drive down Tchoupatoulis to the Winn Dixie so we can get more."

"A small bottle."

"Alice, I know how to buy a bottle of vinegar for us. If there's one thing I know how to do, it's pick out vinegar. Wait in the car."

In Jack's car, alone, while Madeline is in the store, I breathe deeply, filling my lungs, then let go. I know how to erase the image of the baby's room; I take Owen's birthday tape out of the glove compartment and slide it into the cassette player on the dashboard.

The tape begins with Owen's voice. "Alice, happy twenty-nine," he says. When I hear his voice, a wave of sadness washes over me. Imagining him does not have the power of the sound of one word from his mouth. Suddenly, the loss of our marriage is absolutely, concretely real.

On the tape, he has spliced in the sound of water, as if he has turned on the faucet in the bath. This detail makes me almost laugh. "The water," he says again, "is in honor of the aquarium." On each birthday tape, Owen mentions the aquarium. Then he goes on. "And our baths. Do you remember our baths together?" I do remember: before the pregnancy, Owen and I took long baths together every night. Our house in Atlanta had an enormous claw-footed tub. We would sit facing each other, our legs in each other's laps, immersed in the hottest water we could stand.

I snap off the tape player and return the cassette to my purse again. Madeline can't know about it. "Owen," I say out loud. I feel my voice breaking in my throat. "I want to come back."

The car door opens. Madeline slides into the seat beside me. "Look, Alice. I bought the biggest bottle of vinegar in the store!" She displays a small brown bag. "I'm kidding. What's wrong with you? Are you crying?"

"Greta Garbo. Rita Hayworth. Marilyn Monroe. Marlene Dietrich." In Jack's car, as we drive up and down Airline Highway, Madeline names her heroines. "Judy Garland. Alice, they're all dead." Her voice is soft, almost a whisper. Then in a low, throaty voice she begins to sing "Fly Me to the Moon."

"Linny, let's go back to the motel."

"No, I told you I don't want to. Keep driving."

All I can think about is Owen's tape. When I hear his voice on the birthday tape, I want to go back to him. I remember his body: the familiar plains and valleys. The topography of his skin. In my head, while my sister is singing, I map out Owen's body like a landscape. The nape of his neck. The smooth skin on his stomach. I touch his mouth with the tips of my fingers. I allow myself to imagine drawing the outline of his body. Owen never liked to be sketched. I used to tell him that if he could record my voice, I ought to be able to draw him, but he always refused.

Madeline loves to be drawn, to be looked at. I glance over at her quickly as I drive, studying her profile, her abstracted expression. Her body is still; her hands are folded in her lap as she sings. I wonder if she's taken more of Jack's pills.

"Are you having your period?" Madeline says, as if she knows I'm thinking about her. "Don't you remember how, when we were teenagers, you, me, and Lily would always have it at the same time? We thought it was ESP, but I read in a magazine that it happens to women who live in the same house. So, I'm having my period now, and I wondered if the trick still works."

I don't remember sharing our periods with Lily. I remember Lily instructing us to diet so that none of us would menstruate. If we did Chicken Fat enough and practiced Agatha's trick, she promised our periods would stop. I haven't had my period since I left the hospital. The doctors assured me that my menstrual function would return. I told them I didn't care if I ever menstruated again, which seemed to surprise them, as if losing my period was in the end my greatest loss.

"If you won't go back to the Crescent Court, we're going some-where else to talk." I turn into the first parking lot we pass: the Airline Highway Feed Store. The entrance has a bright red awning like a movie theater. According to the marquee, the feed store sells birds, seeds, bags of dirt, and half-price Black Cows with extra ice cream.

"I want to have a baby," Madeline says.

"You can't." I take her arm, crooking my finger under her elbow the way Helen once told me the nurses at Beachaven grasp the old people to lead them down the hall. "I mean, you can. But not now."

"Do you know that if you're unhappy during pregnancy, the baby can sense it? Children can be born depressed. I heard that you can kill them that way." Madeline laughs. "If you have a baby, then someone always loves you. If you have a baby, then you have some-one who will care about you forever."

"Linny, we have to talk about finding Lily," I say, pushing my sis-ter into a booth.

The waitress appears to take our order. Before I can speak, Madeline says, "We'll have two glasses of ice water."

"There's a minimum," the waitress says.

"We don't care. We're both on diets," my sister says. Her voice is triumphant. She twirls her short red hair with her finger and sighs, a long, deep, dramatic sigh.

"Linny, you're the one who convinced me to come on this trip to find Lily."

"Don't you like being with me?" Madeline asks, as if she hasn't heard anything I've said. My sister reaches across the table and grasps my hand. "I used to wish she was dead so that you and I could be alone together. Maybe she's dead now."

I am beginning to think that Lily simply provided an excuse for the trip, for the two of us to leave together, for me to walk out on the life I'd created for myself without my sister. I am beginning to think that Madeline knew all along that if she told me she was going off with Jack to look for Lily, I'd leave with her.

"Take a bath with me," Madeline pleads that night back at the Crescent Court. "We don't have to go to Emerald City. Just a normal, regular bath."

My sister and I sit face to face in the water, knees touching, a bottle of vinegar on the edge of the tub. Set against each other, we are each other's mirror image. Except for the fact that I'm heavier since the pregnancy, and she now has red hair, we're still identical. I am Madeline. Madeline is me. She could live my life, and no one would know the difference. I see Madeline married to Owen, going through the pregnancy, meeting Helen, picture her in front of the life-drawing class at Beachaven taking off her clothes to model for the old women.

"Draw me," my sister says, as if she can read my thoughts. "I want you to. Draw me naked right now."

I shake my head. "I don't draw anymore, Linny."

"Maybe I should start drawing." Madeline uncaps the vinegar and takes a small sip.

"Are you doing Agatha's trick? If you are, you should get out of the tub."

"Alice, every time you drink vinegar, you don't have to do the trick. I just drank a little for energy. Don't nag. No one understands about Lily," Madeline says, looking down at the surface of the water. "I don't think you even understand."

"Yes, I do. She didn't know how to be a mother."

"Alice, what are you talking about? She was a wonderful mother!"

"Do you remember the time she hit you? The night we left New Orleans to move to Sarasota she hit you across the face."

"That never happened. Lily would never hit me," Madeline says, cupping her hand to pour water over her leg. "You're lying. You're making it up because you just wish you were alone right now." Her voice is low and sullen. "You don't want to share anything with me," she continues. "When we were little, we shared *everything*."

For a moment, her body is almost still; then with a sudden jerk she rises from the tub and pushes me down. She forces my head under the stream of water from the tap. I've lost my balance. I'm going to drown in a motel room bathtub with only a few inches of water filling my lungs. I shove her away, hands knocking her face, but my sister is stronger. Then as quickly as she grabs me, she frees me from her grasp, and we're separate again.

"Sorry. I didn't mean to do that." Madeline gazes down at the surface of the bath water, at her skin beneath the surface. "I have a confession to make."

I'm still trying to catch my breath. My head hurts where she pushed me down.

"I stole your wedding ring when you took it off for the bath. You don't need it anymore," Madeline says. "You don't want to be married. I could tell."

"I want the ring back now. Give it to me."

"I can't." Madeline ducks her head to avoid my gaze.

"Why?"

"I swallowed it."

"You ate my wedding ring?" Bath water splashes between us as I reach out to grab her arm.

"I didn't say I *ate* it. I *swallowed* it. There's a difference."

"How could you?" I stand up in the tub, water dripping down my body.

"Alice, we can go to the hospital. If I have my stomach pumped, we'll find it." She lowers her voice. "That's what the doctors do when you try to kill yourself, Alice, but you wouldn't know that, would you?" She smiles, closes her eyes, and leans her head against the edge of the bathtub. "You wouldn't know about the time my stomach was pumped, because you weren't there."

"Linny——" I say her name, but I'm too furious with her to continue.

Outside the bathroom, at the door to our motel room, there's a knock, a small thud on the wood. I think I couldn't have heard it, but I hear it again. Twice, three times, and I rise from the tub, covering myself in the two bath towels the motel supplies, aware I'm not leaving one for Madeline. The knocking begins again, more insistently. I crack open the door with the safety chain on.

"Yes?" I whisper, ready to slam the door in the face of whoever is trying to get into our room.

"Jesus Christ, I thought you'd never answer." Outside, standing on the landing, a small suitcase beside her, one hand balanced on her hip, the other holding a lit cigarette, is Helen.

26

"To save money, we'll live in the car," Lily told us. I nodded. Madeline hadn't spoken in five days, since we left New Orleans. She slumped in the backseat, against the door, her eyes closed. I was worried, but Lily acted as if nothing was wrong.

I pleaded with my sister. "I know you're mad about what she did to Emerald City. Linny, I didn't do it. You can be mad at Lily, but talk to me. *Please*."

My sister refused to look at me.

Each day, Madeline and I waited in parking lots while Lily went inside stores and offices. She said she was setting up our new life. At Winn Dixie, she bought us bottles of water and boxes of saltines, which we ate in the backseat. Madeline chewed the crackers with her eyes shut. My body was cramped and aching, but all of my energy was focused on her. I wondered how long my sister could continue her silence. I never knew she had so much discipline and restraint.

The landscape of Florida was unlike Louisiana. Sarasota was clean. All the buildings were new. Shopping malls stretched out long and flat, and everything was made of stucco painted white, surrounded by palm trees. Instead of humidity and the sour smell of the Mississippi, the weather in Sarasota was clear and bright. Occasionally, if I rolled down the car window, I could smell the Gulf of Mexico. In the Winn Dixie parking lot, I watched old people shop, couples holding each others' arms, men and women alone. Tourist families walked together into the grocery store, or drove toward the beach in rented cars. I wondered if any of the families had ever been to New Orleans and stayed at the Star Dust. I no longer had my sketchbook, so I couldn't draw them.

The third day we were in Sarasota, Lily said, "I'll show you where we're going to live."

I expected her to drive out Tamiami Trail, toward the airport, to the kind of neighborhood where we'd always lived: a strip of old motels where people stayed the night only as a last resort. I figured Sarasota must have its own version of the Star Dust Motel. Instead she drove us to a neighborhood of vacant lots and trailers by the bay and pulled the car up to the curb in front of a house. She turned off the ignition. The stucco house was large, missing front steps. At the front, all the windows were boarded up. The boards on one of the front windows were covered with pink spray-painted letters spelling out "Dawn and Joe 4-Ever." The painted stucco was weathered, so faded that the house was no color at all, as if it had been bleached. Stuck in the scrub grass of the front lawn were two signs: CONDEMNED and FOR SALE.

"We're going to live here," Lily announced.

Madeline's eyes flashed open.

"We're supposed to live in a motel," I said.

"I have a little money saved. I want us to live in a house."

Her words shocked me—*money, saved, house*—words that had never been part of our vocabulary. People like the three of us didn't live in houses. We all knew that houses were for ordinary families. Families had possessions that filled their homes: dishes, furniture, books. All we owned were Judy Garland records. Our clothes fit into a single suitcase.

"Isn't it expensive?" I asked. Lily's salary at the Star Dust was minimum wage, supplemented by tips, which Lily complained she rarely received. Our room in the Star Dust had been free, but I couldn't see how, besides stealing, she could have accumulated the money to buy a house. I wished Madeline would speak. "This house probably costs a lot," I said, although I had no idea how much any house would cost.

Lily drummed her fingers on the steering wheel. "Alice, don't you think I've already thought about the cost? Everything's arranged." The three of us were starting over in a new city, in a permanent, real home: how could it be? "The house was cheap because it's condemned," Lily said. "Nobody wants it."

This house could be a home. Madeline and I could invite other girls over to spend the night. I extended the fantasy. When we graduated from high school, we could go away to college like the other girls and come back to visit Lily in the house at Thanksgiving and Christmas. I could already picture myself at art school in another city, visiting twice a year.

For the first time in five days, Madeline spoke. Her eyes were open, and I heard her whisper: "There's no place like home. There's no place like home."

The words made me shiver, but Lily continued, "A long time ago, rich people lived in this house. The house even had a movie theater. The theater's gone now. It's just a room. Anyway, I knew you girls would like to live in a house with a movie theater." Never, in the nearly eighteen years I had lived with her, had Lily articulated any knowledge that my sister and I had our own needs or desires. We were a family now. We were her daughters.

"There's no place like home. There's no place like home."

Lily turned to me. "Alice, I want to talk to you. I saw your pictures. When I got your stuff together for the move, I found those dirty drawings you did of men. I threw them out."

"There's no place like home."

After ten years of my hiding them in the dresser drawer in our room, Lily had found my drawings of the fathers. She had searched through my belongings.

"You shouldn't be thinking about——" Lily paused and I knew she didn't want to say the word *sex*, because it was a word she never said, a word that revealed its power through its absence.

"I want you to promise you won't draw those pictures anymore," Lily said.

"Never," I said.

Madeline's mouth moved, as her chant grew louder and louder, filling the inside of the car. "There's no place like home."

I was willing to give up anything so the three of us could live in this house.

Eight days later, Lily, Madeline, and I moved in. "It's perfect," my sister said when Lily showed us the movie theater that would be our bedroom.

A small tree had grown into the room through a broken window. Its long branches scattered leaves over the floor. At the back was a small stage, where once a screen must have risen from the floor, the only clue that the room had been a theater. As if there had never been an audience, there were no seats or aisles. Madeline and I slept on the floor, in army sleeping bags from Goodwill. The floor was uncomfortable, cold cement, but what was strangest was not sleeping in the same room as Lily. I was used to seeing her bed beside our own, her dark blond hair spread on the pillow, her body turned away from us. Although I used to wish Madeline and I had our own room, I missed Lily now. She had her own bedroom down the hall. Several of the boards in the hall floor were missing, and we had to step carefully when we entered her room.

"We'll live like this when we grow up," Madeline said one night as we lay in our sleeping bags. "We'll have a house together, a double one. I'll have my own movie theater on my own side, and you'll have yours. But we'll sleep on your side, in your bedroom."

I lay on my side, playing with a pile of dead yellow leaves that had dropped from the tree onto the floor. A warm wind blew in the broken window, brushing my face. "I might want to have my own house." I said it carefully, knowing Madeline would be mad.

She laughed. "Then I'll live with Lily. You can visit."

Each night, my sister fell asleep before I did. I lay awake watching the sky outside the window, thinking about Lily and how our lives had been suddenly, magically transformed. I wished she'd brought us to Sarasota earlier. I didn't know why we'd spent most of our lives at the Star Dust if we could afford a house in another city.

At the Star Dust, Lily had worn her maid's uniform or, when she came home at the end of the day, her nightgown. In Sarasota, she bought T-shirts and jeans and shorts, and she pulled her hair back in a pony tail. She looked younger, prettier. She resembled one of the mothers in the families that used to stop for the night at the Star Dust. New clothes for Lily were part of our new life. Her new jobs were also part of it, one job cleaning offices in a building downtown at night and another as a hostess at a Big Boy two miles up Tamiami Trail.

Lily would no longer do Agatha's trick. She bought us each a bottle of Ipecac syrup instead. She no longer sat with us while we crouched over the toilet, waiting for the food to leave our bodies. That ritual was over. Now she left us to vomit together without her while she went to work.

* * *

Instead of adventure stories about boys, I read *Little Women* again and again the first weeks we lived in the house. When Lily had packed our belongings the night we left, *Little Women* was the only book of mine she'd brought, a copy from the children's room at the Airline Highway public library with a clear plastic cover and pages of illustrations. In Sarasota, when I read it, I loved the passages I used to hate: the scenes with Marmee and her girls. Marmee brushed her daughters' hair against their backs each night, while they sat at her feet in matching white nightdresses. In their house, with darkness settling outside in the snow, the daughters felt safe.

In my favorite scene, the March sisters enacted *Pilgrim's Progress*, running through their mother's house from the cellar to the attic, from the City of Destruction to the Celestial City. They tied sacks to their backs to symbolize their burdens as they ran up and down the stairs. At the top, they were allowed to eat cake and milk. Marmee approved of all their games. I always pictured Madeline as Beth, the weak, sick sister, and I wanted to be Jo, the spirited, adventurous sister. Our mother would love each of us, neither more than the other. I turned quickly past the book's watercolor illustrations of the characters and pictured Marmee as a young woman with long blond hair like Lily.

"You two need clothes," Lily said one day, from the doorway of the movie theater. "You don't have anything to wear."

Madeline and I planned to start school at Christ the King next week. We had one semester of high school left before we'd graduate. "Don't they have uniforms at school?" I asked. At Our Lady of the Seven Sorrows, we'd worn plaid skirts, white blouses, and white socks, and I'd imagined the outfits would be the same.

"Yes, but I want you girls to have other clothes besides the uniforms."

I was worried about money. "We don't need clothes."

Madeline sat up. "I know how we can get new clothes without money."

I already knew what she'd say. "Linny, we don't want to——" I couldn't say the word *steal* in front of Lily. I'd never asked Madeline if she'd been taking things from guest rooms secretly after I'd stopped, if she'd been responsible for getting Lily fired.

"It's garbage night," Madeline said, tossing her hair. "And I know where the best garbage is in Sarasota."

That night, the three of us drove out to Longboat Key. Madeline directed us, telling Lily, "Turn here. A sharp right after this." Lily stopped the car at the end of a dark street by the Gulf.

"How do you know how to get here?" I asked.

"Oh, I've been out here a few times by myself," my sister said. "You don't know everything I do, Alice." I couldn't remember Madeline ever leaving the house alone since we'd moved in. "The garbage men on this street come tomorrow morning," Madeline said. I wanted to ask how my sister knew this information. "Rich people live here. Let's get out and look through the trash and see what we can find."

"You two go. I'll wait," Lily said.

"Come on, Alice," Madeline said, yanking my hand.

I followed her out of the car. "How did you know where to go?" I asked again.

"You're not my mother. Quit it."

"We said we weren't going to take things anymore."

"This is different." Her voice was firm and confident. "Now follow me."

On the street, the houses were large, built from pale bricks, with lighted driveways and gates bordering each yard. I tried to stay close to the hedges that lined the sidewalk. Farther down the street, behind a black gate, a dog began to bark. I followed my sister. I tried to breathe.

But I wanted to run away alone, leaving Lily and Madeline behind.

Madeline led me to a row of metal trash cans. She opened one and set the lid on the grass and began to search. "Go on," she whispered, gesturing to another can. "What's wrong with you?"

"Nothing." I squeezed my eyes shut and dug my hands into the trash can. At first I kept looking up at the house, listening for alarms and police sirens, but then I began to forget about my fears and concentrated on finding new clothes. New clothes would signify my new life. I'd be transformed into another kind of girl, beautiful and elegant. After a layer of ripped paper towels and chicken bones, I found a silk scarf, patterned with red and black diamonds. I held it up to the glow of the street light.

"Good," Madeline said. "I like it."

Next, under fruit peelings, I found the first dress, a ripped green silk decorated with ribbon. We worked quickly, just as we had when we stole from guest rooms at the Star Dust, our hands reaching down, grabbing for what we wanted. We separated out the good clothes into a pile on the grass beside the curb. Madeline was right: it was a different kind of stealing. The clothes we found in the garbage cans on Longboat Key were far superior to what my sister and I had taken from rooms in the Star Dust. Those were the possessions of ordinary children. These were the belongings of rich women who discarded blouses, skirts, and dresses when they grew tired of them.

Garbage night became a ritual: on the nights before the garbage men picked up in the city, Lily drove us to Longboat Key, to the streets of stone mansions beside the water. While Lily kept the car running, we searched the trash cans. Once, in front of a three-story house, my sister found a large plastic bag of little girl's clothes, expensive dresses with Peter Pan collars and ruffled sleeves. She threw the bag back into the trash can. She said we didn't need the clothes because we weren't children anymore. I didn't tell

Madeline that I wanted the little girl's clothes. I could no longer wear those dresses, but I wanted to take them home with me. We left the bag untouched on the curb and continued down the dark street, looking for worn-out feather boas, old tiaras, high-heeled shoes, as Lily's car moved slowly beside us.

On garbage nights, when we came home, Lily let us sleep with her in her bed. We lay beside her, and I imagined the bed was a raft in a sea of darkness. I pictured Marmee and her daughters floating off to the Celestial City together. The bed was a ship that would carry us through the night.

On the first day of twelfth grade at Christ the King School, Madeline lay in her sleeping bag on the floor of the movie theater. She wore a long ripped nightgown from the Longboat Key trash, pink silk with a lace collar. Her hair was pulled into two braids to look like Dorothy. "I'm asleep in the poppy field," she said. "The wicked witch drugged me."

I stood over her, dressed in my school uniform. "Get up, Linny. If we don't leave now, we'll be late."

"I'm not going."

"No, you are. Get up."

"There's nothing you can say to make me go to school." Madeline turned over onto her back and crossed her arms over her chest.

"Linny, we're going to graduate in less than five months. You shouldn't quit now when we're so close to the end."

"Judy Garland did her schoolwork on the set. MGM had its own school. Do you remember who was in her class? Lana Turner, Elizabeth Taylor—"

Lily walked into the room, dressed in her Big Boy uniform. "Make her go," I said.

"I don't need to go to school." Madeline looked at Lily. "You didn't finish high school."

I wanted to yell at Lily, *Don't you want to stop her?* I knew that if the three of us were still in New Orleans, at the Star Dust, Lily would have agreed with me. Now, although she seemed less angry with us, she didn't seem to care what we did. She no longer told us family stories. She didn't play Judy Garland songs.

"Let your sister quit." Lily turned from us and walked out of the room.

"See. She understands because she never went back." Sunlight from the broken window flickered on Madeline's face, shadows of leaves falling over her hair.

"Lily had us. She couldn't go back. The school had a rule."

Madeline stood up and buttoned a black beaded sweater over the nightgown. "Alice, do you really think that if I quit school I'd end up like her? I have other plans."

By myself, at Christ the King, I took Home Economics. The class was taught by Sister Anne, a seventy-year-old nun who used to be an English teacher at the school and now would not retire. Sophomore year was spent on cooking, junior year on cleaning and household tasks, but Sister Anne said senior year was the most important. "We'll be learning how to be mothers," she explained.

For the first weeks of the semester, Sister Anne stood at the front of the art room where the class was held and directed us, while we held rubber dolls the size of newborn babies. We practiced feeding the dolls with bottles and bathing them in tiny plastic tubs.

To me, the dolls were grotesque. In the bathtub, the skin on my doll was slick and cold. I wondered what would happen if I pushed its face down under the shallow water. When I held the doll to my chest as instructed for burping, I didn't feel I was practicing for the future. Instead, I was ten years old again. I could never forget that this was simply a game of pretend, like so many other games I had played in my life.

The other girls cracked their gum and lifted the dolls high in the air, cooing to them as if they were real. My doll refused to become anything but a doll.

The girls at Christ the King School always made jokes to one another about their stomachs being puffed after they'd eaten lunch. "A bun in the oven?" they'd whisper, giggling, poking at each other's ribs. It was a game. "Preggers?" Their laughter hung in the air after they left the locker room. I was glad not to be included in their game. Naturally, none of them was actually pregnant. The one pregnant girl in our class had been a source of shame; she was forced to leave school in the middle of her senior year, just as Lily had done years before.

Without Madeline to walk from class to class with me, to share my locker, I was more alone than ever. The girls stood in knots in the yard, whispering. I remembered what Lily had told us on our late-night drives about the girls at her school, Sacred Heart, and I tried to convince myself I resembled her in my chosen isolation. But I didn't want to be like Lily.

In the girls' bathroom, I hid in the stall, the door locked behind me. The girls were preoccupied with the games of love and romance: how to trick a boy into asking you on a date, how to slow dance without letting your dance partner get to "second base."

"I think George likes me," one girl said to another. "He wants to go all the way."

Her friend nodded, popped her gum, and clutched her math book to her chest. "If you do it standing up, nothing will happen, you know. You can't get pregnant that way."

Through the crack between the bathroom door and the wall, I watched the other girls standing in front of the mirror, combing their hair, comparing themselves with one another: who had prettier hair, nicer clothes, who was skinnier. The only person I had ever compared myself with was Madeline.

"The paper dolls are gone, so we'll become the girls," Madeline said. "We'll go into Emerald City ourselves."

On the stage in the movie theater, Madeline wanted to enact our secret world. During garbage nights, we'd accumulated a small costume collection, all party dresses. Madeline hung the dresses in the closet beside my Christ the King uniforms. We had always shared clothes, but now the uniforms were mine, and my sister wore nothing but costumes.

Now that Madeline wasn't in school, I became her only connection to the outside world. She rarely left the house. She was almost eighteen and yet immersed in the world of childhood. "I can't do this without you. I can't do this alone." Over and over, she begged me to be Ginger Love.

"Red Rover, Red Rover. Let Ginger Love come over," Madeline called from the stage. I walked slowly toward her, across the room.

"We're too old for this," I whispered. "Red Rover, Red Rover. Let Judy Garland come over." With those words, Madeline ran across the room, flinging her arms around me, knocking me over. Collapsed on top of me, she was laughing. "Call me Judy Garland," she said, still giggling. "Call me by her name."

In the garbage on Longboat Key, Madeline found a Nancy Drew lunch box, rusted, with a broken latch. Although she never read the books about the girl detective, she asked me to relate as many of the plots as I could remember, and she copied them down. My sister made list after list of the most important stories and scenes. *The Password to Larkspur Lane. The Secret of the Old Clock.*

"Nancy Drew doesn't have a mother. She was raised by the kindly housekeeper Hannah Gruen," Madeline said one night as we got ready for bed.

I turned away from her, facing the wall, and undressed. "I know. I read the books."

"If you loved me, you'd let me be Nancy Drew and you'd be Hannah."

"Linny, we're too old."

"Lily doesn't tell us we're too old," she said. "She's happy that we're happy. She told me that she's glad I quit high school."

"I don't believe you." I folded my dress into the smallest possible square.

In the end, after I'd related all the plots of the Nancy Drew books I'd read, Nancy Drew dropped out of her own story. "We don't need her," Madeline said, and she rewrote the narrative. Madeline was Judy Garland, and I was Hannah Gruen, taking care of the girl detective on the MGM lot like a mother would, cooking vinegar soup for her, binding her breasts to her body so she'd look like a child, brushing her titian hair.

Madeline never wanted to be anyone but Judy Garland now. In the bathroom mirror, Madeline outlined her lips with red, and I stood behind her. I didn't wear a costume. Even with Madeline's lipstick and my pale face, we matched, and I could tell we'd both gained weight. Now, no matter how much we dieted, we had breasts and hips, as if none of our tricks from New Orleans worked in Sarasota. Every night, we each measured out three teaspoons of Ipecac, but the dark brown syrup didn't help us like Agatha's vinegar trick.

One afternoon when I walked out of Home Ec class, I found Madeline waiting for me in the bushes that bordered the school-yard of Christ the King. "Alice." She stepped forward, toward me, and grabbed my wrist so hard I dropped my book bag in the dirt. She wore a rhinestone tiara and a purple dress from garbage nights. She didn't look at the other girls running past us to catch their bus or be picked up by their mothers whose cars were waiting at the curb. The girls were talking and laughing, their short plaid uniform skirts brushing their knees. No one at the school knew I had a twin sister.

"I've been in Emerald City all day." My sister was breathless, as if she'd been running.

Without planning it, I pushed her down the sidewalk, away from the school building. I hoped no one was looking at us.

"Didn't you hear me? I said I went to Emerald City by myself. I went without you."

"Just walk." I wanted to get Madeline home as quickly as possible.

"Alice!" She stood still. "Do you know that MGM capped Judy Garland's teeth and made her wear a girdle because she was too old for the part of Dorothy? The studio put a mannequin of a fat woman in her dressing room with a sign that said, 'DO YOU WANT TO LOOK LIKE THIS DUMMY?' So Judy Garland did the only thing she could do. She went on the MGM diet." Her voice became softer; she paused between each word. "Chicken soup. Black coffee. Cigarettes." Madeline smiled. "And pills. Pills for everything. Pills to sleep, to wake up. Pills. Pills. Pills."

I knew these facts about Judy Garland's life because Lily had told them to us many times, but my sister was relating them to me as if I'd never heard them, and I was suddenly full of fear. *Pills.* I didn't know why she repeated the word. I studied Madeline as she stood in front of me on the sidewalk, sunlight slanting between us. A heat rash had spread over her neck, against her collar. The hem of her purple costume dragged along the ground. Her arms were thin, folded over her chest. She looked like an old woman.

27

"Well, well," Helen says. "I didn't expect to see you again." Framed by the doorway of our motel room, she wears a housedress and basketball socks, and her white hair is flat on one side and puffed into a tangle on the other. But she's smiling.

I wrench the metal chain off the door and open it as wide as I can. I hug her, and she hugs me back. "How did you know I was here?"

"You called me, Alice, don't you remember? You told me the name of the motel. You even said it was on Airline Highway. I once came to New Orleans in the fifties, so I remembered the city's layout. I'm a pretty good detective."

"How did you get to New Orleans?"

"On the bus. I heard a lot of people's life stories, especially when we went through Mississippi. Most of them fell asleep as we left Alabama. I sat by an old man on his way to visit his mother. He must have been eighty, so I figure she was at least a hundred and ten. Can I come in?"

As Helen enters the motel room, I remember Madeline in the bathtub and feel a small shudder of nervousness. Please stay in the bathroom, I plead silently to her. Don't come out until I've decided what to do. Inside the room, Helen studies my appearance. I yank the towels over my breasts, below my thighs, wishing I'd gotten dressed before I answered the door.

"Don't worry. The last time I saw you, you were naked in front of our entire art class." Helen sits down on the edge of Madeline's bed. "What in God's name did you do to your hair?"

"I cut it," I yank the strands around my ears, as if I can lengthen it by pulling it.

"You didn't cut it. Madeline did. Am I right?"

I don't respond to her question. "Let me just throw on some clothes." I rifle through the suitcase of Helen's clothes. Turning my back on her, I drop the towel and pull on an acetate blouse printed with huge blue flowers and a straight skirt. One piece of the skirt's clasp is missing; I fasten the waistband with a safety pin. "When did you last wear this?" I ask, to turn the conversation away from Madeline.

"I don't remember," she says, but I know she does. "Where's your sister?"

I point toward the closed bathroom door.

"Alice, sit down." Helen lights another cigarette and crosses her legs. The basketball socks slip down to her ankles, baring her skinny white calves. "I want to talk to you. That's why I came here." She takes a drag and blows a smoke ring. "Owen called me."

Owen. No one but Madeline has said his name in the three weeks since we left Sarasota, and to hear Helen pronounce the word is a shock. As soon as she says it, I hear his voice again on the birthday tape—"Alice, happy twenty-nine"—and tears begin to leak into my eyes. I force myself to speak. "Did he tell you to come find me?"

"No, coming here was my idea. He said he was worried about you. He said you never even called him. Is that true, Alice? You haven't tried to contact him once? You called me, for heaven's sake. Why didn't you call him?"

"I called him once, but I hung up." I look down at the carpet between my legs, trying to focus my attention on a long brown stain. Behind my eyes, a wall of tears is pressing closer.

"I told him that I knew where you were. He said New Orleans was where he suspected you and Madeline would go. Alice, until last week, I'd never met him, but when I said I wanted to come find you, he came to Beachaven and bought me a bus ticket to come to New Orleans. He said he didn't think you'd want to see him, but you'd talk to me."

If Owen had come to New Orleans, I tell myself, I would have talked to him, I would have let him walk into the room and wrap his arms around me and take me back to our life together.

The bathroom door flings open, smashing the wall. Wearing a Chinese silk robe that once belonged to Helen, Madeline walks to stand in the center of the room, posing, pointing one finger straight at Helen. "Who's that?"

"Linny, this is my friend Helen." My voice is unsteady.

"What's she doing here?" Madeline sets both hands on her hips.

"I'm here to help you," Helen says.

"Alice, could I speak to you alone?" Madeline sweeps across the room, grabs me and pulls me back into the bathroom. She pauses in the doorway between the rooms and stares at Helen. "It's an emergency." She draws out the word as if she enjoys the feeling of it on her tongue.

"She's ruining our trip," Madeline whispers as we stand in the bathroom together. "Everything's wrong now."

"Stop it, Linny." I fold wet towels over the shower curtain.

"She's here because she's my friend, and she's worried about me." I've decided it's better not to mention to Madeline that Owen is behind Helen's appearance, that he asked her to come here.

"And you told me I shouldn't be thinking about Jack." Madeline walks out of the bathroom and slams the door. A few seconds later, I hear another slam as she leaves the motel room.

I had always envisioned Helen and Madeline getting along. I thought first of the costumes, the clothes Helen gave me this summer, that my sister and I have been wearing, the kind of clothes Madeline loves. But how could I forget that no third person except Lily can ever enter the equation? It's *Madeline + Alice + Lily = A Family* or nothing at all.

When I come out of the bathroom, Helen is still sitting on the side of Madeline's bed. She looks less confident now. Her hands are folded in her lap, and she has stubbed out her cigarette. "Should I not be here? Tell the truth."

"No. I'm glad to see you. I want you here." My position is familiar: making excuses for Madeline. I'm trying not to think about how my sister will stay out all night with strange men, as she did when we spent the night at Adventureland, because any man my sister finds in New Orleans would be worse than the one she spent the night with in St. Petersburg. And what if this time she took Jack's car? I should have run after Madeline, chased her across the parking lot and begged her to come back to the motel room. I'd promise Madeline that Helen would leave on the next bus back to Florida and we'd be alone together again.

Suddenly, the door to the room bangs open, and Madeline walks in, holding a can of Barqs root beer. "Why are you staring at me?" she says.

"I thought you were leaving."

"Why would I leave? Honestly, Alice, you're such an alarmist." She turns to Helen, as if she's confiding in an old friend. "My sister has fears of abandonment. Our whole life, I've always been the calmer one." She drinks her root beer. "Ask anyone." Madeline lies down on the bed, stretching her arms over her head. "I'm exhausted. I'm going to take a nap."

"Should we leave?" Helen whispers. I've always thought of Helen as tough, unflappable, but my sister seems to unsettle her. I shake my head, and Helen continues, "You haven't made any progress on the search, have you?"

I don't know if I should tell Helen how little my sister and I have accomplished on this trip. Madeline's chest rises and falls, her breathing sounds perfectly regular, but I know her sleep must be fake.

"I thought about your search all through Alabama last night. Looking for Lily is the wrong way to go about it. The person you should try to find is Agatha," Helen says.

I withdraw my attention from Madeline and stare at Helen. "How do you know about Agatha?"

"When he came to see me, Owen told me about everyone. He filled me in on all the stories about your family."

"Owen doesn't know the stories," Madeline says under her breath, but loud enough so that I hear.

"Lily might not want to see you, but Agatha would. I know old people. If there's anyone I know, it's them."

Madeline raises her head and stares at Helen. "And how do you suppose we're going to find Agatha? I'm sure she's dead by now."

"It's simple. Go to Lily's old house, where she lived with Agatha."

"We went to the house before you got here." Madeline sits up and smiles at Helen. The smile seems to be a threat.

"We didn't go inside. We didn't even knock on the door," I say. "We just looked at it."

"So maybe Agatha still lives there," Helen says.

The plan is too easy: we could go to Lily's old house, knock on the door, and we'd find Agatha. Could the best way to find Lily be the one my sister and I have been ignoring all along?

"You're wrong. This will never work," Madeline says. "We've been looking for Lily for more than a week, and we haven't found her yet."

For the first time since Madeline and I left Sarasota, I feel excited. Helen has given the trip a focus, a goal, and an end. I dress carefully, in a prim black dress with a polka-dot collar, black tights, low-heeled black shoes. "I wore those clothes to church on Sundays," Helen says, smiling with approval.

"So what?" Lying in bed, my sister lights a cigarette. Since Helen came, Madeline has confiscated most of her cigarettes. Without asking, she took the pack from Helen's purse. Helen said nothing.

I put on Helen's jet bead earrings. Clip-ons, they pinch my ears, giving off a dull pain, a symmetrical double ache on each side of my head. I brush my hair flat against my head and secure the side pieces with bobby pins. I want to look like a good girl, a nice girl, some-one Agatha or Lily or whoever we can find will immediately want to welcome into their family.

Helen and I are ready to go, but I can't convince Madeline to get out of bed. "I'm tired," she says, as I pull the covers off her body. Each time, she pulls them back. "I'm exhausted. Leave me alone."

"We're leaving, Linny."

"Go. You know you're not going to find her. You know she's dead."

"Maybe she is. I want to know."

"You don't need me anyway, Alice. You've got her." She points at Helen.

"Wait here for us," I say. "Don't leave this room."

Helen and I drive to Agatha's house. Our trip is a reversal of the tour Madeline and I used to take with Lily during our late-night drives. I know I should not be taking Helen with me on this trip; I should be with my sister.

For the first time, in daylight, I study the neighborhood where Lily grew up. The houses are huge, with gabled porches and many floors, all newly renovated and painted fresh pastel colors: salmon pink, mint green, periwinkle blue. I remember one of my painting teachers at the Ringling Art School telling the class that these colors have only appeared in tubes and cans of paint in the last twenty years.

"Where's the house?" Helen asks.

"Here." I pull the car up to the curb in front of the house. A rusted car is propped on cinder blocks in the front yard.

"Agatha would never leave a car out like that," I say.

"You never know. Old people can surprise you." Helen laughs, but I don't want to joke. My heart pounds in my chest. I'm sweating through Helen's dress. To calm down, I place my hand on my stomach. When I realize what I've done, I quickly remove my hand. It's a reflex from pregnancy, a gesture I haven't used in months. I used to believe that my hand ensured the baby would be safe.

I can't find a doorbell, so I knock lightly on the door. Once, twice, then three times for luck. No answer. "Knock again," Helen says. "Maybe she can't hear you."

The door opens, and a gray-haired man wearing gym shorts and no shirt says, "Yes?" He doesn't try to hide the fact that he's annoyed.

My voice chokes in my throat. "You don't know me. I'm Alice. I'm—" I can't finish the sentence. Of course the people who live in this house won't know who I am.

"We don't want any of whatever you're selling."

Behind the man, a woman appears. She must be in her late sixties or early seventies. Her hair is piled on her head, dyed blond, very light, the color Madeline calls platinum. For a moment, I believe that these people are Lily's parents, that their car never plunged off the side of the bridge. Maybe their death was a piece of the family story Lily invented.

"We're looking for someone," Helen says.

Maybe the Skylark never smashed the guardrail and dropped into the dark water of the Mississippi. I ask, "Did you have a daughter?"

"Yes. But you couldn't have known our daughter," the woman says slowly. "She died."

"I'm sorry." I swallow hard. But something makes me step closer to the couple. "When did your daughter die?"

"Years ago. She was in high school. Why do you want to know?" the man asks. "Why did you come around to bother us?"

"I'm sorry," I say again, staring at the wooden door frame that separates us from the couple. These people aren't Lily's parents. Lily's parents are dead.

"Please forgive my granddaughter," Helen says. "She's upset because we've been looking for someone we can't find." She smiles at the couple; they don't smile back. "There was an old woman who lived here once," Helen says. "We don't know when she might have moved. Her name is Agatha Bantorvya. She lived here with her granddaughter."

"I think I've heard that an old woman lived here, but that was two owners ago. We moved here when our daughter died, and before that another family owned the house," the woman says.

"Do you know where she could be now?" I ask.

"No. I think I remember something about a nursing home. But this was several years ago."

"Thank you," I whisper. "I'm sorry about your daughter." As I walk down the path away from them, I say, "I lost my daughter too."

In the car, Helen and I sit silently. I don't put the key in the ignition or start the car.

"Do you think I would have been a good mother?" When I say it, the question surprises me. I didn't know I was thinking about the pregnancy; I thought I was thinking about finding Lily.

"Bad mother, good mother. No one has any idea what either one is." She snorts in disgust. "Tell me, Alice, what do you think it means to be a good mother?"

But suddenly I can't speak because I'm crying. I'm crying for Lily. I'm crying for Madeline. I'm crying for my daughter.

"Tell me, why did you leave Sarasota on this trip with Madeline?"

"We were looking for Lily. You know that."

"Alice, I don't know you very well, but I know you're not impulsive. You're careful. If you were going to conduct a real search, you would have gone about it completely differently. If you were really looking for your mother, don't you think you would have gone alone?"

"This was how Madeline wanted to do it," I say. "I did it the way Madeline wanted."

"Why?" Helen says.

"Because that's how we are. That's how I am."

"Why?" Helen says again. Her voice is gentle.

I finally say what I never say, to anyone. "Because Madeline's sick."

Helen reaches across the car and takes my hand, pulling me toward her. I lean against her, as if I were a child, and she slides her arms over my shoulders. Helen and I are the same size, and her grip on my body is precarious. Being held by her is an unfamiliar sensation. The position is uncomfortable, but I don't move.

"You're going to be okay," Helen says. "I know."

At the Crescent Court Motel, Madeline is still lying on the bed. "Oh, you're back," she says in a flat voice that shows she doesn't care we ever left. "Helen, can I have your last cigarette?"

"That's rude," I say, but Helen nods.

She walks to the bed opposite Madeline, sits down, and opens the New Orleans phone book. "Nursing homes," she says slowly, scanning the pages. Her finger moves up and down the black columns. "I'm going to call them all."

"What is she doing, Alice?" Madeline sits up, the unlit cigarette stuck in her mouth.

"Calling around to find Agatha," I say.

"Oh, please. If the phone book worked, Jack and I would have found Lily."

"Come on, Linny. Give this a chance," Helen says.

Madeline rises from the bed. "Don't you ever, ever call me by that name," Madeline says, her voice hissing. "That's the name my sister calls me. No one but Alice is allowed to call me that."

28

On a hot day in the middle of the New Orleans summer, in July,
Agatha takes her daughter to the Ringling Brothers Circus downtown.
Stephan has refused to go; he says he has no money for this trip, and
the circus is an unnecessary luxury their child doesn't need. The afternoon before the circus opens is half-price day. They will watch the
dress rehearsal. All summer, Agatha has been secretly afraid she might
be pregnant again. She drinks vinegar five times a day, chipping tiny
pieces of ice off the block of ice in the kitchen with a spoon for meals.
The beginning of pregnancy, when she waits for the new baby to suddenly, inexplicably leave her body, is the worst. None of the doctors at
the Hotel Dieu Hospital can tell her why the deaths are occurring. As
often as she can now, she pushes Stephan away because she cannot bear
to go through this experience again.

"We have a child," she tells him. "Please. It is enough."

When she refuses him, he knows the reason, but she can see
that he's still angry. Sometimes he won't talk to her the next day.
Finally, one night at the end of June, Agatha tells her husband to

find a prostitute if that is all he wants from her. "I mean it," she says, her back facing him in the dark. "I don't mind."

After that scene, she never asks him if he's looked for another woman or not. It doesn't matter, she tells herself. By allowing him to seek his satisfaction elsewhere, she has protected herself from suffering. Agnes would understand her predicament, but she hasn't heard anything from Agnes in two years. The rest of the family does not write, but Agnes's silence concerns her. When she and Stephan first came to the United States, letters from her sister arrived every week. Now contact with the village is impossible unless she meets someone who is going over to Hungary, and no one ever seems to make the journey back.

At the Ringling Brothers Circus tent, her daughter holds her hand, afraid. Two men dressed as pygmies take their tickets at the entrance to the canvas tent. Agatha can see the line of greasepaint on their foreheads where the skin of their faces meets their wigs, and she knows their grass skirts are costumes, but her daughter's grip on her hand tightens.

Inside the tent, Agatha realizes that to see the attractions advertised on playbills on the walls—the bearded lady, the tattooed child, the skeleton man so thin you can see through his body—she will have to pay more money, money she doesn't have. For half price you don't see the real circus show. The afternoon is a trick.

Agatha and her daughter have only paid enough money to study the exhibits in the center of the tent. Agatha decides she will tell the child that this exhibit is the circus, a lie but a necessary one. She leads the girl to the glass showcase at the back of the tent. The first object she sees, the only one she looks at, is a jar of green fluid and two fetuses. Her daughter begins to cry. A label explains what they have found, an exhibit Agatha knows that Agnes would have loved: Siamese twins, joined at the chest, with a fused liver, a shared heart.

29

The receptionist at the front desk of the Poor Clares Nursing Home recognizes the name Bantorvya. Helen discovers this fact after her thirteenth phone call. No one else is helpful because all the homes have confidentiality policies that prevent, as each head nurse carefully explains to Helen, the release of any patient's name.

"Of course Agatha would go to a Catholic nursing home," I say.

"Not just a Catholic home. A place run by nuns," Helen says. "The Poor Clares are the sisters of the Benedictines."

"Isn't this great, Linny? We've found her." I smile at Madeline, but she won't look at me. She stares at herself in the mirror on the bathroom door, checking her outfit for the visit to the nursing home: Helen's mock Jackie Kennedy suit, blue gabardine with gold buttons.

"Won't you be hot wearing that?" I ask.

"This is what I want to wear." Madeline drops her voice, steps closer to me. "You're mad because I look better than you." I'm wearing a light summer suit Helen wore at Fourth of July parties, wrinkled pink linen. As usual, the skirt binds my waist and puffs around my stomach.

"Girls," Helen says, then stops. She chuckles. "Well, you're not girls, and I'm not your mother. Argue all you want." For the first time since Helen arrived in New Orleans, the tension between us breaks, and we all laugh.

With Madeline in the passenger seat and Helen in the back, I drive Jack's car to the Poor Clares Home. Although I don't tell anyone, I'm filled with dread.

"I think she'll recognize us when she sees us," Madeline says. "The question is whether or not she knows we're twins."

"She may not know who we are, Linny."

"Alice, she's going to tell us where to find Lily."

"We're here," I say. My voice is shaking.

A sign in front of the building reads THE POOR CLARES NURSING HOME. This nursing home is unlike Beachaven; it resembles a nineteenth-century asylum, surrounded by a high stone wall. As soon as I see it, I envision Madeline in the hospital, on the psychiatric ward, where the nurses take away her jewelry and hold her down. Then I flash to the present, to my sister who stands at my side, between Helen and me, in front of the nursing home.

She shakes the sleeve of my dress like a child. "I want to go in."

The lobby is empty. The front hall is long and dimly lit. The home has none of Beachaven's false cheeriness or pretense that it's not a nursing home. No one would ever string a tissue garland from the ceiling or teach arts and crafts. From each side, doors open to residents' rooms, and I hear the sound of television after television. Game shows. Soap operas. Talk shows. The voices of Oprah Winfrey and Sally Jesse Raphael echo off the walls, where every few feet is a small suffering Jesus on the cross, his hands and feet covered in blood.

Madeline walks ahead. At the first nurses' station, my sister stops.

"Yes?" A tired-looking nun looks up from the desk.

"I'm looking for someone who might be here," Madeline says.

"We're the great-granddaughters of someone who we think might be here," I explain. "Agatha Bantorvya. We heard there's someone with that last name here. We don't know if it's her." I feel a small shudder of fear when I say the name.

"She was here, yes."

Madeline stares straight at the nun, stepping closer. "What do you mean?"

"Agatha Bantorvya was a patient here, but she's not now. She's on the ninth floor." The nun glances at me, then back at Madeline. "The floor for the difficult patients. The ones who can't live here with the others. We sent her up there last year."

Helen is already starting to walk down the hall. "Come on, girls."

We follow Helen. In the elevator, Madeline clutches my hands in her own. "Alice, she's in the mental hospital. I know she's in the mental hospital."

The ninth floor is even darker than the lobby, and all the doors to the rooms are closed. No nuns patrol the halls or work at the nurses' station. "Here it is. Oh God. Here she is," Madeline points to the placard outside a room by the bathroom. AGATHA BAN-TORVYA. Madeline traces the letters with her fingertips, then staggers, falling against the wall. One ankle twists behind her.

"You have to pull yourself together, Linny," I whisper. "We can't go in there if you can't calm down."

"Judy Garland, Ginger Love," Madeline says. She makes the sign of the cross over her chest.

The door to Agatha's room swings open. Inside, all the shades are pulled to darkness, and the smell of camphor hangs in the air. A small white bundle lies in the bed. The first part of Agatha I notice is her arms, thin, speckled with age, tied down. Next, I see her face, small and wrinkled, turned to one side as if a nurse had moved it there. Her large brown eyes stare at us. I'm afraid to approach the bed. I step back into the shadowed corner of the room. Helen stands beside the door.

Madeline runs to the bed. "Agatha," she says. "We're here to rescue you." My sister buries her face in the pillow beside Agatha's head. I can't tell if she's crying. Agatha says nothing. Then Madeline begins to speak. "Judy Garland's mother played the piano in the orchestra pit at the New Grand Theater, the movie palace her father owned. The Gumm sisters were dressed in Spanish costumes. They had little brimmed hats hung with bells. Judy Garland was Baby Gumm, and she was an Egyptian princess. She came on stage in a hatbox and jumped out." Madeline raises her head and looks at Agatha. "I got that story from you. Lily told us and you told her."

"Linny," I whisper, "I don't think she can hear you."

"No, she can. Try one, Alice. Do Liza and Judy."

I can feel Helen's gaze on me as I begin the story. "Liza and Judy sang 'For Me and My Gal' at a party for Gene Kelly. Two doctors came to the party to check on Judy Garland, pretending to be musicians . . ." My voice falters. "Please, Linny, she can't hear any of this. I don't want to finish."

"She can too. I know she hears us. Agatha, Agatha." Madeline presses her face to the cheek of the woman in the bed.

The door to the room creaks open, and another nun enters with a tray of needles and vials. She doesn't seem shocked to see the three of us standing in the room. "Are you relatives?" Her voice is soft and kind.

"Yes," I say.

"You must be related to the woman who used to visit Mrs. Bantorvya. She came all the time. Until the accident, she was here almost every day. I can't remember her name though. Lisa?"

"Lily," Madeline whispers. She stands up and walks slowly toward me.

"What accident?" I ask.

"A car accident. I heard it was a suicide. She drove off a bridge. I don't know the details, but enough money was left over to keep Mrs. Bantorvya here. Since the granddaughter died, though, she's taken a turn for the worse. She hasn't spoken since then."

"How long ago did the granddaughter die?" I ask. Madeline is almost beside me now.

"Last year," the nun says. "Did you know her well?"

"No," Madeline says. Her eyes are squeezed shut; her face is contorted into an expression of pain. "No." She drops to the floor, falls on her arm, her head knocking the tile. She lies crumpled at the side of Agatha's bed.

"Linny," I bend down, holding her. "Linny. It's okay. I'm here."

Helen tells the nurse, "That woman was their mother."

In the car on the way back to the Crescent Court, Madeline vomits. I stop and try to clean her face with a napkin, but her head lolls to the side, and she pushes me away.

"I'll sit with her," Helen says, and I help my sister into the backseat.

Now at last Madeline and I have an answer: Lily is dead. Agatha, who could have been the missing link in the story, can't talk to us.

When I was younger, I used to wonder what would have happened if Lily had not left Agatha. What if she'd gone to one of the homes for unwed mothers instead of moving into a motel alone? I think of the house where Lily grew up, the house she would never let us enter. I close my eyes and envision myself inside, walking through the dark rooms, touching the walls with my fingertips, tracing with my hands every surface of the furniture, the floors, as if looking for clues about the people who once lived in the house. But in the end they are all lost to me, indecipherable.

"I'm going back to Sarasota," Helen says after I've put Madeline to bed in the motel. I gave my sister three of the sleeping pills I found in the lining of her purse, breaking my own rule about drugs because I want her to sleep all day.

"Please don't leave."

"No, I think this is a time for you and your sister to be alone. This is something you two need to go through together."

I don't know if I want to go through it alone with Madeline, but I don't tell Helen. The sheets are pulled over my sister; only the ends of her red hair are visible on the pillow. Her stillness terrifies me.

Helen hugs me. "Good luck, Alice. Remember what I said."

"Thank you," I say, and I hear her voice in my head, *You're going to be okay.*

I watch Helen walk to the end of the parking lot. At the edge of Airline Highway, she sticks out her thumb like a hitchhiker and turns her face up to the sun.

Now, finally, as I sit on the bed beside my sleeping sister in the Crescent Court Motel, I remember what I have tried to forget.

"Girls, come sit on my lap," Lily said one morning as she stood in the doorway of the movie theater, and I knew something was wrong. Her voice was soft and gentle, coaxing. She wore new clothes, a white suit I had never seen before. I didn't remember stealing the suit from anyone's trash.

I sat up in my sleeping bag and unzipped the side. "We're almost eighteen. We don't want to sit on your lap," I said.

"Get dressed," Lily said, as if she hadn't heard what I said. She turned around and left.

Madeline and I dressed, side by side, in silence. Then we walked down the hall. As soon as I saw the front hall, I knew the danger we were in. A suitcase and Lily's old pink ballet bag sat there. I stopped when I saw them, but Madeline walked on toward Lily.

Lily opened her arms and drew us to her. Her embrace was unfamiliar. Her hands were clumsy against our backs as she pulled us together against her chest. I felt a fluttering behind my back, in my pocket, as if she were pressing something into my jeans. When she released us, I felt in the pocket and touched a thick envelope. Lily stood before us, her hands clasped, her fingers twisting together and then apart.

"You girls are practically adults," she began. "You're grown up now. And so it's time for me to explain some things to you."

We waited. I held my breath, although I knew what was about to happen.

"It's time for me to start taking care of myself," she went on. "You two don't need me anymore."

"No!" Madeline ran out of the front hall, back toward our room.

There was a long pause.

"Alice, I want you to watch over your sister for a while," Lily began. You have to take care of her. I want you to understand that."

"For how long? When are you coming back?"

She didn't answer. "Madeline isn't like you."

"When are you coming back?" I repeated.

"You know, I left home when I was younger than you. Agatha was like my mother, and I never saw her again."

"Where are you going?" I could hear the panic rising in my voice. If she could sense my fear, maybe she would stay. "What if we need to call you? Can you give us your phone number?" I wanted to continue the conversation, as if I could convince her to stay with us by the power of my words, which had always failed with her before.

"You'll be fine," she said. "Don't worry so much, sweetheart."

Sweetheart. It was the first time Lily had ever used an endearment for me. The word sounded stilted, totally wrong, like a punishment. It was the most horrible word she had ever said to me.

I turned around and began walking down the hall.

"Where are you going?" Lily said.

"I need to be with Madeline."

This was a lie. I could not face my sister yet. Luckily, she wasn't in our room. I went into the movie theater and sat down alone. I thought back over the past months, looking for the signs. In the four months we had lived in the house on Siesta Key, Lily had not been impatient with us. She did not admonish us anymore. I pinched myself hard on the inside of my arm to keep from crying, as if the pain I inflicted on myself could drown out my sadness. Lily had left it up to me to tell Madeline she was leaving. I knew the truth: Lily was waiting for us to grow up, not as most mothers do, with a sense of sadness that their daughters will leave them, but with the hope that as soon as we were old enough, she would finally be free to leave us. I remembered the envelope Lily had slid into my pocket. Carefully, I slit it open. It was full of money, thirty twenty-dollar bills. It was Lily's last gift, a sign that her departure was permanent and final.

Downstairs, the front door closed. Lily was gone.

I looked up. Madeline stood in the doorway. She'd put her night-gown back on. I pulled her to me. "Linny," I began, trying to hide my own tears. I knew I needed to be strong for Madeline. From this moment on, she was my responsibility. That morning marked the end of my childhood and, at the same time, my unspoken permission for my sister to continue hers. Without knowing it at the time, at that moment I gave her permission to stay a child forever.

"Don't say it," Madeline told me. I held her on my lap, her head crooked against my shoulder, her body nestled into mine.

"Lily is dead. Lily is dead. Lily is dead." Madeline is awake now. She repeats these three sentences over and over like a song. She rocks back and forth on the bed.

"Why don't we go to sleep, Linny? We can talk in the morning."

"I've been in bed all day. You knocked me out with those drugs. What I want to do is pray. Let's pray for Agatha, Alice. Now I lay me down to sleep, I pray the Lord my soul to keep, If I should die before I wake, I pray the Lord my soul to take."

"Linny, we're not going to die," I say, switching off the bedside lamp and pulling the sheet over my chest so that the fabric separates me from my sister.

Madeline moves closer to me. I can feel her breath on my face. She is breathing too quickly. "You never know." Madeline smiles. "If you don't say it, you could be sorry."

I turn away from her to face the wall, but I can't protect myself from her tonight. She continues talking.

"I'm dead. Look at me, Alice. I'm already dead."

I know she wants me to turn back to her, to focus my attention on her.

Her voice continues, disembodied, drawing me closer to her in the dark. "Have you seen those drawings on the sidewalk? Sometimes they're on the news. They're drawings to mark the site of murders. The police trace around someone's body when they're dead. A chalk outline, I think. I'm just like that, Alice. I'm dead."

I sit up and turn on the light. "Okay, Linny," I say, trying to keep my voice from sounding alarmed. "I'm awake. I'm here."

"Alice, I know you want to leave," Madeline says, then stops. Her voice is imperious, a distinct threat. "You can't leave me."

"I'm not leaving you, Linny. Of course I'm not leaving you." I want to soothe my sister with my words, but she will not allow it.

"I'm never going back. I don't have any reason to go back."

"Linny——" I begin, but I can't finish my sentence.

"Alice," my sister says suddenly, "pretend you're my mother." She reaches for me, winds her arms around my neck and pulls me against her. Her head drops. Her mouth fumbles against my chest, and I realize she is searching for my breast.

I struggle to be free of her, but Madeline is strong. She wraps her arms around my ribs tightly so I can barely breathe.

"Pretend I'm Owen." She buries her head in my chest.

With all my strength, I shove my sister away from me.

"Don't you love me? Don't you love me at all?" Her voice rises as she moves away from me. "Do you know what my intake form at the hospital said? I saw it, by accident. The doctor had written at the top of the page, 'The patient is very attractive.' Do you think he was right? Do you think I'm attractive?" my sister asks. Her voice is breaking.

"Linny, of course——"

"In the hospital, they took care of me. They cared about me. Do you know that they cared about me more than you ever could?" Her voice rises.

I look down at the bedspread in order to avoid her face.

"The only place besides the hospital where I was ever happy was Emerald City. I was safe in Emerald City, Alice, and you were the one who wouldn't go there anymore. You made it disappear. You made them disappear. You killed them, Alice. That's why there's no more Judy Garland and Ginger Love."

"Judy Garland killed herself. And there never was any Ginger Love. We made her up." I'm trying to speak calmly.

"I think Agatha heard me when I talked about Judy Garland, don't you? I know she did." She pauses. "What do you think it would be like to drown?" she asks. "To be buried under ice?"

"I don't know," I say carefully, deliberately. If I hear the sound of my own voice, I will know I have some control over what's happening to my sister.

"You don't know. I'll tell you something you don't know," Madeline says. "If one twin commits suicide, the other twin has a twenty-five-percent chance of dying too. It's a fact." She sits up and takes my hands. "Alice, I have an idea. Let's become blood brothers," she says, holding my hands. "Prick your finger and then do mine," Madeline tells me. "Do you have a needle? How about a pin?" Before I can stop her, she has yanked out one of her earrings and is stabbing at her finger with the post of the earring, with the point of the silver wire. "You have to do it hard," she says.

A drop of red spots her finger. She holds it out to me, an offering. "Let's mix our blood," she says. "So if I died, you'd die too."

"Linny," I speak softly, as if my voice can calm her. "I want to go to bed. Tomorrow we can talk about all of this. Please."

Suddenly, my sister grabs my shoulders. "Alice, there's only one thing for us to do. We don't have to go back or stay here." Her eyes are unnaturally bright, glowing in the dark, like an animal's. "Let's die together."

Fear fills my chest. I jerk free from her embrace. "No!"

"What do you have to go back for? What do you have to live for? If we die, you can be with your baby. The three of us will be together. We'll be a family. Don't you believe in the afterlife?"

I stare at Madeline, afraid that if I say the wrong words, something terrible will happen. I must measure my sentences carefully, pick the right phrases. "Linny," I start, my voice wavering.

"Are you afraid? Why are you always afraid? I brought the pills I told you about this summer, the ones I collected in the Miss Wonderful box. I knew when I left that we might have to follow my plan."

"Linny, calm down." I realize immediately that it is the wrong thing to say.

My sister jumps out of bed and begins pulling on Helen's clothes with abrupt, violent motions. When she yanks Helen's cocktail dress over her head, I hear the fabric ripping. "I hate you!" she screams. "You never listen to me. You don't care about me at all."

"Linny," I say again and I reach for her.

As my hand extends to meet hers, as my fingers uncurl to grasp her own, Madeline hits me in the face. The shock of her slap knocks me off the bed and back against the wall. My skin burns. I can't see for a minute, but then my vision clears and Madeline is standing over me and she is screaming, loud, violent shrieks.

"Why are you always here?" my sister says, her voice hissing through her teeth. "Why can't you ever leave me alone?"

30

Lily is dead, and now I remember another story I want to forget.

I ask to be unconscious when she is born. The obstetrician tells me not to use that word, but the other word is no better—when she is *delivered*.

"Put me out," I tell the doctor when it is clear that the induction of labor will finally succeed. I watch the narrow tube suspended from the bag above my head drip the liquid that will fill my veins and save me. It's too late for her.

"We can't do that. It would be too dangerous. If we do that, you won't push and we need you to push to ensure that the placenta comes out. You don't want an infection, do you?" the obstetrician says.

"I don't care if I get an infection," I say. "I don't care if I die from an infection. I don't want to be awake."

"She doesn't mean that," Owen assures the doctor. "She doesn't know what she's saying."

"I understand. This has been a very difficult situation," the obstetrician says.

You don't know what pain is, I thought. *None of you do.*

"After the procedure," the doctor says, with a glance in my direction to see if the term is acceptable, then addressing Owen, "we can discuss the various options."

"What options?" I'm tired of being treated as if I am not in the room. "What options?"

"In terms of the body," she says gently. "Cremation is a choice many women make."

"Why do we have to deal with the body?" Owen asks, his voice rising. "Haven't we been through enough?"

"I'm afraid it's a Georgia state law. Fetuses in gestation for over twenty-five weeks must have a grave."

"We don't want that—" Owen starts, but I interrupt him.

"Yes, we do." He looks at me with confusion. I know he's trying to protect me. "I do," I say. "I want a grave." For the first time all day, my voice is steady. "Let's go ahead and do this. Let's get the procedure over with."

I refuse to allow Owen in the delivery room with me, which I know hurts him. "Alice, please don't do this to me," he says in a low voice. "Don't shut me out. Please. I don't understand you, Alice. I want to help you. I want to share this with you."

I shake my head.

The labor is only forty-five minutes long. I am trying to think between the pain, in the interstices, as if I can have another, separate life that occurs between the contractions. I have always been told that pain comes over you in waves, rushing and then receding, but this pain makes itself known to me in jolts that split my body open at the root. I know that I will not recover.

Finally, I pretend I'm Madeline. The birth is a shock treatment in the hospital where I have to go when my sister leaves me to start a new life with someone else. I feel as if I am dying, but I have a trick: oblivion. My mind is being wiped clean. "Think of a chalk-board," the psychiatrist tells me as he swabs my forehead with alcohol. The metal is cold. "Then picture it being wiped perfectly clean." Over and over again I imagine this emptiness, this erasure, until my voice sticks in my throat and I cannot cry out and my daughter has left my body and entered the world for the first and last time.

When it's over, as everyone told me to expect, there is no cry from her or an intake of breath from the nurses or an exclamation of the fact that she is a girl.

Instead, there is a terrible space, a silence.

Then she's gone.

I want to touch her. I ask if I can hold her, but I am not allowed.

31

"Take me to the hospital," Madeline says. She packs her suitcase without looking at me.

Past midnight, Madeline and I stand together at the entrance to Charity Hospital in the dark. A suitcase full of Helen's clothes sits on the sidewalk between us, beside the stack of Judy Garland records and Lily's scrapbook. My sister is making her hands into tight, balled fists.

"I don't want you to do this," I say. "Come back with me. I'll go wherever you want to go." My face aches where my sister hit me. The skin on my cheek hurts when I speak.

Madeline is silent.

"I won't leave you. I won't go back to Sarasota if you don't want me to."

Nothing.

Then she says, "Do you know why Lily left? I want to tell you. She left because she hated you. She told me, Alice. She didn't want to be your mother anymore."

I know my sister must be inventing this. I can no longer believe anything she says. "Linny, let me help you. Let me take care of you."

"You don't know how to take care of me," Madeline says in her coldest voice.

Then she opens her hands, and for a moment I think she'll offer a gesture of forgiveness, an embrace that will change everything. Pieces of paper flutter from her fingers to the sidewalk. Madeline leaves the scrapbook on the ground. She picks up the suitcase and the stack of records and walks through the double doors that lead into the hospital. When I bend down to pick up the pieces, I see that Madeline has ripped up a photograph, the photograph Lily took of us twenty-nine years ago in which we lie side by side, perfectly identical. On the sidewalk, our faces are torn apart, our bodies broken.

32

When Lily left, we ate. Glazed donuts. Candy bars. Eclairs. Hamburgers dripping with mayonnaise. The first week without her, each morning Madeline and I walked down to the end of our street, to the strip of fast-food restaurants on Tamiami Trail, the places Lily had always forbidden us to go. I wanted to go down the right side of the road in order: Taco Bell. Tastee Freeze. Best-O-Burgers. Mister Donut. We tracked each neon sign. My sister and I decided we would each make one rule for our new life. The order of the restaurants was mine. Madeline's restriction was our silence. "I don't want to talk about anything but food," she said, and I agreed.

"A single can of Coke contains more than ten tablespoons of sugar," Madeline said as we walked down the highway. The statistic about Coke was a fact told to us by Lily, but we didn't discuss that.

Cars rushed by us on the highway. A man shouted, "Hey, twins, want to play with me?" from the window of a pickup truck. I remembered Lily telling us to walk on the opposite side of the highway from the direction that cars were heading in order to avoid men's comments and leers.

"Per ounce, cheese contains more fat calories than chocolate," I said in a toneless voice.

"A croissant contains more fat than five pats of butter."

Our conversations about food were a relief because they weren't conversations. We didn't need to listen to each other. The most important part of our new way of talking was remembering not to mention Lily or her absence.

We sat side by side at the pink and white counter at Mister Donut, ordering one donut after another, from the right side of the racks to the left. Crullers. Butternut. Jelly-filled. Our fingers were sticky with sugar, and we didn't care. We ate without speaking. We ate without looking at each other. At night, at home, when I decided it was too dangerous for us to walk the Trail, Madeline and I drank Coke after Coke and ate potato chips. When we ran out of chips and soft drinks, we filled a bucket with tap water and took turns holding it up to our mouths until our stomachs were much too full.

"Water can add as much as ten pounds to your weight," I said.

"We could be pregnant," my sister said, as we studied our new bodies in the mirror.

I stood sideways, my T-shirt pulled up over my chest, pretending to be pregnant.

Madeline and I hadn't spoken it out loud, but we had formed an understanding: there would be no more vinegar tricks. No Ipecac. No toothbrush tapping the soft tissue at the back of the throat. Wherever Lily was now, I knew that she would imagine us practicing the techniques she'd taught us. She would know that she could count on us to carry out her old routines. She would be surprised that we had refused, but the truth was that I was afraid to enact Lily's rituals without her. I believed that the tricks could easily go wrong when practiced by the two of us alone. We needed Lily as a guide. I knew that if Madeline or I started throwing up without her, we would have made a terrible mistake.

Each morning my sister and I weighed ourselves, as we used to do in our old life, on Lily's small bathroom scale. I managed to gain four pounds in five days. Madeline gained three. I would never be a ballet dancer. I would never be an actress. I would never have a boyfriend. If Lily could see us, I thought, she'd be sick. If she knew what we were doing, she would definitely not come back.

"Look," my sister said, pulling up her dress to show me her stomach after a weigh-in. She pinched a layer of skin between her fingers. "I'm disgusting." She sounded triumphant.

"Soon I won't be able to wear my jeans," I said. When I rested my hand on my stomach, it hurt. Even the skin felt stretched and painful. However, I knew that this pain was good. I deserved it. I knew that Madeline and I found a perverse happiness in referring to our new grotesque bodies. For the first time, our bodies truly belonged to us, and we could punish them freely without intervention. The new punishments were our own, and they were harder than the tests Lily had assigned. Yet if our new punishments were a race, I was winning. I gained weight more quickly than my sister, as if my body had been waiting for this chance to expand and fail me. As if I were always, secretly, the worse daughter in Lily's eyes. For most of our childhood, I had eaten more than Madeline, and now I could fill my stomach faster, with better results. The danger was that if I ate too much and gained too much weight, my sister and I would no longer match.

"You're fatter," Madeline told me as we shared a bag of sugar cookies, lying on the floor of the movie theater together, with the shades pulled down so that no one could see us, in the dark. It was her only comment about the new difference between us. I looked down at my stomach, rounded in an arc even as I stretched my body flat, and felt a wave of panic.

I was growing larger, but what I wanted most was to disappear.

"A pint of ice cream is made with a quart of whole milk and lard," I said.

Eating filled our time while we pretended to be deciding what to do. Or I pretended. With the move to Sarasota, and now Lily's departure, signifying the end of childhood, the balance of power in our family had shifted. Madeline was no longer the leader, the one who planned our stealing and our escapes. For the first time, she expected me to be in charge. I had no ideas about our future, but I knew we were in danger if we did not have a plan.

In Lily's double bed where Madeline and I now slept at night, I turned my body to the right and to the left, on my side and on my back, hoping to find a position in which my stomach didn't ache. A bitterness rose in my throat, although I hadn't allowed myself to vomit. I swallowed over and over. I went into the bathroom and brushed my teeth again and again, but the taste remained at the back of my throat like a warning.

Beside me, Madeline fell into a deep, untroubled sleep immediately, her arms wrapped around her body, hugging herself, lying close to me. Occasionally, in the night, she would turn toward me and throw her arm over mine, as if she were checking to make sure that I was still there. I knew she figured I would fix our life. For hours each night, as I lay in Lily's bed, our situation and its various possible hopeless outcomes ran through my head. It might be some time before anyone noticed Lily was gone, as she had not had a regular job. No friends we knew of. No lover.

The first week without Lily, I dreamed of Reid Alistair every night. In the first dream, the scene was the recess yard at Mater Dolorosa, a crowd of girls playing four-square. My sister and I were children again. The other girls were middle-aged women, with graying hair and strings of pearls looped around their necks. The main action of the dream consisted of my trying to make them include Madeline in the game. Reid Alistair stood at the edge of the schoolyard. He smoked a cigarette. He wore a white leotard, and he had a dancer's body, thin and lithe, and sandy-colored hair falling in a wave over his forehead. He looked like a handsome boy some other girl my age would want to meet. I nudged Madeline and directed her gaze toward him, but neither of us walked over to meet him, as if we were afraid. A daughter shouldn't be awkward around her father. A father should want to talk to his daughters. Something was wrong. The problem was Madeline. I wanted Reid Alistair all to myself. I didn't want this man to spend time with my sister, as if she could steal him from me.

I wanted to ask him: Do you ever think of Lily? Do you know who we are?

I paid the bills—water, gas, electric—using the money from Lily's envelope. She'd left a hundred dollars in her checking account too, and I signed her name on her checks in my neatest handwriting. Then when Lily's money was gone, I told my sister that we would have to live without lights and take cold baths. I tried to make myself believe that we were living an adventure, like the boy in *Sole Survivor*, but I knew my sister and I were in trouble. Lily had told me to take care of Madeline.

One afternoon, when I came home from school, Madeline was waiting for me on the front steps, dressed in a long pink dress with a train. "I want to go to Christ the King."

"You're coming to school?" I wasn't sure that the nuns would allow Madeline to start twelfth grade several months late.

"No, I want to go to the church."

Because Madeline didn't want any of the nuns affiliated with the school to see her, we skipped the regular services and took the bus to the church in the middle of the afternoon, after the healing mass and before the start of evening prayer. Christ the King was dark and empty, the smell of incense still faint in the air. Our steps echoed in the vestibule. As soon as we reached the pew, Madeline dropped to her knees, head bowed in her hands.

"We need to steal something," my sister whispered, without raising her head. "I know we're out of money." Madeline looked up and smiled. The smile, I knew immediately, was dangerous. "I know what I could sell." She sat up at the pew and lifted her hands above her head like a ballet dancer. "Me!"

"Don't be silly," I said sternly, although her suggestion was alarming.

"Alice, I could do it. I've seen the women downtown. You just stand on the side of Lemon Street after dark and wait. When a car drives up, you ask the man inside if he wants a date."

"Forget it," I said. "I'm not letting you do that."

"I've heard you can make a hundred dollars in an hour. Most of them just want a blow job." Madeline rose from the pew. "I can do whatever I want." She walked quickly ahead of me out of the church.

That night, while Madeline slept in Lily's bed, I walked through the house, in the dark, dragging my fingertips on the walls. In front of the hall closet, I studied our clothes. A long velvet skirt. A holster of cap guns. A stained fedora. All found in other people's trash. The only thing Lily had left behind was an old nightgown, washed so many times the cotton was shiny, ripped under one arm.

Lily had been gone for three weeks. I still waited for her to call. Several times a day, at first, I picked up the receiver when the phone had not rung, as if expecting her to say my name. *Alice.* In the first few weeks without Lily, our eating habits gave us a new life. But trying to gain weight had become an expense we could no longer afford. We discovered fifty more dollars hidden in Lily's underwear drawer. Now that money was gone. We needed money. We needed jobs. I realized that Madeline would never look for a job. It would be up to me to find money. To get a job, I would have to tell more lies about my age, about where I lived.

I sat down on the floor in the dark hall, my arms balanced on my knees. I knew now that Lily had always intended to leave. She was simply waiting until we grew up and she was no longer legally responsible for us. And in the end, she couldn't even wait until we turned eighteen. She left us several months early. Her decision about her own departure was what led to our sudden move to Florida in the middle of the night. She had tricked us into thinking we could live as a family in a house.

In the morning, as soon as the sky filled with light, I woke my sister. "Linny, we're going to the movies. Get up." I pulled my sister out of bed. "It's John Wayne Week."

"I hate John Wayne," Madeline said. "Leave me alone."

"No." I handed her my own clothes, a pair of shorts and a T-shirt. "And you're not wearing a costume."

"I hate Westerns," Madeline said as we stood outside the Crossroads Theater, at the shopping mall. Although I knew we needed to ration our remaining money, we were sharing a cup of coffee I'd bought in the mall, passing it back and forth between us. Coffee was what adults drank. "Why can't we go to musicals, like the kind of movies we used to see at the Joy Theater?"

"They don't show those here. What difference does it make, Linny? It's a movie. You love movies."

"John Wayne is not the same as Judy Garland. Do you know how easy it would be to sneak in through that side door?"

"We are not doing that anymore. No stealing." I knew a good way to convince my sister of my point: a threat. "Linny, if the police catch us for anything, they'll take one of us away." I stepped closer to her and lowered my voice for effect. "Do you want to live by yourself?"

Madeline stared back, her eyes level, unblinking. "You're being mean."

"I want you to be realistic."

"If you're so concerned with being realistic, why are we waiting in line to see some dumb movie?"

In the theater, John Wayne fired his gun at a row of Indians and they fell over, one at a time, in order. My sister kept her eyes on the screen, followed every image. Meanwhile I tried to focus on our future. Lily had set up a new life in another state. She probably rarely thought of us, except to experience relief that we were gone from her life. John Wayne fired his gun into the horizon.

On the walk home from the John Wayne movie, we saw a new sign. A billboard on a side street off the Trail read SELL YOUR BLOOD. FAST MONEY. "That's it!" Madeline said, grabbing my hand, squeezing my fingers tightly. "We can do this!" She pulled me across the street and into the plasma center.

When we signed a list on a clipboard at the front desk, we told the first lie: we signed fake names. "Pretend you're married," Madeline whispered. "Make up a new last name." I chose Anderson. Madeline signed herself as Madeline Bantorvya.

Next, we said we were eighteen.

"Driver's licenses?" the nurse asked.

"Why?" Madeline asked in an imperious voice.

"I have to ask for identification," the nurse told her. "It's my job."

"Actually, we don't drive," my sister said. "Our husbands usually drive us places if we need to go somewhere. Do you know that we've been married the exact same length of time? We had a double wedding." My sister and I were once again back to our life of lies, which I had sworn to her and to myself would never happen. *No stealing*, I repeated silently to myself. *After today no lies.*

The nurse appraised us skeptically but said nothing.

We would be given thirty dollars each. There were more forms to sign. Another nurse weighed us and took our blood pressure. "We've never had twins come in before," she said. "My husband was a twin."

Madeline flashed a smile. I said nothing.

The nurse explained that we must be able to wait in the plasma center for an hour after our blood was drawn to ensure that we had no side effects. "So if you have to get to work later today, you'd better come back on a day when you're free."

"Oh, no. We're free." Madeline smiled again.

Cots covered with white sheets lined the back wall. The nurse said, "You can lie down over there afterward if you feel faint." I wanted to lie down on one of those cots now. I wanted to sleep for the rest of the afternoon. "Now I just need to weigh you, and we'll get started."

Our weights were high, one hundred and twenty-five for my sister and one hundred and thirty for me. I had never weighed this much in my life, but the nurse seemed pleased. "Women under one hundred and five pounds are not permitted to give blood."

Behind the white curtain on the left side of the room, my sister and I lay down on identical stretchers, side by side. Madeline's expression was excited. Her eyes were bright. I forced myself to watch when the nurse pushed the thick needle into my arm. Then I let myself sink into my own thoughts. Without Lily, there was no routine at all beyond our bad eating habits. I knew that my sister and I were unanchored, that we were floating. I could not leave Madeline now. I was almost eighteen, and I was supposed to be able to declare myself an adult and go out into the world.

After about fifteen minutes, a doctor stopped on our side of the room to monitor our IVs. "Hello," Madeline said, turning her face to the side on the stretcher and smiling broadly. She spoke in the voice she employed when she tried to convince me to steal, a coaxing voice, full of promise and invitation. Only this time my sister was not talking to me, and hearing the voice filled me with alarm. The doctor nodded briefly at her and continued checking the tube that ran into her arm. Madeline stretched her other arm across her body and touched his hand. "Hello," she said again. Her fingers stroked his skin. He did not move his hand away, but he looked at her with an expression of puzzled interest, no doubt amazed at her boldness.

"Linny," I said, in a half-whisper. "Quit that."

She removed her hand from the doctor's arm. "I have to do what my sister says," she said, smiling.

After the doctor moved on to the front of the room, I turned to her. "What are you doing?"

"Relax." She closed her eyes and pressed her hands together over her chest. Then she said, "Hey, do I look like I'm dead?"

33

Agatha receives a telegram in New Orleans—"AGNES VERY SICK. YOU MUST KNOW."

The final story will be told later, in a letter that will arrive in a few months, relating that Agnes has left home to find her own cure for her sickness. She has decided that all she can do is cure herself. This is not a vinegar trick. With coins sewn in the hem of her dress, the story told in the village relates, Agnes began walking toward America. The village storytellers say that Agnes has always been wrong in the head. She forgets that countries have borders, and a wide ocean separates the continents. Agnes is stupid, the villagers will say later. On the road leading to the border, Agnes lies down on the grass. She is tired, but content because she has left home and is on her way to somewhere else. She has begun a journey.

In Lily's story, Agnes gives herself up. She gives up. But now I don't know if this is the truth. I go back to the story to make it my own.

I bring back Agnes and Agatha from the past, the dead, or

wherever they have been waiting. Agatha is beautiful: an old woman in a black silk dress. Her hair has faded to a dull gray rust. She is surprised to see her sister.

Where has Agnes been? Where was she during the long years in America when Agatha was suffering through her pregnancies alone?

Agnes is still a child. The years apart from her twin have not aged her. Her hair is a bright auburn, her face unlined. She cannot speak English, but she knows how to sing. In the hospital, the nurses taught the young girls songs, nursery rhymes, and various national anthems for countries that no longer exist as independent nations.

Madeline is watching; I know that my sister is pleased. She opens Agnes's suitcase packed at the hospital and slips into her clothes. The white gown patterned with faint blue flowers gapes open at the back. She fastens Agnes's paper name bracelet to her wrist. She is ready for the future to unfold like the past.

Yet I know now that I can't save her. In her story, Madeline would say that the four of us could live together: two sets of twins. Four women. In a new house in another village in another country. A house filled with light and air and space. Missing walls, no staircase to connect the floors.

In Madeline's story, we would live with Judy Garland and Ginger Love. In the movie theater, Judy Garland sings "After You've Gone," wearing a sailor dress, her breasts taped to her chest, her heart fluttering, her hands shaking from too much Dexedrine, the small green pills, MGM's favorite drug. Ginger Love takes her hand, links their arms together. The world outside Emerald City has nothing to offer them.

No. I want to leave that house behind. The women float through the house like ghosts.

34

That night, after we sold our blood for the first time, I wanted to punish my sister. "I want to tell you something, Linny. We're not going to Emerald City ever again. This is it."

Madeline was arranging costumes on Lily's bed, matching shoes to hats, spreading a skirt flat. She wore Lily's nightgown, the one with the rip under the arm. She didn't seem particularly concerned about what I'd just said. "We'll see." Then she said, "Tonight, we're going to be Agnes and Agatha." Our great-grandmother and her sister had never been characters in our performances in the past. "We've never brought them to Emerald City."

"Linny, come on," I said. "What did I just tell you?"

"This is the last play ever. I've already got it planned. You're Agnes and I'm Agatha." I was surprised that Madeline gave me Agnes. I knew she must have wanted to play the sick sister, the one who was abandoned.

"Okay, But I meant what I said. This is it." We were Agnes and Agatha on the stage in the movie theater, bath towels wound around our heads to imitate babushkas, lipstick painted in circles on our cheeks. We shook our skirts and pretended the wooden floor of the stage was a field. As I stood on stage, waiting for her to run back from the village to the farm, I knew that I was tired of the games and tricks we'd used to get through our childhood.

"Okay, that's enough. Let's do the escape," Madeline said.

She untied the towel and removed it from her head, then began to pull her dress off. "I'll be Lily." Her dress crumpled at her ankles, Madeline stood naked on the stage, the square of gauze from the plasma center taped to her bare arm.——I had ripped off mine as soon as we came home. The weight we'd gained had not shown up on her as it had on me. Her stomach was only slightly rounded. "You're the daughter," she said. "You have to play both of us."

I nodded. I would agree to whatever she said. If there was a future for me, for her, for us, I knew it would consist of my trying to create and maintain her happiness while I watched myself fail over and over again at my own. But I knew that this game was dangerous.

"I'm also the director," Madeline said. "I'll tell you what to do." She pointed to the edge of the stage. "Lie down there and pretend you're sleeping. You won't know I'm leaving until I'm gone. It's a surprise."

I didn't want to act out the scene, but I knew I could not refuse my sister. I followed her orders helplessly. I stretched out on the edge of the stage. I felt like crying because I knew that with each stage direction I took from Madeline, I was falling further and further down into this life with her. She and I would be alone together for the rest of our lives.

Madeline wanted to make the departure scene more dramatic. She said we needed a ladder of knotted sheets from Lily's bed that she would use to crawl out the window in the middle of the night.

"I'm leaving now," she said. "I'm telling you that I'm leaving."

I stood silently in front of her. I was unsure of how I was supposed to play both her and me.

"Go on," she told me. "Aren't you sad that I'm leaving? You don't look sad. I'm going to the hospital. Now, when I walk toward the door, I want you to start to cry."

Every three weeks, on Tuesdays, as often as the plasma center would allow, Madeline and I sold our blood. Each time, Madeline flirted with the doctor on duty. She was waiting for him to ask her on a date. "Or at least to go in the back room," she said. "Remember what I said about the blow job? I think he already likes me enough for that."

"Stop it!" I told her, and I meant it, although I'd also had an impossible fantasy that the doctor would fall in love with her and take her away. She'd live with him in his house. I was sure it was a mansion by the water. He could keep her safe.

"I'll give him a discount," Madeline said, laughing. "I won't make him pay full price."

Soon after we gave plasma for the first time, another doctor, the doctor who managed the plasma center, had called. Madeline answered the phone; I listened to her half of the conversation.

"Oh. Thanks!" She lay on the floor of the movie theater, winding the phone cord around her wrist. "It's so nice of you to call me."

"What is it?" I said, when she hung up.

"I know he's interested. See, he called me at home. That's the first step."

"I want to know what he said, Linny."

"He called to tell us both something about our blood. He wanted to inform us our blood type was negative. He hoped we'd continue coming in to donate because negative blood types are rare. Our blood is needed." Later, I understood that Madeline hadn't told me everything he said: He'd explained that our antibodies were needed for the treatment called RhoGAM given to Rh-negative women during their first pregnancies. The procedure would involve going to Sarasota General Hospital, letting our blood be removed so the antibodies could be taken out, and then waiting until our blood was replaced. Later, I knew that she didn't tell me the full story because she was afraid of the hospital.

"He's not interested in you. He called to talk about blood."

"He's not interested in *our* blood, Alice. He didn't want to talk to you. He's interested in *me*."

Already, I envisioned years of the same scene: Madeline and I stretched out on identical cots at the plasma center, needles stuck in our arms, staring at the ceiling. Madeline would flirt with each doctor who came over to check on our progress. I would lie silently beside her, pretending not to see what was going on.

The next week was our eighteenth birthday, and I found an old theater that was playing *Babes in Arms*, one of Judy Garland's earliest movies, which came out the same year as *The Wizard of Oz*, at an early afternoon show. "Linny, my birthday present to you is that you can sneak into the theater from the side door." Several days before, I had gone to the theater to figure out a way for my sister to sneak in and found the side door.

Madeline smiled. "My present to you is two boxes of sourballs," she said. "I was saving them for the movie, but you might as well know." My sister and I were back to our old weights again; the days of eating in the Tamiami Trail restaurants were over. Sourballs were the candy from our Joy Theater days.

I'd forgotten that *Babes in Arms* was a Busby Berkeley film, one of Lily's favorites. Threatened with the state work school, the sons and daughters of vaudeville performers put on a show to raise money for their parents. Judy Garland was Mickey Rooney's girlfriend, Patsy Barton. In one of the early scenes, Mickey Rooney asks Judy Garland, "Do you ever feel older than your folks?" I remember how

I'd once liked the way the children in the film must become adults, but now the transformation seemed forced and horrible to me. Judy Garland and Betty Jaynes sang together: "To look at us you'd never dream the two of us were twins. In fact, it's quite ridiculously odd. . . ." The song was "I Like Opera, I Like Swing." I remembered Madeline and Lily singing it in the car on the late-night drives in New Orleans. "We're really just like two peas in a pod!"

When *The End* flashed on the screen in curving script, I stood up. Madeline walked out of the theater without a word.

I was the first to speak. "Well, are you glad we got to see Judy Garland on our birthday?" I wanted to ask, *Did the movie make you think of Lily?*

"I like the later movies better," Madeline said. "I'm sick of Mickey Rooney."

"Maybe you're tired of Judy Garland."

"No! You never understand what I'm saying anymore, Alice."

As we walked the rest of the way home in silence, I thought of how I'd graduated from Christ the King only weeks ago, and how, without telling my sister, I'd applied to Manatee Community College. I'd received a letter from the registrar saying I could start classes in the fall, and a letter from the financial aid office telling me I'd been awarded a Pell Grant. I knew I should have tried to apply to a better college, a real four-year college, as the nuns at Christ the King had told me to do. They'd said I could get into any number of schools, even on the East Coast. They said I should apply to art schools. I had a brochure about the Rhode Island School of Design hidden in my drawer. But I couldn't leave my sister. What I wanted to do instead was to leave without leaving, to make a separate life for myself here. I would learn discipline. I would start drawing every day. I would devote myself with great attention to a task. I would draw myself out of this life with Madeline.

* * *

After we got home, I took out a stack of my old drawings, the ones Lily had not destroyed, the ones I'd done of Judy Garland in the Joy Theater years ago, which I'd hidden beneath my clothes.

In the first, Judy Garland is a woman dressed as a little girl. She's probably seventeen. She wears a sailor dress, with a wide white collar, and Mary-Jane shoes. Lily had told us that when she made films for MGM in her teens, her breasts were taped to her chest because the studio didn't want her to look old. This is the version of Judy Garland that Lily prefers: the child star who appeared in film after film.

My second drawing depicts Judy Garland as an adult. This one is based on Lily's description of the Orpheum concert. The skin around her eyes is wrinkled, her chin sags, and she teeters at the edge of the stage I've sketched below. She wears a high-necked dress to hide the scar from the time she cut her throat with a water glass. I imagine that she's forty or so. Pills are sewn into the hem of her dress. This is the Judy Garland Madeline loves: the addict who tries to hide her secret self from the crowd who adores her.

In the third picture, which I never finished, Judy Garland is in character. She's Dorothy in *The Wizard of Oz*. I didn't complete all the checks on her gingham dress. I only filled in one of the ruby slippers. But she is on her way down the road toward Emerald City. I never drew the Tin Man, the Scarecrow, or the Cowardly Lion because I liked to have Judy Garland on her journey by herself. This is the Judy Garland I would choose: the girl attempting an escape.

For hours, I sat with the pictures. When I looked at those drawings, I rejected that past. I would look for a different world. That afternoon, I planned the first steps that would lead me away from Madeline. As the afternoon ended, and darkness filled the movie theater, I thought, *What if I hadn't had a sister? What if I hadn't been a twin?*

35

The first night without Madeline in the Crescent Court Motel, I sleep in Helen's white nightgown, curled up in a corner of the wide bed. The right side of the double bed seems vast and empty; several times, I wake up in the middle of the night alone and wonder where I am. But the person I am missing isn't Madeline. It's Owen, his body beside me, his hand on my back, his leg thrown over mine. In the morning, I stand up and lower my shoulders between my knees until the blood rushes to my head and I'm dizzy and awake, then dress in the last outfit from Helen's box: a jade-green princess dress with an empire waist and a matching scarf. I wrap the scarf around my head twice so that it covers my short hair. Although my cheek where Madeline hit me is still tender, there's no bruise, no evidence of what she did. I stuff my dress from the previous night, the dress I was wearing when Madeline went into the hospital, into the toilet, shutting the lid.

In my biography of Frida Kahlo, I remember reading that instead of making quick sketches on scraps of paper, she drew everything that passed through her head in the black-and-white copybooks that Mexican children used in school. The notebooks would save her, she said, in moments when she felt empty. I was struck by that word. I understood it, *empty*. I have always thought I'll feel comfortable, finally, when I feel that. But now I see that emptiness solves nothing.

I take out Lily's scrapbook. Sitting on the motel room floor, I turn the pages, as I have so many times before, looking at the *carte de visites* of Agnes and Agatha and the clippings about Judy Garland's childhood successes. I look at the sonogram image from the ultrasound. I have no pictures of Madeline; she tore up the only shot. I can't arrange the pictures into any kind of order, not a narrative or even a group of objects within an imaginary frame. Carefully, I unfold the drawing Helen made of Owen. His expression is sad.

I want to call him, but I'm afraid.

In the parking lot, I unlock the door of Jack's car and start the engine.

I'll spend this day alone driving, deciding what I should do next.

For the first time, today, I take my daughter with me. I place Frida on the empty side beside me in the car. She is only three weeks old, too young to be out with me like this without a car seat, so I strap her small body with the seat belt, as if she is a prisoner. She doesn't cry. I kiss her forehead; her warm skin that smells like talcum powder and milk.

I take my daughter for a tour of my own childhood. We're silent together as I drive. The most important thing I must do is not look at her, or she could disappear. First, I drive to Agatha's old house, where Lily, as a teenager, chose to run away to give birth to us. The shutters of the house are still closed to sunlight, and the car sits on the lawn. I picture the couple inside, the incomplete family, missing their daughter. Then I drive to the Poor Clares Nursing Home and stare up at the window where I tell myself Agatha must be. I should go inside to see her, but I don't.

Next I drive out to the Star Dust Motel. Leaving Frida in the car, I walk over the vacant lot to the pool. At the edge of the pool, I sit down on the ground. I kneel, as if I'm in church and could pray by pressing my face to the dirt.

Why did my daughter die? Why did my own mother leave me?

I can't let myself believe what my sister told me as we stood in front of the hospital. Lily left us both. I can never tell my sister the truth: how, during my last conversation with her, Lily told me to take care of my sister because she could never live on her own. Madeline has invented her own version of events in which she can never be the one who is left behind. I am Madeline. Madeline is me. Now the equation no longer works.

The difference between us is suddenly clear: I am the one who lives in the outside world.

When I return to the car, the baby is gone.

The way Lily taught us, I go out to the New Orleans airport to decide what to do and where to go. I sit in a black metal chair just as the three of us did when Lily decided to take us to Sarasota, when she began to get ready to leave us. At the end of Terminal D, the Eastern Airlines gate is deserted; the airline hasn't flown in several years. The only sign of life is a man pushing a large broom across the floor at midnight, sweeping the dirty carpet in a desultory fashion. He glances at me, acknowledges my presence with a nod.

At 7 A.M., I call our rented house in Sarasota from the pay

phone by the service desk. As I thought, there's no answer. Next, I dial Dr. Levy's office. The phone rings five times before the answering machine picks up, and I hear her smooth flat voice: "You have reached the doctor's office. Please leave a message. If it is a life-threatening emergency, hang up and dial 911." I set the phone back in its cradle. I remember that Dr. Levy once said, in one of her few statements during my therapy with her, that the primary psychological problem with anticipating our own death is that we can't bear the thought of the world going on without us. Since we found out that Lily died, since Madeline went into the hospital, the part of my life I've tried to keep at bay is coming closer.

I close my eyes, lean back in my chair, and remember Madeline as Judy Garland, chanting "There's no place like home. There's no place like home." She was mumbling in her sleep, her head tossing on the pillow. She could click the heels of her red shoes three times and be transported to the place where she really belonged. Now I long for that. But Dorothy was a child. She didn't have to create a childhood home; it was already there for her, ready and waiting. Agatha would have called it the Old Country, the village she left. Lily taught us that home is always temporary, a motel, a stopping place where we live before she leaves us. She must have found her own home somewhere in the end. Home. My daughter knew it as my body.

I remember reading a newspaper article my sister sent me last year about Japanese memorial parks. Aborted fetuses in Japan must have graves, an idea that used to sicken me, but the graves are treated with care. Parents bring their other children to the graves to see them. When someone asks how many children a mother has and one of her children lies in a grave, she includes that child in her number. According to this system, I still have and will always have a child.

I have to see where she lives now.

*   *   *

My hands shake as I dial the phone number of Charity Hospital. I ask for the receptionist on the fifth floor, then I say Madeline's name. The receptionist says, "You'll have to call back tomorrow at nine."

"I can't," I say. "It's a family emergency. I have to talk to my sister."

"Alice." I hear Madeline's voice. My face flushes, as if she could see me.

"How did you know it would be me?"

"No one else would call me." I am listening intently to my sister's voice, as I have my whole life, waiting for the familiar signs: her dreamy exhaustion, her lassitude, her bursts of anger. Then I tell myself, *stop listening.*

"How are you?" I say.

She ignores my question. "When I get out of here, I'm going away for a while."

"Where?"

"I think California. There's a nurse I met here who's been telling me about it. I'll drive out there and if I like it, I might stay. I like traveling. I like to be in the car. You know, Alice, the happiest time of my life was when we were on those Judy Garland drives with Lily in New Orleans."

"Madeline," I say. I am not going to call her Linny. I am not going to say, *you don't have a car to take you there, you can't live there alone.* "I can't come with you."

"What made you think I was asking you to? You always want to be included in everything I do. Can't you ever do anything alone?"

My sister's version of reality is wrong. I've always known it, but I've never forced myself to see it. I say nothing.

"Do you think you could send me some clothes? Something lacy, fancy? You can choose."

"Madeline, I have to go." This is the first time in my life I have ever hung up the phone in a conversation with my sister. I hold the receiver after I've completed the action. The reason for our search had nothing to do with Lily. It was about re-creating childhood, holding onto that past. My efforts to return to the past took me in the wrong direction. And now I see that there is no heaven for dead children that we can enter because there is no heaven. We have to learn to live without it.

36

I imagine Madeline in Charity Hospital in New Orleans. I would like to believe that my sister is searching for a telephone to call me. The nurses on Ward Five keep quarters in their skirt pockets and dole them out to the patients who are the most quiet, who do not disturb the others. These are the women who sit in front of the television with heavy eyelids because they are sedated, Thorazine running through their veins and making them into good patients. When the metal clamps touch their foreheads for the electroshock, they are calm.

In the hospital, day and night are indistinguishable. Is it morning or late afternoon when my sister hides in the freight elevator in order to go all the way downstairs? Is it evening? In the basement, a cleaning woman pushes a sweep broom over the floor. She wears tennis shoes covered in blue paper like a surgeon. Walkman earphones play rap music and drown out all sound. She doesn't notice Madeline. Madeline walks in the basement's empty halls, past the boiler room where the humming silver generator keeps the hospital full of light and motion. She hums to herself under her breath, a happy Judy Garland song, "Meet Me in St. Louis."

Something is wrong: my sister is in the basement, but I'm upstairs.

I wait for her in her room on the fifth floor. There's no indication that the room is hers—no souvenirs or photographs or mementos. The bed is made, sheets stretched tightly across the mattress. In a corner above the room, bolted to the wall, a television plays cartoons. The pink suitcase is missing. I'm selfish, as proved by the fact that what I am truly looking for here is a sign that my sister loves me.

In every story, there is the good sister and the bad sister, the one who leaves and the one who stays, Judy Garland and Ginger Love. The one who leaves the other behind and goes out into the world in search of her new life. I don't want Madeline to believe the connection between us is broken, although I'm ready to sever it. We repeat the logic of a mother and a child. I want my sister to yearn for me, to hope, to grieve, but I will give her up.

37

I drive back to Atlanta in one day, eight hours of driving with two stops for gas. On the way, I listen to Owen's birthday tape over and over. When I listened to it before, I never made it to the end to find Judy Garland.

Owen has taped a version of "Over the Rainbow" from when she was an adult. The flourishes and trills from childhood are gone. Her voice is soft: "away above the chimney tops, that's where you'll find me . . ." There are long silences between the lines of the song. I recognize the version—from the *Palace Two-A-Day* album, 1952, one of Lily's favorites—because it's the one in which, in the middle of the song, Judy Garland begins to cry.

Although I never understood Lily, I heard her story again and again. She told us her story until we could tell it back to her, but in the end she told us lies. Together, Madeline and I kept Lily with us. Between us, through our silence, Owen and I kept the baby safe. If I didn't talk about her, I thought I could remain with her. If we were silent, he and I and our daughter could remain together. All my life, this had been my definition of family: two of us trying to hold the absent third. Two of us who thought we could save the one who was already lost to us.

Do I need to remember or do I need to forget? When will I finally feel as if I am safe? I press Rewind to hear the song again. Judy Garland's voice breaks on the line "skies are blue." Then I take the scrapbook from my purse and open it carefully on the seat beside me. I pull over to the shoulder of the interstate.

On all the brittle pages, there isn't a single photograph of Lily, Madeline, and me together. No document marks us as a family. *Madeline + Alice + Lily = A Family* is not an equation that ever existed. First, I tear out the birth certificate from the last page where Lily kept it for so many years. Madeline tore up the photograph of the two of us, side by side; I tear up our birth certificate. I tear up the conclusion of the story. Once the birth certificate is gone, I page through the scrapbook backward. I tear out the remaining memories of the past that for years have defined the boundaries of our lives. It's not our past, my sister's and mine, but Lily's version of it. The only stories about her life are the ones that she invented. I can invent my own. I imagine a new art project. A piece about all of us: Madeline, Lily, Agnes and Agatha, my daughter.

A story in which no one wants to die.

In Atlanta, on the way to our house, I drive through miles of suburbs, then hit the city, crossing under the maze of highways that marks downtown. The afternoon is bright and almost cool, as if the summer heat is already starting to burn off the sidewalks and roads, as if fall could be here already.

I park in front of our house. Owen's car is there, parked in the driveway. I was right: he has come home. "There's no place like home," I remember my sister saying when Lily showed us the house she'd found. "There's no place like home." Here's the place I call home, the house I left to save my sister and find my mother. The house stares back at me, ordinary brick, refusing to become magic.

I open the car door and walk slowly up the gravel path to the front door.

Instead of using my key, I ring the doorbell. When Owen opens the door, I can't read the expression on his face, but he is wearing a short-sleeved blue cotton shirt that I don't recognize. I always thought I knew all of his clothes. Under the shirt, he wears a gray T-shirt with Georgia Tech Track and Field inscribed on the front in faded letters. I remember that shirt. I used to wear it on the nights we stayed up all night working in the kitchen. I loved the T-shirt because it smelled like him.

In the past few weeks, since I returned to Sarasota, I have imagined him so often, I have pictured our encounters so frequently, yet to see him is a shock.

"I missed you," I say before I can stop myself. These are not the first words I wanted to say.

I wait for him to make a comment about my short hair or my strange green dress or the absence of my wedding ring. He takes my suitcase from my hand; his eyes linger on my face. "Alice," he says.

"We didn't find Lily," I say.

"I know. Helen told me." He gestures toward the doorway and into the house as if he is inviting me to come in. Being invited into my own house feels odd, yet I follow him inside.

The front hall and the living room look exactly the same. We stand facing each other in the middle of the room. Part of me was afraid Owen would not want to speak to me at all. I thought he would pack up my clothes, my books, my art supplies, ready for me to take them from the house. I thought he would want to leave me. Part of me also hoped that we could fall into each other's arms and he could forgive me for everything, as in an old movie, right before the credits flashed on the screen. Instead we both sit down, and there's a long pause.

"Madeline's in the hospital," I say.

"You shut me out," he says, and his voice is low and filled with sadness. "You haven't had a real conversation with me since we went to Sarasota. All you talk about is your sister and what you have to do to save her. You told me you've been thinking about your childhood, but you didn't tell me what you've been thinking. You have your own world, and Madeline is part of it, but you won't let me in."

"That's over." I stumble over my words, unable to think of what I want to say. "I want to talk to you." I remember how I talked to him when we first met, how he was the only person besides my sister I had ever been able to talk to, how I told him our stories with ease and fluency. He touched my body, and my tongue loosened, words came to me, and I talked and I talked.

"You can't just say you will. We have to sit down and do it." He stops for a moment, then he says, "We have to talk about the baby."

"I can't," I whisper.

"You and I were going to be her parents."

"Please, stop." I want to stuff my fingers in my ears like a child who can seal herself off from the world.

"We were supposed to share her life. Can't we share her death?"

My body begins to shake. My voice catches in my throat. "I don't know."

Owen bends over me; the sleeves of his blue shirt open like the wings of a bird as he reaches for me, as if he could enclose me inside his body, but he doesn't take me in his arms as he would have a few weeks ago. He just looks at me.

Silence falls between us. I am searching for the one statement I can make so that everything will be okay. And there is none.

"I'm ready to see the grave," I say. "Will you come with me?"

Like Helen, I take out the phone book and prepare to scan the lists of names. One by one, I plan to call all the cemeteries in Atlanta, following the alphabetized list in the yellow pages in order. Owen says, "I know where it is, Alice. I've been there."

We drive out to the Garden of Memories at the end of the afternoon. At the cemetery gate, an elderly woman in a yellow dress stops each car to ask the number of the grave. "Area sixteen," Owen says.

She smiles as if to wish me a good trip. "Down to the right, dear."

Babyland is marked off by a picket fence like a playground, but it covers several acres of grass. Owen walks beside me. I study the names imprinted on the small flat stones in the rows, each one the size of a paperback book. Edith Virginia Porter, February 13, 1987–February 15, 1987. Mary Elizabeth Levine, December 1, 1988–December 2, 1988. Mark Taylor, August 19, 1989–August 20, 1989. None of them lived longer than three days. The smallest stones do not have names at all: Baby Todd, Baby Randolph.

If I could pray, I would kneel down at the smallest graves with no names. "Hail Mary, full of grace," I'd begin, and I imagine Mary swooping down from heaven like an enormous bird to gather me in her arms, her soft blue wings. Agatha would say that Mother Mary, who loves all children, loves these children more than the rest. She kisses me on the lips and pulls me up with her, to the highest part of the sky.

"Alice," Owen says, and he touches my arm.

Where are the stories about these children? I think of the women who write in Baby's First Year books before the birth, who keep journals of their babies' movements inside their bodies. They have husbands who videotape the first, second, and third trimester doctors' appointments, preserving the slow motion of the sonogram over their wives' skin forever. These babies will grow up with the stories, reading their mothers' words and watching the tapes; each baby will know that her mother wanted to remember the time when she inhabited her body.

The woman at the cemetery gate must think I am some child's mother, and I am. We are our parents. No other parents are visiting today.

Owen stops walking. "Alice, here it is," he says.

We're standing in front of the small square of ground I've been afraid of all summer. *Frida Carson-Wilhem, April 31, 1993.* Until now, there hasn't been an object for my grief. I've grieved for her as if she'd lived, but she did live. I've been afraid the world will forget her, that I'll forget her, because no one knew her except me, and I knew her through my body.

Owen knew her too. At the hospital, after the labor was over, the doctor in charge signed the death certificate. Owen was told we had to deal with the body, and he did everything without me. Then I didn't want to know what had happened to the baby, but now I want to hear the story. I try to imagine the coffin. A plain metal box, the size of the milk boxes on other people's porches when I was a child. Those milk boxes, where chilled white bottles were left and taken, used to signify normality, an ordinary family. A house where nothing bad could happen. None of those children would ever die.

Owen takes my hand. I wrap my fingers around his.

Light drains from the sky. I pick some dandelions by the fence, and we leave them on her grave. On the way out of the cemetery, I look back only once, to see the field of small, flat stones, before we drive toward home.